Also by Dana Dratch

Confessions of a Red Herring

Seeing Red

DANA DRATCH

KENSINGTON BOOKS

www.kensingtonbooks.com

KENSINGTON BOOKS are published by

Kensington Publishing Corp.
119 West 40th Street
New York, NY 10018

All Kensington titles, imprints and distributed lines are available at special quantity discounts for bulk purchases for sales promotion, premiums, fund-raising, educational or institutional use. Special book excerpts or customized printings can also be created to fit specific needs. For details, write or phone the office of the Kensington Special Sales Manager. Kensington Publishing Corp., 119 West 40th Street, New York, NY 10018. Attn.: Special Sales Department. Phone: 1-800-221-2647.

Kensington and the K logo Reg. U.S. Pat. & TM Off.

ISBN-13: 978-1-4967-1658-3
ISBN-10: 1-4967-1658-2
First Kensington Mass Market Edition: June 2019

ISBN-13: 978-1-4967-1659-0 (e-book)
ISBN-10: 1-4967-1659-0 (e-book)

10 9 8 7 6 5 4 3 2 1

Printed in the United States of America

To my parents,
for a childhood filled with love and books.

Chapter 1

Lightning split the sky as I dashed up the sidewalk. Not the smartest time to be carrying a metal-framed umbrella. Not the smartest time to be wearing my best navy-blue dressy dress and three-inch sling-backs, either. But if I didn't want to arrive at Ian's cocktail party looking like an extra from *Titanic*, I needed the bumbershoot. And a sponge.

Mother Nature was venting some serious rage. My neighbor's elegant mixer was supposed to have been held outside, weather permitting. But this weather was definitely not permitting.

At this rate, we were going to be trading drinks on the patio under twinkling lights for huddling around hurricane lamps in the basement.

The power had gone off three times just in the hour it took me to get ready. When I left, my brother Nick was on the couch trying to watch a basketball game. Lucy, our puppy, was cowering under a blanket next to him. All I could see was her tail.

Thunderstorms freaked her out. Nick figured it was a holdover from her previous life as a stray. With no place to come in out of the weather, the noise and pelting rain must have been particularly terrifying to such a small, defenseless creature.

"See, nothing to worry about," he said, slipping a treat to the lump under the blanket. "You should be more worried about taking the 76ers and the points. I expect better from you."

"I put my golf umbrella by the door," he called to me. "It's big and deep, and it'll keep you dry. And from the looks of what's going on outside, you're gonna need it."

"Ooh, University of Arizona—very stylish," I said, unsnapping the clasp while carefully keeping it closed in the house.

"Consider yourself lucky. I was saving it for the Domino's guy. If you're not home by midnight, should Lucy and I come looking for you?"

"If I'm not home by midnight, send a rowboat. The party's only supposed to go a couple of hours. And that was before Ian had to move it indoors. So he might cut things short."

"Yeah, the local weather guys are practically wetting themselves. We've got Storm Watch '19 on Channel 6, predictions of multiple tornado warnings on Channel 10, and big promises for hail the size of golf balls on Channel 12."

"Why is it always golf balls? Why not walnuts? Or Christmas tree ornaments? Or Ping-Pong balls?"

"Would you be afraid of Ping-Pong balls? They know if they're gonna grab your attention, it has to sound scary." He gently stroked the blanket lump.

"But it's not scary at all, is it, Lucy? Is it? Not when we're all warm and dry."

I shut the front door, pausing on the porch to open Nick's umbrella. Thunder and lightning clapped almost simultaneously.

Inside, Lucy howled. I knew exactly how she felt.

As I jogged across the street and up the front walk to Ian's stately Victorian—now officially a B&B christened the Cotswolds Inn—the wind picked up. Rain was pinging off the umbrella. Or maybe it really was hail.

Suddenly, the heavy oak door swung open.

"Such a nasty night out, miss—come in and get dry." Harkins.

Decked out in a gray chalk-stripe suit, white vest, and matching tie, he was playing the role of stereotypical English butler to the hilt. Complete with white gloves.

I'm guessing none of the guests knew what I knew: Harkins was also Ian's father. And co-owner of the Cotswolds Inn.

He took the umbrella, expertly toweled it off with a chamois that appeared out of nowhere, folded it, and slipped it soundlessly into a caddy by the door. All in less time than it took me to step inside. The man was a wonder.

"Just this way, miss," he said with a small smile. "The guests are enjoying cocktails in the study." He dropped his voice to barely above a whisper, "And Ian will be so very glad you've arrived."

"The study" turned out to be an old-fashioned library. Complete with two-story oak bookshelves lining the walls. They put my do-it-yourself Ikea bookcases to shame.

People clustered around the room, laughing and talking, drinks in hand. A fire crackled in the fireplace. And lively '30s-era jazz played in the background—courtesy of some unseen electronic wizardry. If I hadn't just run through a thunderstorm, I'd never have known that all hell was breaking loose outside. Clearly, these folks didn't. Too bad I hadn't brought Lucy.

Ian and several others looked over as I walked in. My face went hot. And probably pink.

The curse of the redhead.

"Alex, hullo! So glad you could make it," Ian said, coming toward me. "You look smashing. Can I get you a drink? We just opened a lovely bottle of champagne."

Decked out in a black tux, British ex-pat Ian Sterling could have given James Bond a run for his money. I felt my heart beat a little faster. But maybe it was just from sprinting up the sidewalk.

"That would be wonderful, thank you," I said gratefully.

As he hoisted a champagne bottle out of its silver ice bucket, I noticed the woman glued to his elbow. Our neighbor Lydia Stewart.

While I'd opted for a short, dressy dress, Lydia looked like she'd stepped out of the pages of *Vogue*: Pale and wraithlike in a full-length, strapless, black taffeta ball gown with a bell skirt. Sporting a couple of diamond earrings that could double as chandeliers. Knowing Lydia, they were real diamonds.

And the dress probably cost more than I earned in a year.

Unlike me, she was bone-dry. Not even a drop of rain on her shoes. *How did she do that?* the practical part of my brain wondered. Had she booked a room here for the night? Or did she have more permanent accommodations?

I quickly shook off that last thought and accepted the champagne flute from my smiling host.

"Alex lives in the neighborhood, and she's a writer," he announced to the room. To me, he said, "So, working on any interesting stories lately?"

For most anyone else, that would be schmoozing. But with Ian, I sensed that he really was interested. Not just in me—in everyone. In the couple of months that he'd lived across the street, I'd noticed he had a quick mind and great people skills. If he wasn't an innkeeper, he'd have made a great reporter. Or a top-notch spy.

Unfortunately, the one assignment I did have was top secret. So I demurred. "Not really. I just finished up a story for *Metropolitan Bride*, and I'm meeting with another editor tomorrow morning for a new assignment. Fingers crossed."

"A bridal magazine?" Lydia sniffed. "That's ironic, isn't it? What do they say—'Always the bridesmaid, never the bride'? I wonder if that applies to bridal writers, too? Like the old adage 'Those who can't, write.'"

"I believe you'll find the correct quote is 'Those who can't, teach,'" said a distinguished sixty-plus

6 *Dana Dratch*

man in a sharp blue blazer, cradling a lowball glass in his hand.

"Oh, stuff and nonsense, as you well know," said the older woman seated near him on a vintage leather sofa. They both laughed.

"I'm afraid we've spent a good part of our lives in academia," the man explained. "I'm William Prestwick—Bill. This is my wife, Emily." With that, Emily waved her champagne flute and smiled.

"Escaped just in the nick of time," she said. "Now we can travel and enjoy life—instead of droning on in front of a gaggle of tots who don't even have the good manners to look up from their electronic whatchamacallits."

"The Prestwicks are staying here at the inn for the week," Ian interjected.

"Lovely place," said Emily, as the lights flickered.

I noticed that Harkins had slipped in and was surreptitiously placing heavy silver candelabras filled with thick new tapers all around the room.

Well, a power outage would be one way to end a party early.

"Cute dress," Lydia said, sidling up to me. "Did you make it yourself?"

"Scarlett O'Hara called—she wants her coffin lining back," I replied, just loud enough for her to hear.

Lydia's jaw dropped.

"So, are you guys seeing the sights or visiting family?" I asked, settling in next to Emily Prestwick.

"Definitely the sights," she said. "We're from

Boston, but we've been to Washington many times for conferences."

"We wanted to come for once when we weren't on anyone's schedule but our own," Bill added.

"We were going to stay at one of the big hotels in the city, but then Bill found this place online. It just seemed too perfect. An old Victorian house with an English garden and afternoon tea."

"Ems is a professor of architecture and housing. I'm botany."

"Home and garden," I said.

"Exactly," said Emily, raising her glass.

I looked around the room. Lydia had quickly flitted back to Ian's side and was regaling a group of listeners with a story. Or boring them to death. Hard to tell.

I actually recognized a few of the faces here tonight. But most were unfamiliar. Ian had been hosting these little get-togethers fairly regularly since the inn opened a few weeks ago. He'd invite all of the inn's guests, a neighbor or two, and some of the local bigwigs—especially the ones who could steer a little business his way. Chamber of commerce and visitors bureau types. When possible, he'd also sprinkle in a few movers and shakers. A semi-celebrity. An author, professor, or corporate honcho in town for whatever. Or a politician happy to escape the Beltway rubber-chicken dinner circuit, for even a few hours.

"Adds a little dazzle to the proceedings," Ian confided once.

He'd invited me several times, but this was the

first chance I'd had to actually attend anything since his garden party grand opening. When I'd inadvertently shown up with a couple of killers in tow. Followed by a phalanx of squad cars. And an ambulance. Long story.

I'd also discovered that freelancer hours were as bad as staff reporter hours. But the money was a lot less predictable. I was wasting half my time begging editors to send checks and the other half pleading with creditors to give me extensions on bills.

So the idea of spending an evening idly sipping cocktails and making small talk seemed frivolous. But Nick and my best friend, Trip, had made a united assault on my current lack of anything resembling a social life.

I gave in when Trip floated the idea of using the event to make a few contacts for my fledgling freelance writing business. "You might even scare up a story or two," he drawled. "Besides, when's the last time you left the house for anything but work?"

"Does the grocery store count?"

"You're going," Trip concluded.

I had to admit, it did feel nice to get dressed up for a change.

"So, I recognize a few of the local people here for the party. But who's staying at the inn?" I asked Emily.

"It's a nice crowd," she said. "See that couple on the little settee? They're on their honeymoon. Paul and Georgie Something-or-other. They seem nice, but we haven't seen that much of them."

"That's because we've been spending a lot of

our time out and about, Ems," Bill said. "The honeymooners have been staying close to home. Not locked in their room, mind you. Enjoying the inn. Teas, meals, walks in the garden. You've probably seen them around the neighborhood."

A normal person might have. Other than mugging the mailman daily for missing checks, I wasn't seeing much of my neighbors lately. While I let Lucy out for regular "breaks" in the backyard, Nick was the one taking her on long walks.

"Very possibly," I said, noncommittally.

"There's another woman we haven't seen much," said Emily. "Always wears a silk scarf around her head and big sunglasses. Very glamorous. Rumor is she's some kind of movie actress. Takes meals in her room. Didn't even come to the party."

"I heard she's recovering from a bit of the nip and tuck, if you know what I mean," Bill said.

"Oh, Bill, you are a horrid gossip," his wife chided, laughing. "Don't pay any attention to him."

The lights blinked again, followed by a couple of bright flashes outside. But neither Bill nor the Depression-era jazz missed a beat.

"Well, if I were interested in that kind of thing, this would be the place," he reasoned. "Away from the city, first-rate food, and lots of peace and quiet. Just the ticket."

"Even if it's true, it's none of our business," Emily said. "But it's all very mysterious. Oh, and your friend in the black dress is staying here. But that's just for tonight."

"Not if she has her way, it's not," Bill countered.

"She's been looking at that poor innkeeper the way a hungry freshman looks at a vending machine. Then there's that other fellow. The large African American gent? Never caught his name. Haven't seen much of him, either, come to think of it."

"Other fellow?" I asked, happy to change the subject from Lydia.

"Oh, he's here," Bill said, sounding a little surprised. "Sitting behind you, next to the window. Talking to our host, as a matter of fact."

I twisted around in my seat. That's when I spotted him.

He saw me simultaneously. His eyes smiled, crinkling slightly. His mouth didn't.

So what was Rubicon Jones doing here?

His friends called him Rube. Everyone else called him Mr. Jones. And most people, given a choice, stayed out of his way.

Rube looked like a linebacker. He dressed like a gansta rapper. And he lived like a Medici prince.

We'd crossed paths when I was working for the paper. The subject of the story—an addict fresh out of treatment—had been a longtime customer of a local, low-level dealer. Rumor was that the dealer's dealer got the stuff from Rube. Others claimed he was also running girls, guns, numbers—or a combination of all three.

No matter how hard I searched, I couldn't find a link. Turns out, there wasn't one.

But there was a secret.

Rubicon Jones wasn't a drug kingpin, a gun-runner, or even a thug. Rubicon Jones wrote romance novels. Some of the best-selling page-turners on the market. And the man was a machine. He was cranking them out and raking in some serious money.

As Victoria Hightower, he authored a series of Regency bodice rippers. As Marisa St. John, he penned contemporary, Afrocentric romances. As Prudence Penobscot, he wrote a wildly successful line of second-chance-at-love novels. And those were just the ones I knew about.

Even though Rube had moved his mom into his palatial new home in Georgetown, she firmly believed that family ties were lifelong bonds. So his money supported a network of relatives. And his reputation as a major league crime lord meant no one would ever mess with Mrs. Jones when she visited the old neighborhood.

Only Rube, his mother, and their accountant knew the truth.

It was a great story. So great I didn't write it.

It would have ruined the guy's life. And a week later, no one would have cared.

Besides, my beat was crime. And it's not like he was a crooked congressman or coke-snorting mayor.

I smiled and turned back to Bill and Emily just as Paul and Georgie walked over. She had on an electric-green sundress and sandals. He'd opted for summer linen—coral shirt and oatmeal slacks. And a sprig of something that looked like baby's breath in his lapel. Beach casual.

"Plenty of room over here," Emily said, sliding over.

"I'm Paul. Paul Gerrard. This is my bride, Georgie."

"We just got married this week," she said, breathlessly.

"Ah, yes, the honeymooners. Bill and Emily Prestwick," Bill said, gesturing toward himself and his wife with his lowball glass. Despite his loquaciousness, I noticed his glass still held a good two fingers of scotch. Maybe it wasn't his first?

"I'm Alex. I live across the street," I said, smiling.

"We were filling Alex in on who's who tonight," Bill said. "Oh, Ems, there's that musician," he added, snapping his fingers. "The one all the kids like."

"Johnny Jericho! I forgot about him. Sweet boy. Beautiful manners. Pulled out the chair for me at tea. I imagine he's playing a concert somewhere around here this evening. I hope it's indoors."

Johnny Jericho, also known as the prince of punk, was headlining at the Arena. His biggest danger tonight wasn't hail or lightning. It was throngs of screaming, head-banging fans. Which probably explained why he was staying out in the burbs.

"He'll be fine," I said. "The venue is definitely indoors. I wonder how he heard about this place?"

"Word of mouth. From a supermodel, no less," Bill said with a chuckle.

"Anastasia?" I asked, fearing I already knew the answer. My sister—who I called Annie and the world knew as the glamorous Anastasia—had booked in for exactly two nights a few weeks ago. Just long enough to broker a delicate detente between me and our mother and, apparently, recommend the place to a few of her more famous friends.

"Yup, that's the one. Word is she stayed here and loved it. You and I got in just in time, Ems. Pretty soon it's going to be all jet-setters and glitterati. They won't have room for the likes of us."

I noticed a quick look between Paul and Georgie.

"Are you Johnny Jericho fans?" I asked.

"No," Paul said flatly. "And if I'd known that he was staying here, I'd have booked us somewhere else. I want a nice relaxing honeymoon. Not a bunch of noisy rockers trashing the hotel."

"The wedding was a little stressful," Georgie explained. "We just wanted to get away for a few days."

Paul the pill. She could have done so much better.

"So who else is here?" I asked.

"There was a businessman checking in this afternoon," Georgie said. "I didn't actually meet him. But I think he's in insurance."

"If you haven't met him, how do you know he's in insurance?" Paul quizzed.

"Well, he was trying to sell a policy to the butler," said Georgie. "I heard him."

"That's awfully nervy of him," said Emily.

"Is he here tonight?" Bill surveyed the room, squinting.

"I haven't seen him since," Georgie said, shrugging her shoulders.

"Oh, and don't forget to tell her about the ghost, Ems," Bill prodded.

"The ghost?" I asked.

"Oh, Bill, that was a cat, and you know it. Really."

"I heard it. In the small hours of the morning. Just ask your friend in the big black dress . . . ," he said, pointing.

"Lydia?" I said.

"Her family built this house," he continued. "Originally, it was some kind of a ritzy boarding school. When the school closed, another wealthy family bought it. Later lost the mother in childbirth. Right here in this house. The baby, too. Anyway, according to the legend, every so often, when it's very dark and very quiet, you can still hear the infant's ghost crying for its mother. Damn sad."

"Superstitious claptrap," Emily said.

"I know what I heard, and it wasn't a cat," Bill insisted.

"Well, it wasn't a ghost, either," his wife huffed.

"From what I've learned, ghost stories are just excuses for old wiring and substandard plumbing," said Paul. "With what we're shelling out, that better not be the case here."

"Technically, my parents are shelling out, Paulie," said Georgie. "It's their credit card."

"Because your father insisted on claiming the reward points," Paul said, standing suddenly. "I'm getting a drink."

As he strode off, Harkins appeared silently to our left. I was beginning to suspect Harkins did everything silently.

"Caviar? Canapés?" he inquired politely.

"Have you heard about the Legend of the Ghost Baby?" Bill asked, helping himself to a canapé.

"Bill, honestly," his wife said, nabbing a cracker with caviar and cream.

I followed suit. Curiosity was definitely not killing my appetite. And this was getting good.

Harkins looked around quickly. "Without speaking out of turn, sir, there were a few tales of some rather . . . odd . . . noises over the past months, as the house was being readied," he relayed in a hushed voice. "While I don't believe I've heard it myself, some of the craftsmen described it as sounding rather like an infant. But I am quite certain there is a rational explanation. It is a very old house."

With that, he straightened and took his tray to another cluster of guests nearby.

Bill fixed Emily with a triumphant grin. "I told you. I was right! There is a ghost baby."

"There's a baby all right, and he's sitting right in front of me. How about topping off my champagne glass? Georgie, would you like a drink? The bubbly is marvelous."

"What the heck," Georgie said. "It's a party. Sure, I'll have a glass."

A peel of thunder shook the house. It felt like a cannon had gone off in the next room. The lights went out. And a string of lightning strikes strobed, giving our movements an eerie stop-action effect.

Everyone stopped talking at once. And the cheery music suddenly felt slightly malevolent.

"All right, everyone," Ian announced calmly as he and Harkins set about lighting the tapers. "Nothing to worry about. Just a little power interruption. We can chat and sip by candlelight. And the electric should be back on momentarily. In the meantime, I'm opening another bottle of champagne. And we certainly don't need electricity for that!"

The guests laughed in good-natured appreciation.

A few minutes later, as Emily, Georgie, and I chatted in the cheery glow, I felt a gentle tap on my shoulder. I turned. Ian smiled down at me. He'd removed the jacket and rolled up his shirtsleeves.

"Could I possibly beg your assistance?" he asked, sotto voce.

"Of course," I said, without thinking.

"Come with me."

When we'd passed into the candlelit lobby, he pulled open a drawer and retrieved a large flashlight.

"The truth is, I'm afraid, that we may have blown a fuse. My father can keep the party rolling with food and drink, but I need to check the fuse box in the cellar. And if you're up for it, I could use someone to hold the flashlight."

"Of course," I said. "Lead the way."

Was it weird that I was giddy he'd chosen me over Lydia? Of course, a trip to the basement would have turned her designer dress into a giant dust rag.

He opened a narrow side door. "Normally, I would hold this and let you proceed. But the stairs are rather steep, so it's probably better if I go first. Be sure to grab the handrail—it's good and solid."

Damn. Was he chivalrous or what? Except for the very real threat of falling down the stairs in heels and breaking my neck, this was seriously romantic.

Or maybe Trip was right and I just needed to get out more.

We descended downward slowly, carefully navigating the steep steps. They'd be tough going, even with lights. In the dark, they were downright treacherous.

"Does this happen often?" I asked, assaulting the banister with a death grip.

"I'm afraid I've had to do this a few times in the past few months. Though not since we opened. I really thought we'd gotten the electrical issues sorted."

"Maybe it was just the lightning. That last strike sounded pretty close." Poor Lucy was probably hiding under the couch.

"And it is a pretty old house," I said, remembering Bill Prestwick's ghost story. Phantoms couldn't flip switches, right?

"Here we go," Ian said, as we reached the landing. He turned, offering his hand with a flourish. "Mind your step."

Of course, my heart was doing that weird fluttery thing.

"Should be right arouuuund here," he said, shining the flashlight. "What on earth?"

In the dim glow, I didn't see it at first. Then Ian stepped back, focusing the light on the wall. The door to the fuse panel was hanging wide open.

"It shouldn't be like that. We keep it shut."

"Has anyone else been down here? Maintenance guys? Deliveries for the party?"

"We haven't had any workmen here since we opened. And all the deliveries for the party went into the kitchen. The only things I keep down here are some antiques that need reworking, a few bits and bobs for the inn, and our wine collection."

Ian leaned in and took a closer look. "Good Lord, someone's flipped all the breakers."

"Could a lightning strike have done that?"

"Doubtful. It would take out a circuit or two, but not everything. I had a new electrical system installed, along with a lot of new wiring and a state-of-the-art fuse box."

"Sabotage?"

"I don't want to use that word. But this didn't happen by accident. It doesn't make sense."

"Can you call an electrician?"

"No need," he said, handing me the flashlight. "I'll flip a few switches, and we should be good as new. What I don't understand is why the generator didn't engage. It doesn't provide full power, but at least we wouldn't be standing here in the dark."

Behind me, against the wall, I spied a chest freezer. Like the one my parents had in the garage for all of two weeks when I was a kid. Dad brought it home one day. He'd found it at a yard sale and swore we could save a bundle by stocking up on roasts and chops.

Mom hated it. I don't know which offended her more: the fact that it had been someone else's castoff or the idea of keeping food in the garage. She ditched it the first time Dad left on a business trip. He pretended not to notice.

"Hopefully the stuff in the freezer will keep," I said, shifting the light from one hand to the other.

"Oh, that's not set up yet. Hasn't even been plugged in," Ian said, absentmindedly, as he studied the diagram on the panel.

I reached out and put my palm on the freezer lid. Cold.

"So who would want to throw a monkey wrench into your party?" I asked. I could think of one person who might want everyone else to leave early. But I couldn't picture her clawing her way through a basement to make it happen.

"That's a puzzle. No one can get in from outside. And everyone here was at the party."

Not everyone, I thought, remembering Georgie's story about the odd insurance salesman. The reclusive actress could have done it too, but why? Unless she wasn't an actress at all. A vengeful ex who was handy with tools? Come to think of it, how much did I really know about Ian? I studied him in the glow of the flashlight.

Head tilted to one side, he squinted at the panel, his mouth set in a grim line. A lone lock of dark hair had slipped onto his forehead. In the close air of the basement, I could smell his cologne. Woodsy and masculine.

Why tell me the freezer wasn't working when it obviously was? Could Harkins have plugged it in without telling him? Maybe the mystery marauder had done it. But why plug in a freezer, then cut the power?

"Cross your fingers and say a prayer," Ian said, looking over at me. With that, he flipped several switches. The lights flashed on, and we heard a loud cheer from upstairs.

"Let there be light," I said.

"*Fiat lux*," he agreed, grinning. Then Ian leaned in slowly and kissed me.

That fluttery thing turned into a spark. For a split second, I thought we'd backed into the fuse box.

As we parted, Ian smiled broadly and took my hand, leading me back up the stairs. "I think you and I have earned ourselves a glass of champagne. Shall we?"

Chapter 2

For my money, the real trouble started the next morning when I walked into the kitchen and found a baby.

Just after sunrise and still bleary-eyed, I made straight for the stainless-steel coffeepot that lives on the counter near the sink. After Ian's cocktail party last night—and a little bubbly a deux—I'd returned home and gone from Cinderella-at-the-ball to sweatpants in record time. Then I'd stayed up 'til two finishing a freelance story that was due this morning. In a few hours, I was off to meet another editor about a temporary gig that would (hopefully) pay the bills for the next six weeks. I was drained but happy.

That's when I saw it. Resting on the kitchen table. Ensconced in one of those plastic car-seat things, like a mollusk in its shell. I flipped on the kitchen light, blinked hard, and looked again.

Still there.

"Holy crap!"

The butcher-block counter was solid. I touched the coffeepot, which was cold. I smelled chocolate and butter—the scent of freshly baked chocolate chip cookies. And I was surrounded by stainless-steel cooling racks holding dozens of the cookies my younger brother, Nick, had spent most of the night baking for a client. So this wasn't another weird stress dream.

I grabbed a cookie, then cautiously took a step closer. The downy blue blanket tucked around it— him?—moved rhythmically, rapidly, up and down. Between the blanket and his white knit cap, only the circle of a little pink face was exposed, along with two small, balled-up fists resting near his chin. Like a miniature pugilist. His eyes were closed tight.

I scanned the table. No note. No clues. Nada.

I looked under the table: nothing but Lucy's water dish.

Nearby, the kitchen door was locked and double-bolted.

I walked into the living room eating the cookie as I went. The front door was also locked and double-bolted.

I padded to Nick's door and knocked.

Silence.

I knocked harder.

"Go away!"

"You left something on the kitchen table."

"Yeah, cookies. Go away!"

I could hear the *click* of Lucy's nails on the hard-wood floors. Then rustling near the door. "Rowr? Rowwwwrrr! Rowr!"

"I meant the other thing," I called through the door. "The baby."

"Gotta sleep! Go away!"

"Rowr! Rowr!" Lucy chimed in, scratching at the door.

"Nick, this is an emergency!" I yelled, pounding on the door. "Get up! Now!"

"Is the house on fire?"

"Yes!"

Two minutes later, the three of us—Nick, Lucy, and I—stood in the kitchen eyeing our little intruder.

"So you really didn't put him there?" I asked quietly.

"Un-uh," he said, smoothing down a bad case of blond bedhead with his left hand. "I mean, the cookies are mine, but that's it."

Reflexively, I brushed the telltale crumbs off my pink bathrobe. "The doors are all locked and bolted from the inside. I checked."

"Anybody else have a key?" he asked.

Nick was living with me temporarily. After a sudden career change and relocation from Arizona by way of Vegas. Followed by an even more sudden engagement that had recently crashed and burned.

That was about the same time I'd launched my new freelance career. Which sounded a lot better on LinkedIn than saying I'd been accused of murder and fired.

We Vlodnacheks had kinda had a rough couple of months.

But, hey, we land on our feet. I was already getting steady assignments and making enough to keep the bills paid. Provided I didn't develop any expensive habits, like cable TV or eating out.

And Nick's new venture, a bakery he ran from our kitchen, was growing like kudzu. His hours were as bad as mine, but his clients were a lot quicker with the paychecks.

"Two keys: yours and mine," I answered. "You didn't happen to hand any out, did you? Mom? Annie? Brandon the Burnout? That cute girl at the Yogurt Hut?"

"No way. This is my sanctum sanctorum. My fortress of solitude. My . . ."

"Got it, no extra keys," I said. With any luck, his ex-business partner, Brandon, was at least two thousand miles away. And after what had happened with Gabby, Nick was still nursing a broken heart. Despite the best efforts of a large chunk of suburban DC's female population.

"What about Trip?" he asked, meaning my best friend and former news editor, Chase Wentworth Cabot III. "Trip" to his friends.

"Uh, no. And besides, Trip doesn't go around playing stork and dropping off babies in the middle of the night."

"Are you sure? 'Cause what I'm seeing would indicate otherwise."

"Trust me, you couldn't get him to deliver a newspaper at this hour, much less a baby."

"So where'd it come from?" Nick asked.

"Didn't Mom and Dad have that talk with you?"

"OK, we know where it came from. But how did it end up here?"

"He," I corrected. "He's wearing blue. That means he's a boy."

"You want to test that hypothesis?" Nick challenged.

"Not really," I admitted. "I'd rather figure out why he's here. And how he got in."

We'd had a break-in four weeks ago. My ex-boss. Head of the P.R. firm that wooed me away from a twelve-year stint at the newspaper, then fired me after three months. And tried to frame me for murder. Long story. But after the dust settled, I'd beefed up security and had the old doors, doorframes, and dead bolts professionally replaced with top-of-the-line gear. It was hideously expensive. And the insurance company only paid a fraction of the bill. But I slept great.

When I had the time.

"Man, you are the only person I know so tapped out that crooks are now breaking in to leave stuff," Nick said.

"Should we call the cops?" I asked.

"I don't think he's got a record. Plus, I'm pretty sure they don't make handcuffs that small."

"Yeah, but he'd have the world's cutest mug shot," I said, studying the tiny sleeping stranger, who suddenly puckered his mouth and made suckling motions. "Seriously, somebody's got to be missing him."

"Somebody actually thought he'd be better off here," Nick countered.

That stopped us both cold.

"So we should find out who he is and what's

going on before we return him," I said, thinking out loud.

"And in the meantime, we—and whoever left him here—will know he's safe," Nick said.

"If we don't get arrested for kidnapping. Why do I think that's the same thing you said when you guys found Lucy?"

Hearing her name, Lucy looked up expectantly. Nick grabbed a bone-shaped treat out of the big mason jar on the counter and offered it to her. She dropped to the floor and held it delicately between her two front paws, crunching contentedly.

"She'd been abandoned," he said softly, wiping his hand on his pajama bottoms. "She was foraging out of trash cans in an alley. This little guy was left warm and dry in a safe place."

"A locked kitchen that smells like cookies?"

"Works for me," he said, grabbing two tollhouses from a nearby rack and tossing one at me.

"He must be loved," I said between bites. "Not only did they beat out those dead bolts to get him in here, but that car seat looks expensive. And he's got that rosy, healthy, chubby-baby thing going."

"So if his family left him here, we're not kidnapping him," Nick reasoned. "We're just babysitting."

"Some babysitter I am. I'm eating cookies for breakfast."

Chapter 3

Since I had to go into DC to meet with an editor—and Nick didn't have to deliver the cookies until this afternoon—he got the first shift of baby-sitting duty.

Better him than me.

I was in bumper-to-bumper traffic when my cell rang. I pulled it out and checked the number: the very editor I was heading to meet. I prayed she wasn't canceling the assignment and hit TALK.

"Hello, this is Alex Vlodnachek."

"Alex, this is Maya. There's been a change of plans."

My heart sank. I really needed the money from this gig. Fixing and reinforcing the doors on the house had put a serious dent in my wallet. Which was one of the reasons I was still driving a grimy, blue station wagon with "slut" carved on one side and "bitch" on the other, along with a nice big X etched on the hood. Another long story.

As a freelancer, you never knew when your paychecks were going to show up. Or dry up. So I had a few months' worth of mortgage payments squirreled away in savings. And I wanted to keep it that way.

"We want you to meet Marty," she said finally.

"Meet Marty?"

"Hmm, yes," she said, already sounding bored with this conversation. Or distracted. Which, in a newsroom, could signal the presence of anything from a hangnail to a hand grenade. Or, more likely, someone had just arrived with food.

I went into salesmanship mode—an aspect of my new career that I truly hated. "Well, of course, I'd love to meet Marty," I said heartily, simultaneously wondering *Who's Marty?*

"Oh good, I'm glad I don't have to read you in on that part of it, then," she said, sounding vaguely relieved.

"So, should I meet you guys at the paper at nine?" I asked, fingers crossed.

"No, St. Edna's. And if you have any questions, just give me a call." And with that, she hung up.

OK, so instead of going to a newspaper conference room, I was heading to a hospital. One that was about ten miles in the opposite direction. But, hey, at least they hadn't canceled.

After an off-ramp detour, two gas stations, and three sets of directions, I was pretty sure I was, literally, on the right road. And when I picked up a trail of little blue HOSPITAL signs, I followed them like bread crumbs. As I passed a guy in a hospital gown tethered to an IV shuffling down the side of the road puffing on a cigarette, I figured I must be close.

And I was right. At the next big intersection, there it was: St. Edna's Medical Center. It was massive. Kinda like the health-care version of a shopping mall on steroids. Spread over acres with dozens of wings and parking lots everywhere.

I still had no idea who the mysterious Marty was, where we were supposed to meet—or whether Marty was a man or a woman. I didn't even know Marty's last name.

But, hey, if reporters had all the answers up front, we couldn't call it "news."

I reasoned that if there had been some kind of blood-soaked emergency, Marty wouldn't be taking a meeting. So I skipped the E.R. portico in favor of the hospital's main entrance and snagged a spot only a few rows from the front door. On the end of an aisle next to a small tree, "bitch" would be hidden by the black SUV to my right, but "slut" would be on full display.

Nick had volunteered a couple of times to cover the words (and the X) with a can of Krylon. At first, I was afraid it would make my already-ancient station wagon look like it should be up on blocks in someone's overgrown backyard. But with the glances and comments I was getting from potential clients, family members, and total strangers—not to mention my neighbors—I had to admit, I was warming to the idea. Even if he couldn't match the paint.

I figured whoever Marty was, I could have him (or her) paged to meet me in the cafeteria. So I strolled up to the front desk.

"Hi," I said to a twentysomething African American guy in navy scrubs who was manning several large phone panels and a computer terminal. "I need to have someone paged."

"In-patient, out-patient, or staff?" he asked, without even looking up.

Dr. Marty? Nurse Marty? Marty the comfort dog?

"In-patient," I said, hoping I'd guessed correctly. At one-in-three, my odds weren't great. But I had to start somewhere.

"Down the hallway to the right, take your first right—and follow the green line to the nurses' station. If the patient isn't critical or in ICU, they'll help you out."

"And where's the cafeteria?"

"Come back up here and keep going down that hallway," he said, pointing left. "Then just keep walking until you smell scorched breakfast potatoes and rubber eggs."

"Sounds delicious."

"It smells better than it tastes. Trust me, stick with the ice cream. Or the Jell-O."

"Will do. And thanks."

When I got to the nurses' station, it was bedlam. "Justin, call security!" a short, squat brunette nurse yelled from behind a centralized desk, cradling a phone in one hand. "The old guy got loose again!"

"Again? Are you sure?" a lanky blond nurse hollered as he sprinted down the hall and into one of the rooms. He reappeared seconds later, looking perplexed. "Hey, I told Dr. Bell last time we should chain him to the bed."

"He's supposed to walk," the first nurse said. "He's just not supposed to walk *out*."

"Don't tell me, tell Bell. He is gonna kill us. Did you page the cafeteria?"

"No, because this is my first shift, and I'm a damn candy striper," she said. "Of course I paged the cafeteria. Right after I checked the supply closet and the meditation garden. He's gone, Justin. G-O-N-E gone. And I'm on hold for security."

"That means he's getting liquor or smokes," Justin said, wiping sweat from his forehead. "Flip a coin."

"Uh, I hate to interrupt, but I'm here for Marty," I said softly to the female nurse.

"Hang on, Justin!" she yelled, slamming down the phone. "Do you have him?" she asked frantically. "Do you know where he is?"

"He isn't attached to an IV by any chance, is he?" I asked, flashing back to the lone figure ambling down the side of the road.

"Only for the last twenty-four hours. He kept getting dehydrated. And *someone* thought it might keep him near his room," she said, giving Justin some serious side-eye. "Where is he?"

"Uh, he's fine. He's just getting some air. But I can get him back to his room, if that would help."

"Honey, you have no idea how much that would help. The hours are lousy, and the pay is worse, but I need this job."

I knew the feeling.

Chapter 4

Marty hadn't moved much from where I'd seen him earlier. Now he was sitting on a tree stump, sucking on a cigarette for all he was worth. Still attached to the IV.

I had to pull a U-ey at the next light (legal) to get around to his side of the road. As I rolled up, he was stamping out one butt and firing up his next one. The man was a smokestack. I didn't know whether to be impressed by his tenacity or alarmed by the grip of his habit. With the next couple of mortgage payments in mind, I opted for friendly-but-neutral.

I pulled off on the shoulder next to him and threw open the passenger-side door. The one that said "bitch."

"Are you Marty?" I hollered over the traffic.

"Who . . . wants . . . to know?" he challenged, between drags. He punctuated the question with a wet, phlegmy cough.

"I'm Alex Vlodnachek," I yelled. "I was supposed to meet you at the hospital. Maya sent me."

He got up off the stump and shuffled over, IV rack in tow. When he made it to the car, he put one hand on the doorframe, leaning heavily.

"Vlod the Impaler? Hey, nice to meet you, kid. Really liked the piece you did on Coleman & Walters. I met Everett Coleman a couple of times. Total weasel." With that, he let loose with another long, wet cough. When he finished, he wiped his mouth with the back of his hand, popped the cigarette in, and took a long drag.

Cars whipped by, announcing their seventy-mile-an-hour recklessness with staccato horn blasts. Like I couldn't feel the Chevy rock every time one of them roared past.

"Look, why don't I give you a ride back to St. Edna's and we can talk. We could go to the cafeteria or sit out in the garden, if that's better."

"Don't get me started on the cafeteria. Is there a burger joint around here? We could hit the drive-thru. I'd kill for a bacon cheeseburger and some onion rings. And a large chocolate shake."

"Uh, it's not even ten a.m. And shouldn't you be getting back? They're kind of freaked out that you left."

"So the warden knows I went over the wall?"

"Uh, yeah."

"Which one of 'em was it?"

"Short, plump brunette and tall, skinny blond guy with a scraggly five o'clock shadow. Both in green scrubs."

"Arlene and Justin. Arlene's the worst. That

woman's got eyes in the back of her head. A cross between the Hydra and a German field marshal."

"They're worried they're gonna get fired."

"Oh hell, she's supporting three kids on that job," Marty said, finally climbing into the car. "Little one's gonna cost a fortune in orthodontia. Huge overbite. I've seen the pictures. Looks just like a beaver."

"So you want to go back?"

"For the time being." He grabbed the IV pole, chucked it into the backseat, and pulled the door shut with a heavy *thunk*. He rolled down the window, flicked out some ash, and took another long drag. "But you owe me a bacon cheeseburger."

"That's a deal." I figured my chances of smuggling food in were a lot better than his of getting out again. Especially with Arlene and Justin on the case.

"So what exactly are you in for?"

"Ten-thousand-mile tune-up. And I'm getting a new knee. Titanium joint. I keep asking what they'll give me for the old one as a trade-in." He laughed, and it turned into another cough.

I was thinking they should have been less worried about his knee and more concerned with his lungs. But I don't have an MD after my name.

"Look, kid, I don't want to be the bearer of bad news, but someone wrote something nasty on the side of your car."

"It's French for 'Uber.' So how are you connected to Aunt Margie?" I asked, checking the mirror and pulling smoothly back into traffic.

Aunt Margie was the advice columnist for the

Washington Sentinel. Whether you were a teenager with a crush on your mom's hot best friend or a grandma who secretly hated one of your grown kids, everybody wanted commonsense coaching from Aunt Margie. From her tone and the thumbnail photo that ran alongside her column, I'd always pictured her as a classic screen dame straight out of a 1940s screwball comedy—a cross between Auntie Mame, Eve Arden, and Rosalind Russell. And DC could be divided into two camps: those who admitted to reading Aunt Margie every morning, and those who were lying.

So imagine my surprise when I'd gotten a phone call last week from one of the *Sentinel*'s editors informing me that Aunt Margie was going on a six-week holiday and asking if I wanted the gig.

At the time, I felt like I was on the ledge of a forty-story building looking straight down. Aunt Margie was leaving some pretty big stilettos to fill. Even temporarily.

As a freelancer, though, I'd learned you never say "no" right away. Not if you want to make the mortgage.

And the money was good. Obscenely good. But who was I to be giving advice? My life was a mess. From one month to the next, I didn't know if I could even pay my bills. And except for weekly lectures, my own mother wasn't speaking to me.

I didn't know which would be worse: if no one took me seriously or if someone actually did.

But Aunt Margie herself offered me a lifeline. Or, more accurately, training wheels. Maya informed me that I would select and answer the letters, but before they were published, Aunt Margie would read and edit my answers. Heavily, if necessary. Because, according to Maya, she wanted her responses to reflect "that sparkling perspective that was uniquely Aunt Margie."

I'd always read her column. But the past week I'd read little else. The *Sentinel*'s digital archives went back about twenty years. I didn't just scan every Aunt Margie column I could get my hands on—I studied them. Tore them apart. Dissected them—not just for word choice, cadence, and tone—but to see exactly how her mind worked. Even under that microscope, Aunt Margie didn't disappoint. The woman was a marvel. Smart, sassy, succinct, sometimes sarcastic—and so very practical.

I'd discovered her in elementary school, right alongside the comics. And while I never actually wrote in, she helped me navigate junior high and high school. Not to mention my first newspaper job. Which, ironically, was a lot like high school.

"I'm Aunt Margie."

"Huh?" Red taillights flashed ahead of me, and I slammed on the brakes. We both lurched forward hard. "I'm sorry—you're what?"

"Hey, nobody wants to get their personal advice from a middle-aged guy with two divorces under his belt, ink stains on his cuffs, and a taste for the good single-malt he can't afford. So 'Marty' became 'Margie.' And poof, here we are thirty years later."

My head was spinning. It might have been fumes from the stop-and-go traffic. It could have been the fog of cigarette smoke. Or the fact that one of the cherished girl-power icons of my young adulthood was sitting in my passenger seat sporting an overgrowth of ear hair, an open-backed hospital gown over khakis, and black Crocks with socks.

Margie wasn't a glamorous, well-preserved modern-day incarnation of Eve Arden or Rosalind Russell. Marty looked like a gnome. Short with sparse, wispy white hair, a beachball-sized belly, and a cancer stick continuously clutched in his right hand.

It was like finding out that Santa wasn't real. If you'd believed in Santa for twenty-plus years. And consulted him regularly for advice.

"And I gotta say, I discovered I have a knack for it," he said. "Margie's a good old broad. The more I got to know her, the better the writing got."

"But you're Margie?" I said slowly, not totally comprehending. Maybe Margie was a real person— a friend, a neighbor, his actual aunt—and he just polished up the prose?

"Look, kid, what you've got to understand is that Margie is an attitude. A character. A way of looking at the world. None of us is really Margie. We just let her take over our brains for a little while. And let me tell you, the old gal's good people. She won't let you down."

I was beginning to wonder if his knee was the only thing Marty's doctors were evaluating. Luckily, we were back at St. Edna's. And I was even more relieved than the first time I'd found the place.

Chapter 5

When I pulled into my driveway three hours later, there was a white county van at the curb. I could hear Nick shouting from inside the house.

The baby!

Had one of the neighbors called social services? Were they taking the little guy before we could find out who he was or where he was from? What if we couldn't get him home to his family?

This was my fault! I should have stayed home. I never should have saddled Nick with this alone. What was I thinking?

I ran up the walk, nearly colliding with a chubby guy with heavily gelled dark hair and thick, black-framed glasses lugging a big black-leather shoulder tote.

"You're a blackmailing, bribe-taking little roach!" Nick hollered, running down the walkway in bare feet, waving a large wooden spoon.

The guy turned, tapped his clipboard, and smiled.

"I hope you can calm him down. I'd hate to add assault charges to what he's already facing."

"This isn't over, Simmons!" Nick shouted from behind me.

For his part, Simmons skipped the sidewalk and waddled quickly down the lawn. I looked at the van. Was our little guy in there?

"The baby!" I hissed. "Nick—where's the baby?"

"He's in my room. He's fine."

After Simmons jumped in and hit the door locks, he rolled down the window. "Be seeing you soon, Mr. Vlodnachek," he called in a thin, clear voice. "And I hope you have a license for that mutt. Because I'll be contacting animal control."

Nick broke and ran toward the van. "I'll kill you, you slimy little toad! I will boil that fat little body in oil and serve you on toast!"

Simmons apparently didn't trust that Nick wouldn't be able to pry him out of the van with that spoon. He gunned the engine and sped off down the street.

On the walkway, Lucy sat back on her haunches and howled.

"Hey, come on, you little goofball," Nick said, strolling back up the lawn. "Knock it off."

Instead, Lucy arched her back and took it up half an octave. And a few more decibels. "Ra-ra-ra-ra-aaahh-*oooooo*."

Nick kneeled, ruffling the fur on the top of her head. "It's OK. Calm down. It's ooooo-kay, baby." To me he said, "She's finding her inner wolf. We've been watching the Nature Channel online."

"That explains a lot. OK, if County Guy wasn't here for the baby, what was he here for?"

"Me."

"What are you talking about?"

"The bakery. He shut me down."

"Noooo!"

"Yup," he said, grimacing.

"Why?"

"Simmons is from the health department. I don't have a license, so they closed the kitchen. I'm out of business."

"Jeez, Nick, I'm really sorry. I had no idea you needed a license. I feel awful."

"It's not your fault. I knew. I just kept putting it off until I had a little more money. Besides, I made sure everything was super clean. I mean, if a client gets sick, that's not exactly good for business. But I was just getting started, and I wasn't making much, so I thought I had a little more time."

"What happened?"

"One of my competitors ratted me out."

"Which one?"

"Don't know yet. Simmons wouldn't say. But I'll find out. Then I'm going to have some fun."

"Boil him in oil and serve him on toast?"

"I was up until four a.m. baking. I downloaded a few *Game of Thrones* episodes to stay awake. I think it kinda seeped into my subconscious."

"I tried that with Univision. Flipped it on while I slept, hoping my brain would absorb a little more Español."

"Did it work?"

"Nein. Animal control?"

"Lucy's fully licensed and up-to-date on all her shots. He's just trying to throw his weight around."

Three guys on speed bikes, clad in helmets and racing togs, whizzed down the block. One of them lifted a hand in a wave.

Automatically I waved back.

"Neighbors?" Nick asked.

"Never seen them before," I admitted.

"Empty threats or no, we'd better keep Lucy on the leash when she's out of the backyard for the next few weeks," I said. "Just to be safe."

"Yeah, that's probably smart," he said, giving the pup a full-on tummy scratch. She thumped her tail in delight.

"So what happens to the stuff you've already baked?" I said, remembering the chocolate chip cookies that had populated the kitchen earlier this morning. "Did he confiscate it?"

"He threatened to, but he's not legally allowed. I'm also not allowed to sell any of it."

"So I have a kitchen full of limbo cookies?"

"Yup. Eat 'em or freeze 'em. Doesn't matter to me. Worst part is, if I can't fill this order, I have to give back the deposit. Which I already spent on supplies. And I'm gonna lose what could have been a really good client."

"And by 'good' you mean . . ."

"They eat a lot of cookies, and their checks don't bounce," Nick said.

"OK, I can only guarantee one out of two."

"So I've noticed."

"Hey, what about Ian?" I said, snapping my fingers. "I can't sell them to him. I don't know how, but that little weasel Simmons is wired. What's worse, my next order is actually for Ian," he said, rubbing his forehead. "Damn!"

"No, I mean, what if you set up shop temporarily in Ian's kitchen? He's running a B&B, so the kitchen's fully licensed. Plus, half his business these days depends on booking afternoon teas and fancy luncheons, which means he really needs you. And you know he can't bake."

We'd sampled Ian's attempts at pastry in the not-so-distant past. Let's just say that Lucy, who still raids the occasional trash can, wouldn't touch the stuff.

"I could sweeten the deal," Nick said, gaining momentum. "Give him a discount for the use of his space."

"There you go," I said. "And it's only temporary. Just while you're getting your kitchen certified."

"If Simmons has his way, that'll never happen," Nick said, shaking his head. "You should see the list he gave me."

"Hey, if there's anything I learned in newspapers, it's to take things one crisis at a time. First, you get around the police barricade. Then you worry about what you're going to say to the bomb squad."

"What did you say to the bomb squad?"

"Asked them about the detection dogs. Find the right topic and people talk—they can't help it."

"Well, I'm supposed to deliver the cookies this afternoon, but the actual event isn't 'til lunch tomorrow. If Ian says yes and I can reschedule the delivery, I might still be able to do this."

"You do realize that while you're across the street

baking cookies, I'll be over here putting a dent in the last batch?" I said.

"Not to mention tending to the needs of little James Bond Vlodnachek. I call him J.B."

"For real?"

"I changed his diaper first. I get to name him," Nick said. "And he deserves something cool. It came down to that or Idris Elba Vlodnachek. Besides, if he's going to be living here, we have to call him something."

The guy had a point.

"OK, well, while you go talk to Ian, I'll look after J.B." I said. "After that, we hit the store for supplies. We're going to need a lot more milk."

"For the baby?" Nick asked.

"Him too."

Chapter 6

Twenty minutes later, Nick came through the door with a grin on his face and a bundle of pink mini roses in one hand.

"From your admirer across the street," he said with a flourish and a bow.

"Can I take that as a yes to you bogarting his kitchen?" I asked, taking the bouquet and heading toward the kitchen in search of a vase.

"Hey, as far as he's concerned, I can move in," Nick said, trailing behind me. "But I think the discount I offered him on his orders may have had something to do with it. Plus the fact that his B&B guests are going to smell bread, cakes, and cookies the minute they walk through the door. Your buddy Ian even offered to let me order ingredients through his supplier, as long as I reimburse him. And he gets stuff for a lot less than I've been paying at the warehouse store. I've got to do some math, but even after giving him a cut on the price, I'm going to be clearing more money."

"That's fantastic!"

"His kitchen's got everything. Man, this is going to make it so much easier. And the best part is Simmons and my mystery competitor are gonna plotz. But the place has already been inspected and licensed, so there's not a damn thing they can do."

"At least this buys us some time to get this place retrofitted," I said, filling a big jelly jar with water and settling the flowers in it.

"Yeah, I'm getting the second third of the emu money soon. I figure that should cover most of what I'll need. If you don't mind someone hacking up your kitchen."

Part of the reason Nick moved in: He'd divested himself of his first business. And his first fiancée. Leaving the business had been the easy bit.

It was an emu ranch in the middle of the Arizona desert. Going in, he knew it would be hard work. But he'd enjoyed it—and the emus.

The secret pot patch had been a surprise.

Once Nick found out what his burnout business partner had been up to, he'd destroyed the existing crops, planted some garden-variety vegetables, and arranged to sell the place—lock, stock, and emus— to a local university. They were turning it into a green research station and studying the effects of emu dung as a soil additive. Turned out the stuff was magic as a fertilizer. As his partner had discovered.

While the college reps offered the most for the ranch, they wanted to pay for it in three installments. But they'd also promised to give the emus a comfortable home for life. Nick accepted and made them put that last part in writing.

Naïve he wasn't.

Now he was camped out here, rebuilding his professional life. And recovering from Hurricane Gabrielle. And that last part was gonna be a lot harder.

Suddenly, a high-pitched wailing cut the air. And it was joined by a plaintive howl.

"Oh jeez," I said, sprinting for the living room. J.B. was settled in his carrier on the living room table. His mouth was open wide, his eyes were scrunched shut, and his face was a deep shade of pink.

Lucy, inconsolable, turned his sorrowful solo into a duet.

I reached for the baby, thinking human contact would reassure him. No dice. If anything, the shrieking went up half an octave. And his face turned crimson.

I bounced him gently on my hip. "Hey, little J.B. Are you having a good day? Later we'll go for a nice walk with Lucy and Uncle Nick. Won't that be fun? Won't that be fun?"

Apparently, J.B. did not think that would be fun. J.B. had had it with all of us. He shook his tiny fists, opened his sweet little bow mouth even wider, and screamed until his whole body quaked. I didn't see how so much rage could fit into such a tiny body.

"Try singing to him," Nick suggested.

"Did that work when you changed his diaper?"

"No, he kinda dozed through that. I'd just fed him, and he could barely keep his eyes open."

"What did you feed him?" I hollered over the din. Whatever it was, I was willing to give him more of it now. By the gallon, if necessary. "Row, row, row your boat," I tried gently.

"His mom—or whoever—left a couple of bottles of milk in his carrier. After two of those, he slept like—well—a baby."

"Got any more of that stuff?" I said. "Gently down the streeeeam . . ."

"Nooo," he hollered over the screaming. "There were only two bottles and two diapers. We're out of both."

"I'm pret-ty sure you're only sup-posed to give them one at a time," I sang, loudly.

"Well, J.B. asked for seconds."

"Uh, how exactly did he do that?" I hollered at Nick, while bounce, bounce, bouncing the screeching bundle on my hip. J.B.'s lung power was truly impressive. He didn't even stop to breathe.

"He screamed the minute I took the empty bottle out of his mouth and didn't stop until I popped another one in there. Reminded me a little of Uncle Ernie."

"Nah, Ernie's a happy drunk. C'mon, Captain J.B., row, row, row your boat, gently down that stream . . ." I sang, trying to sound cheerful and kid-friendly.

J.B. wasn't having it. And the pup threw back her head and let out a bloodcurdling howl.

"We need to do some-thing," I sang to the tune of "Row, Row, Row Your Boat." "This is get-ting worse. It sounds like we're mur-der-ing ba-bies and pup-pies. Some-one will call the cops."

"OK, we split 'em up," Nick said. "You take Lucy and hit the grocery store for diapers and formula.

I'll stay here with J.B. until you get back. Then I have to go to Ian's for the rest of the day and bake. Fair?"

"Fair," I said, handing off the squalling, squirming bundle of fury.

For his part, J.B. didn't miss a beat. At least he was an equal opportunity screamer.

"Just the grocery store," Nick shouted over the din. "No fair making extra stops."

"I promise nothing," I replied, grabbing my purse and Lucy's leash. "And get out of my head."

Chapter 7

Even after I pulled into the grocery store parking lot, I swore I could still hear J.B. crying.

On the plus side, I was pretty sure those high-pitched screams had liquified what was left of my earwax. And maybe an eardrum.

I gave Lucy a quick walk through the grass island on the far side of the lot for a last-minute break before we headed into the store. Nevilleson's was one of the few markets left that wasn't part of a chain. And it had a "don't ask, don't tell" policy on emotional support dogs. As long as your pup was well-behaved and your credit card cleared, Nevilleson's didn't care.

"Remember, you've got to be a good little girl," I said to her as we hustled inside.

Lucy looked up at me, puzzled. Like didn't I realize that our little visitor had suddenly lowered the yardstick for good behavior? Substantially.

"Yeah, but J.B. doesn't get to go for fun car rides and groceries," I explained to her. "Because he's not as well-mannered as you are."

I had to admit, the thought of spending the rest of the afternoon with a screaming J.B. had me seriously considering absconding to a nice quiet coffee shop for a few hours. One with a dog-friendly patio. I felt for Nick. By now, he'd probably lost most of his hearing.

I grabbed a cart and hit the dairy aisle. I reached for a half gallon of 2 percent, reconsidered, and grabbed a gallon jug. "Now we look for diapers," I said to Lucy.

I rounded the corner and skidded to a stop. Diapers. An entire aisle of diapers. There must have been ten different brands. And all of those brands had different sizes and types. Daytime diapers. Nighttime diapers. Diapers for travel. Diapers for active babies. Diapers for babies with sensitive skin. Diapers with aloe. Clothlike diapers. Scented diapers. Diapers with cartoon characters.

It was worse than the tampon aisle.

After reading the backs of a dozen different packages, I gave up and dialed Nick. "How much does he weigh?" I shouted into the phone.

"Shhhhh!" he said. "It's your silly aunt Alex. Yes, it is! Yes, it is!"

"Oh my God, did he stop crying?" I was amazed. And a little ashamed.

"Yes, he did. Who's a good boy? Who's a good boy?"

"OK, so what does the good boy weigh?" I asked.

"Should I ask him or just check his driver's license?"

"Apparently, they size diapers by weight," I told him. "No weight, no diapers."

"You don't have to ask me twice. Do you have a bathroom scale?"

"I don't even have a postal scale." With a super-model for a sister, I'd learned early that letting a scale rule your day was no way to enjoy life. And Annie was big on enjoying life.

"Hang on," Nick said, and I heard some shuffling on the other end of the phone. "Let's see. J.B., come to Uncle Nick. Up you go. And down. And up. And down. Now let's sit you down again. That's my man. OK, just an estimate. but I'd say he feels like about twelve pounds."

"Were you doing lifts?"

"Yeah. And he's a lot lighter than the hand weights I've been using at the gym."

"How did you calm him down? Did the singing work?"

"Not exactly."

"OK, as the person who has to sit with him this afternoon, how exactly?"

"I fed him," Nick said.

"You said we didn't have any bottles left."

"We didn't. I had to get creative."

"How creative?"

"I read somewhere that breast milk tastes a lot like vanilla, so . . ."

"Not my fro-yo?!"

"Trust me, it was for a good cause. J.B. is smiling at me right now."

"That's just gas," I replied. "And if it's not now, it will be in fifteen minutes."

"When you're getting bottles, make sure you get

the ones that are BPA-free. Otherwise it could mess up his hormonal development."

"He has hormonal development?"

"According to WebMD. And don't even get me started on diaper rash. If you ever want to see pix that will keep you up nights . . ."

"Does it say anything about how to prevent it?"

"Cornstarch. And zinc oxide cream, if he does get it."

"Hang on, let me write this all down." I remembered his earlier comment and added frozen yogurt to the list. When I looked up, Lucy was sniffing giant cartons of formula across the aisle. "OK, what about the diapers? They've got about a zillion different kinds. Were there any labels on the ones he was wearing—anything that would give us any hints at all?"

"Nada," Nick said.

"What about the tabs—any words or animals or cartoons? Seriously, I'm looking at the Great Wall of Pampers here."

"OK, lemme check. I'm gonna have to wash up after, so I'll have to call you back."

While Nick combed through the trash for clues—or whatever—I scoped out shelves filled with formula. It was almost as bad as the diapers. A dozen different kinds. Formula made with milk, goat milk, soy milk, and rice. Fortified with iron. Fortified with calcium. Liquid. Powdered. Supplemental for breast-feeding. Supplemental for solid food.

How did moms navigate this stuff? I felt like I was taking the final exam for a class I'd never attended.

J.B. was doomed. My brother was at home feeding him ice cream. And I was standing in the baby aisle in a stupor. Whoever J.B.'s mom was, she'd definitely picked the wrong house.

That's when it hit me. Maybe she *had* broken into the wrong home. Was it possible she'd intended to leave J.B. with one of the neighbors—someone who knew him—instead of us?

I knew the Clancys down the block. But not whether they had a friend or relative with a baby and a set of lock picks.

There was crotchety Mr. Rasmussen behind me. But I couldn't picture anyone asking him to care for a goldfish, let alone a child.

Ian lived catty-corner across the street. But no way anyone could have mistaken my tiny bungalow for his elegant Victorian B&B.

And with a couple of dead bolts on every one of my doors, J.B.'s mother had to have been really motivated. Or truly desperate.

The phone in my hand rang. Nick. "Tell me you got something."

"You mean, besides the obvious," he said.

"You're getting extra karma points for this one."

"Actually, it wasn't that bad. I don't know what everyone always complains about. It's like little rabbit pellets. And it hardly smells at all. Anyway, the diaper had sticky tabs with little blue cartoon pandas on them. And there seems to be some thicker padding in the front, not just between the legs and in the back."

I scanned the shelves. Daytime diapers. For boys. Featuring Peter the Panda. Bingo!

"Got it. And you're relatively solid on the twelve-pound thing?"

"Plus or minus a few pounds, yeah. Which reminds me, I've got to get to the gym tomorrow. Oh, and don't forget the wipes. And according to the mommy blogs, we're gonna need a lot of them. Preferably something hypoallergenic."

I whirled around and faced the other side of the aisle. Lucy had curled up on the bottom shelf of the shopping cart, and her eyelids were getting heavy. Hosting our new little guest was stressful for all of us. And I'm guessing the visit from Simmons was no picnic, either.

"Any idea what kind of formula J.B.'s mom used? 'Cause I gotta tell you, it's like Baskin-Robbins out here."

"Not a clue," Nick said. "But the bottles are plastic. And they say 'Gro-Ryt' on the side. I think we should get glass, though. It'll limit his exposure to phthalates and BPA, plus it's dishwasher safe."

"More WebMD?" I asked.

"BabyMama.com," Nick said.

At this rate, I figured he'd be writing his own blog by the end of the week.

Chapter 8

I opened my front door cautiously. Lucy and I looked at each other.

Silence.

The pup trotted in, and I followed, juggling two economy-sized packages of disposable diapers. They were too big even for grocery bags. And I had three more in the car. The damned things cost a fortune. I didn't know how many we were gonna need. But if J.B.'s appetite was any indication, I wanted to be prepared.

Nick was sacked out on the couch. Apparently, J.B. had that effect on people. Once the crying stopped, everyone around him was so weary, they collapsed.

Including J.B. himself.

He was snoozing in his carrier. Only this time it was settled on the low living room table. I prayed he'd sleep until dinner. Or breakfast.

Nick had done his bit. So I unclipped Lucy's

leash. She dashed into the kitchen, and I heard her lapping from her water bowl in the kitchen.

Fifteen minutes later, I'd stocked my linen closet with diapers and my pantry with formula. Hopefully in a variety that our little guest would enjoy.

I'd also cornered the market on glass baby bottles and BPA-free nipples. Although I had absolutely no idea what I was supposed to do with them.

Was it like jeans, where you could wear them a few times before you washed them? I reasoned it was more like wineglasses: wash them first, just to get out any residual dust that might ruin the flavor of your drink. I suspected J.B. might appreciate that. I loaded up the dishwasher, murmured a silent prayer, and hit START.

And wasn't there something about boiling baby bottles—either with or without the formula, then cooling them, so that the meal was sterile? Hopefully, Nick had the 4-1-1 on that part, too.

"Puppies are a lot easier," I said to Lucy, who rotated her ears as she looked up at me with big, black eyes. "Even with scooping the poop."

Minus a few doggie no-nos, like chocolate and onions, Lucy ate pretty much what we did. With some good, nutritional puppy food as a base. Sunday morning scrambled eggs. One-third of any bacon that came into the house. And her all-time favorite: hamburgers. Preferably with Nick grilling.

Next, I grabbed the coffeemaker and made a fresh pot. With J.B. in residence, we were gonna need some extra caffeine.

Nick strolled into the kitchen, yawning and stretching. "I thought I smelled coffee."

"Five more minutes and you would have smelled grilled cheese."

"I'll go back to sleep."

"So how bad was it? And, more important, what tips do you have for me?"

"Keep his tummy full, and he'll sleep through anything."

"Maybe that's why his mother left him here. She couldn't afford the food bills."

"No lie," Nick said, grabbing a frying pan and throwing it onto the stove. I handed him the bread.

"Any chance she was just overwhelmed?" I asked. Or maybe that was simply my personal take on the whole baby thing.

"I dunno. With J.B., it's almost like he knows he's supposed to be somewhere else. With someone else."

"So he thinks we've kidnapped him, and he's trying to alert the proper authorities?"

"OK, not exactly. But, like, babies bond with their parents. Especially their moms. They know their voice and their smell and their touch. It's comforting. Suddenly, he wakes up, and the only person who ever loved him is gone. And to babies, love is survival. I mean, this is the person who does everything for you. 'Cause you can't do it yourself."

"So he recognizes that the person who loves him and feeds him and changes his diapers is gone. And in her place . . ."

"Two of the original three stooges," Nick said,

dropping some butter into the pan and flipping on the burner.

"Yikes," I said. "Kinda puts the scream-fest into perspective."

"Imagine if you woke up in a strange house and all the familiar faces were gone."

"If they were feeding me and doing my laundry, I might be OK with it. Kinda like a spa vacation."

"We've got to reunite him with his mom," Nick said, tossing bread in the pan, along with a few slices of cheese and a couple of generous dollops of salsa. "You're a reporter. How do we do that?"

I'd been thinking of almost nothing else since we'd found the little guy this morning. Was it only this morning? It seemed like a week ago.

"Well, for starters, it would help to know if any young moms are missing. I could talk to one of the police flacks and see what I can learn. But unless we want them rolling up to confiscate little J.B., I'm gonna have to keep it fairly generic. Like I'm working on a story on missing women in general. Or something related to postpartum depression. But if you're OK with it, I'd also like to talk to Trip. We can level with him. And if anyone's gone missing in the last few days, he may have heard something. At the very least, he can keep an ear out."

"Yeah, that sounds good," Nick said, as he flipped the sandwiches.

"I was thinking about it in the store. What if she just got the wrong house?"

"You mean like the time Santa left me that doll with long red hair, so I gave it a crew cut?"

"No, that was you opening the wrong present. The gift tag said 'Alex.'"

"I was three. I couldn't read yet. But you mean, like, one of the neighbors could have been the real target?"

"Yeah, although I don't know who. I hate to admit it, but until Lucy moved in, I'd never even met most of my neighbors."

"Yeah, the little pup is really a social butterfly. Aren't you?" he said to Lucy, whose eyes were riveted on the sizzling frying pan. "So, should we start taking J.B. for walks? See if anyone says anything?"

"You mean besides, 'Gee, I didn't realize you were pregnant—who's the unlucky father?'"

Nick slid the sandwiches onto plates. Then he threw some leftover meat loaf into the pan, followed by a little more butter and a few dashes of various spices.

"Just how hungry are you?" I asked, incredulous.

"This one's for Lucy. She needs some good protein."

"Gotcha. So did those websites you cruised give you any ideas on J.B.'s age? I mean, if we're trying to track backward, it would help to know when he was born."

"You know who'd know?"

"No."

"C'mon, Mom had four kids," he said, pulling out a paper plate and neatly emptying the contents of the pan onto it. "She has to know the difference between a two-month-old and a four-month-old."

He carefully placed the plate on the floor next to our table and dropped the frying pan into the sink.

Lucy was trembling. And the look in her eyes was primal. Like a wolf cub. But she waited until Nick backed off before she pounced.

He grabbed his plate and slid into the chair across from me. "Plus, Mom probably won't turn us in to the cops."

"Don't count on it. Besides, it's been a few decades since her baby was a baby. Physically, anyway."

"You're just afraid she's going to blame all this on you," he said, taking a bite of his sandwich.

"I am, and she will," I said, slicing my sandwich crossways. "Let's use the resources we've got handy first. If we have to call her later . . ."

"Coward."

"Definitely."

Chapter 9

Nick left for Ian's just after lunch. Lucy tried to go with him.

I totally sympathized.

Before he left, I handed him a big glass mason jar. Filled with tollhouse cookies, it had a lopsided red bow on top.

"Is this for snack time, so I can make friends with the other kids?"

"That's a present for Ian. To say 'thank you' for the flowers. And the party invitation."

"'Nuff said."

J.B. was sleeping soundly in his carrier on top of the living room table. I'd even adjusted the blinds so the sun wouldn't hit his face and wake him.

I sat on the sofa next to him, leafing through the notes I'd taken during my meeting with Marty. But I was bracing, just waiting for the alarm to go off. Like in elementary school when they announced fire drill day.

Finally, I couldn't take the silence any longer. I grabbed the phone and dialed Trip.

"Trip Cabot, editor extraordinaire."

"Have you got a minute? It's kind of an odd story."

"Is it weird that I don't even have to ask who this is?"

"You've got caller ID."

"Yeah, but with you I never need it. Besides, I'm not sure I should be speaking to you. Rumor has it you're working for the competition."

Aunt Margie's home paper was the *Washington Sentinel*—the big competitor of my old newspaper, the *Washington Tribune.* Trip hadn't stopped teasing me about it since I took the assignment. He was also the one who'd convinced me I'd be crazy not to do it.

"I promise this has nothing to do with newspapers. What do you know about babies?"

"As much as any happily single gay man living in DC and working eighteen-hour days. That is to say, nothing. Why? Oh God, you're not pregnant, are you?" he whispered.

"Not unless it's the Second Coming." Our running joke was that my love life had been in a bit of a drought. It might have something to do with my recently having been accused of murder and threatened with prison. Or it could be me.

"OK, this stays strictly between us. Someone left a baby at my house."

"You mean, like, they forgot and left it behind after a raucous party?"

"No, I mean like 'broke in in the middle of the night and put him in his carrier on my kitchen table.'"

"Damn. So much for your improved security."

"I know. I feel like calling the locksmith and demanding a refund. Look, has anybody gone missing lately? Someone who might have had a baby within the last six months? Or have any babies been kidnapped?"

"I can keep an ear open. The sad thing is, if the mom is a teenager or living on the street, her disappearance might not have even been reported."

"This doesn't feel like that, somehow," I said, struggling to put what I was sensing into words. "Out in the middle of the burbs? Beating out a couple of dead bolts? And mine isn't exactly the biggest, most expensive house on the block."

"Which is what you'd want, if you were going to play stork with your own baby," he said quietly. "Although, from the outside, your place looks pretty idyllic."

"What do you mean?"

"Two young up-and-comers, a cute puppy, a nice neighborhood," he said.

We both digested that one.

"So you think the mama knows you?" he asked.

"I don't know. Here's what bugs me. I was up until after two working on a story. Nick was in the kitchen baking until four a.m. But when I got up at six, the baby was already there. Asleep in the kitchen, with all the doors locked. That's a pretty small window of time for someone to just get lucky."

"So you think someone was watching you guys?"

"I think they had to be. Plus a car on the street for that long, especially at that hour, would draw attention. At least, I hope it would."

"OK, I've waited as long as I could. What happened with Mr. Cute at the little soirée last night? Spill!"

"We split a bottle of champagne in the kitchen after checking out his fuse box."

"Is that what the kids are calling it these days?"

"No, really, the power went out. I helped—well, I held the flashlight—while he fixed it. Then we went into the kitchen, and he opened a bottle of champagne."

"Very promising start."

"And we kissed."

"Way to bury the lede, Red. So Uncle Trip was right to push you out of the nest?"

"Oh yeah. Although, it would have been a lot better if Lydia Stewart hadn't been popping in every couple of minutes. The woman is relentless. When she couldn't get him out of the kitchen, she told everyone the party had moved, and they all piled in. When I left, Ian was making scrambled eggs for the stragglers."

"Well, technically, I guess they are his paying guests. Sounds like it would have been rude to shoo them away. What you two need is an excursion off-site."

"That's exactly what Ian said when he walked me to the door."

"His door or yours?" he inquired pointedly.

"His front door," I said firmly. "Ian wanted to walk me home. But Harkins had disappeared, and he was afraid to leave a crowd of tipsy guests in the kitchen unsupervised."

"Sounds like New Year's Eve at the Farm," Trip said, referring to the 500-acre estate that was his childhood home. "So where is he taking you?"

"We haven't even had time to compare schedules. I was out of here first thing this morning for the Aunt Margie thing. And now we're taking care of a baby. And trying to find his parents. I hate to say it, but Ian's going to have to take a backseat for a few days."

"From what you've said, I'm guessing the parents either know you or they live near you," Trip concluded. "Any chance the baby could be Nick's? From his life in Arizona?"

Oddly, that thought had never occurred to me. I looked over at the sleeping bundle. Nick did seem to be better with him than I was. But that didn't mean anything. Did it?

"I don't know. And, to be fair, I've never actually seen the little guy with his eyes open."

"He's been there all day."

"Yeah, and he's always sleeping or crying. Either way, eyes shut tight. I couldn't even tell you what color they are. But if he's Nick's or if he belongs to someone we know, why the drop and run? Wouldn't you at least leave a note? Or knock on the door and say, 'Hey, I need someone to watch J.B. for a few hours—can you help me out?'"

"J.B.?"

"James Bond Vlodnachek. Nick's idea."

"OK, we've got to get that kid back to his mom quick, before you two scar him for life."

"You have no idea."

Chapter 10

I refilled my coffee cup, dumped in some milk, then grabbed a plate and five of Nick's chocolate chip cookies. I figured I'd better stockpile calories while J.B. was asleep. When he was awake, there wasn't time to eat. Or hit the bathroom. Or blink.

Next to my feet, Lucy sat up very straight and looked up at me. Pointedly.

Nick had given her a bath in the backyard yesterday morning. So her white tummy and fawn-colored coat were even cleaner than usual. While she was a short-haired dog, she was still very much a puppy. So she still had a lot of her puppy fat and puppy fluff.

"You're absolutely right," I said, reaching for the mason jar that held her favorite bone-shaped treats. "Cookies for me means cookies for you, too. That's only fair."

I pulled out two treats and held out one for her. I figured I'd keep one in reserve for later. But not much later.

That's when we heard it. Three short screeches

followed by one long wail. J.B.'s version of Morse code. Now if I could only figure out what he wanted. And who he was.

I opened the back door, tossed the second dog biscuit into the yard, and looked over at Lucy, who had the other bone-shaped cookie in her mouth. "It's OK," I told her. "Save yourself."

Lucy scampered across the kitchen and hopped down the back steps. I closed the screen but left the door open. Screaming baby or no, I needed to keep an eye on the pup, too. Especially with Simmons lurking around.

I popped into the living room. "It's all right," I tried to reassure J.B. "It's gonna all be OK, little man. Your aunt Alex is here. I'm right here." I unbuckled the car seat and lifted him out. That's when it hit me.

Diaper-changing time.

My brother could say what he wanted about "almost no smell." That's not what I was getting. Either Nick was suffering from severely blocked sinuses, or J.B. was saving his best stuff for me.

I lowered him back into his carrier, buckled him fast, and raced around the house gathering supplies.

With no changing table, I figured the glass-topped coffee table was the way to go. It was big enough, plus the oak frame made it good and solid. And it was easy to clean. If what I was smelling was any indication, that would be crucial.

Fleetingly, I considered wearing rubber gloves. But J.B.'s mom wouldn't have done that. And from what Nick said, this little one needed to know that even though Mama was AWOL, he still had people around who loved him.

Through it all, J.B. wailed. Earsplitting screams. Mouth wide open. Eyes scrunched shut. Face scarlet.

Once I got him onto the table and peeled off the onesie, it took a minute to register what I was seeing. A diaper as reimagined by an industrial engineer who'd never actually seen a baby. Nick.

The outer layer was a white kitchen trash bag that had been wrapped around his little bottom like a burrito. It was fastened neatly on the sides with two pieces of silver duct tape.

Beneath that, acting as the actual diaper, was one of my sunny yellow tea towels.

Forget Nick's neat little pellets. It looked like someone had thrown a grenade into an outhouse. The tea towel had given its all. But it was a lost cause. Under the yellow cloth was a layer of something white and absorbent. A folded puppy pad. Unscented, of course.

I chucked the whole thing—tea towel and all—into the trash. "This is gonna take a lot of baby wipes," I reported to J.B.

He stopped, burped, and stared at me with wide, frightened eyes. They were a beautiful sapphire blue. Then he started crying again.

Given the two ninny nannies looking after him, I didn't blame him one bit.

I wrestled him into the new diaper and fastened it with the panda tabs. And it fit!

Whatever other complaints I might have about Nick, he knew how to weigh a baby.

But the onesie definitely needed a bath. I grabbed

the red cashmere throw from the sofa. It was butter soft. And it would keep the little guy warm for an hour, while I washed his clothes.

I felt for J.B. The closest I'd come to dressing a baby was playing with dolls as a kid. And a small, squirming human is a whole different ball game. I opted for a loose, toga-style wrap. At least it beat the plastic bag burrito.

"You know, you look very stylish," I said, lifting him from the table and settling him into his carrier, all the while carefully supporting his neck. "And this will keep you warm and snug while I wash your little outfit."

Even though he was still screeching, I leaned over and kissed the top of his downy head. He smelled good. Like fresh air.

J.B. stopped howling for a second and opened his eyes. When he saw me, he looked scared and started crying again. This time, instead of screaming, it was soft weeping. With tears. Like he was grieving. He broke my heart. I wanted to sob right along with him.

And somehow, I didn't think this was a problem that a bottle or two of formula was going to solve.

Chapter 11

At eight the next morning, I was on my second pot of coffee. I'd have done better just to run an IV from the pot to my arm.

J.B. never slept more than an hour and a half at a shot. I swear he could sleep and eat at the same time. A couple of times, I fell asleep with him in my arms. When his bottle was empty, he'd start wailing again.

At the beginning of the night, Nick and I took turns with him, dozing in shifts. But between washing bottles, changing diapers, warming formula, burping him, and rocking him, even working as a team, it was all we could do to keep up. Two of us and only one of him. And we were outnumbered.

I was beginning to wonder if his parents had dumped him because they needed a solid night's sleep. But I was willing to forgive and forget if they'd just come claim him.

Sometime around four a.m., exhaustion and sleep deprivation were seriously affecting our judgment.

I actually considered calling our mother for help, while Nick proposed pitching a pup tent in the yard so he could get a nap. And taking Lucy with him.

As I mainlined caffeine this morning, J.B. snoozed in his carrier on the living room table. If he kept to his nocturnal schedule, he'd be up any minute.

Nick had passed out in one of the lawn chairs on the front porch with Lucy at his feet. I didn't have the heart to wake either of them.

I'd planned to start my new job this morning. Maya had e-mailed my first batch of Aunt Margie letters yesterday. But forget giving advice. I could barely string together three words to form a sentence. And that sentence was "I need coffee."

How did real parents do it?

Somehow, I didn't think even Aunt Margie could fix this mess. (And I hazily recalled considering *that* idea around 4:30 this morning.)

So I chugged coffee and hoped for inspiration to strike. Or a meteor.

When the house phone rang, I dove for the kitchen wall. Too late.

"Wah-wah-wah-*waaaaaaah!*" I heard from the living room.

"Uh, hello," I said.

"Jeez, Red, that sounds like a baby." Trip.

"Really? Must be on your end. I don't hear it." I stretched the cord and grabbed my coffee cup, practically pouring the warm liquid straight down my throat.

That's when I noticed that the yellow T-shirt I'd put on this morning was inside out.

"I've got the weekend off," Trip said. "I was thinking about hitting that new Cajun place in Georgetown. I've heard you can make a meal on the dessert cart alone. So naturally I thought of you."

"I'd love to. But I can't. I can't even begin to explain what's going on over here."

"Does it involve a four-letter word that begins with 'B' and ends with 'aby'?"

"Yup."

"Have you had breakfast?" he said.

"At this point, I'm not even sure I had dinner last night."

"I'll bring food. Nick around?"

"Crashing on the front porch. Sat down to read the paper and dozed off."

"A sleeping aid *and* you can wrap fish in it," Trip said. "Show me a website that can do all that."

"Relax. It had nothing to do with the content. He put in a full day baking; then we were both up most of the night. It was kind of an all-hands-on-deck situation."

"Got it. I'll be there in an hour with sustenance. By the way, I have some news you've got to hear."

Chapter 12

Turned out the news Trip brought—along with most of Burger King's breakfast menu—had nothing to do with J.B. or his mother.

"Mira Myles is out," Trip said as he unwrapped his egg-and-cheese sandwich.

"Out of her mind, more like," I said, reaching for the ketchup.

"Which one is Mira Myles?" Nick asked, popping potato nuggets into his mouth.

"She's the one who wrote that column for the *Sentinel* pretty much claiming that I'd killed my former boss," I reminded him. "Later totally discredited. She's also the one who took out the china department of an Arlington home store when her fiancé broke off their engagement."

"Half the stemware department, too," Trip prompted.

"Yeah, once she got going, there was a lot of rage there," I said.

"Oh yeah, I remember seeing the video on the

news," Nick said, smiling. "One of the local bloggers called her the Batshit Bride."

"That's the one," Trip said, slipping Lucy a long strip of crispy bacon. "The boyfriend's family owns the corporation that owns the *Sentinel*. But the real news is that Mira's got it in her head that someone talked her precious Denny into breaking up with her. Someone he chatted with at a bridal registry event."

"Wait a minute," Nick said, snapping his fingers. "Was that the thing you dragged me to when you were doing that bridal story? Was that *you*?"

"Hey, I didn't talk him into anything. I didn't even know who his fiancée was. All I said was, if you're talented enough to win an art scholarship to Florence, the love of your life should be rooting for you. Not discouraging you."

"Well, she's loose," Trip said. "And word has it, she's looking for revenge."

"I didn't even use my own name when I went to that thing. Good luck finding me. Besides, wouldn't it make more sense to go after Denny? He was nuts about her. She could probably win him back."

"Can't leave the jurisdiction," Trip said. "The home store's pressing charges. And Denny's parents had the old family retainer file a restraining order. She can't come within five hundred yards of any of them or their newspaper offices."

"Jeez, she lost her job? She was one of the *Sentinel*'s stars. Mira sold papers."

"The way I hear it, one too many questionable

stories, plus a very public meltdown that made the news . . . ," Trip said.

"Plus she made Denny miserable," I said, troweling strawberry jam onto a buttermilk biscuit.

"Especially that last one," Trip said. "Anyway, thought you should know."

"I'd rather know who J.B.'s mom is and when she's coming to take him home," I said.

"Amen to that," Nick said, as he slipped a paper plate loaded with scrambled eggs topped with crumbled bacon in front of Lucy.

She held herself back until he stood up, but her tail was beating double time. The pup loved bacon and eggs. Especially the bacon.

"Unfortunately, I have exactly nothing on that topic," Trip said. "Zippo, zilch, and nada. One gentleman reported missing two towns over. But he's seventy-three, and his wife suspects he might have hopped a bus to Atlantic City to gamble and hit the buffets. According to our hard-charging crime reporters, no one else in the wind. And definitely no missing babies."

"I've been thinking about it, and if we're going to have J.B. in the house for a couple of days, we're going to need more than diapers and formula," I said. "I've lost track of how many times I've had to wash that little onesie."

"Yeah," Nick said. "The poor little guy's been sleeping in his car seat for at least a full day. That's got to be making him at least a little cranky. What we need is one of those discount baby stores. Like BabyMart or Mega Baby. The blogger moms love

those places. Everything you need in one place.
And the prices are decent."

Trip slid his eyes toward me. Clearly a question.

"Hey, the man knows his babies," I said, reaching
for an egg sandwich. "Thanks to him, we got the
right size diapers, and we're not messing up J.B.'s
hormones with the wrong kind of bottles. Why don't
we go this morning? There's a Mega Baby a couple
of miles from here. Next to that barbecue joint."

"Which explains how you know where it is,"
Trip said.

"I happened to glance out the window while I
was waiting for the cherry cobbler."

Nick shook his head. "I can't. I have to run the
chocolate chip cookies to my client before noon.
And if I wait around and help them clean up after,
she'll cut me a check."

"I have the day off," Trip volunteered. "I was planning to sample a four-course Cajun meal from a
Michelin-starred chef. But I can skip it for a jaunt
to a baby superstore. Talk about a once-in-a-lifetime
opportunity."

"Wait a minute," I said to Nick. "If you're visiting
a client and we're hitting the baby store, who's
watching J.B.?"

Nick and I were so tired and loopy, we'd forgotten why we were tired and loopy.

"I can't take him to the lunch. Schmoozing is
part of the job. And what if he needs a bottle or a
clean diaper?"

"Relax, Red, we'll just take him with us," Trip
said. "It's a baby store. He'll fit right in."

"Yeah, but your Corvette doesn't have a backseat, and J.B. needs to be in the backseat. So we're gonna have to take the Slutmobile. We can't take the Slutmobile to the baby store. They'll think J.B. is a slut-baby."

My best friend looked at me like I'd lost my mind. Then he shook his head, reached into his pocket, and handed off his keys to Nick. "It has a little storage in the jump seat, and the trunk is spotless. Please do not exceed the speed limit."

Nick's face lit up like a five-year-old at Christmas. "Really? Oh, man! Thank you!" He grabbed the keys and practically ran out to the driveway.

"I promise I won't go over fifty-five," he called out from the front door. "And I'll put a tarp down so you don't have to worry about crumbs. Wait 'til they see me in that shiny red Corvette convertible—my competition is going to plotz. I just hope I run into Simmons."

Trip looked at me and dropped his voice, "Not literally, right?"

Groping the bottom of the takeout bag, I found one last, lonely tater tot, popped it into my mouth, and shrugged.

Chapter 13

Cherry cobbler or not, there's no way I could have missed Mega Baby. It took up three-quarters of the upscale shopping center behind the barbecue place. And there was a three-story inflatable baby out front. With a yellow banner proclaiming, "From our bouncing baby to yours."

"If it was a seafood restaurant, would they have a giant inflatable clam out front?" Trip asked, giving it a gimlet eye.

"If Nick gets his kitchen licensed, maybe we can put a giant inflatable cookie on the front lawn," I said, swinging Nick's Hyundai into the closest spot that wasn't marked RESERVED FOR MOMMA. "I'm thinking a thirty-foot cookie might discourage some of the after-hours visitors."

"Tacky kitsch as a form of home security? I like it."

J.B. didn't care one way or the other. J.B. hadn't made a peep since we'd pulled out of the driveway. When I opened the back door, I discovered why: He was sacked out. With a smile on his face. Sweet little guy. Did he think we were taking him home?

He'd fussed when we carried him to the car. I pictured a major wrestling match to get that car seat buckled into the back of Nick's sporty little Hyundai. But Trip made it look like a sleight-of-hand magic trick. A couple of snaps and both J.B. and his car seat were facing backward and strapped in snug and tight.

What did it mean that the men in my life were better mothers than I was?

"So did you ask Nick if the little guy might be his?" Trip asked.

"Not yet. We've kind of had our hands full. Besides, if it was a possibility, don't you think he'd have said something?"

"He might not know it. You women are a strange and secretive species."

"I dunno," I said, pulling a cart from the rack, as Trip settled the carrier with a still sleeping J.B. in the front. "I kinda think there has to be some middle ground between giving birth in secret and dumping your child on the father in the middle of the night. Like suing for child support. Or threatening to tell our mother."

"I've met your mom. That's definitely the way to go."

"No lie."

Mega Baby clearly knew its customer base. There was a bar cart with a giant coffee urn and a stack of hot cups right inside the door. Perfect for zombie moms and dads.

"Ooh, caffeine, I could use some of that," I said, making a beeline for the table.

"If you and Nick Jr. behave yourselves, we'll stop for barbecue," Trip said.

"Do you really think he's Nick's?" I asked, dumping three pods of creamer in my coffee. "Does he remind you of Nick?"

"Not really. The eyes are a different color. And he doesn't have much in the way of hair. But I'm no geneticist. It could be possible."

I had to admit, that thought stopped me cold. Did I just need a few baby blankets, or should I be registering him for a 529 plan and a good college?

"C'mon, Red," he said. "It's like the newsroom. We'll take it a step at a time. It'll be OK."

"You really think so?"

"Hey, you've had him more than twenty-four hours and no E.R. visits. He's fed, he's clean, and he's happy."

"That's because he's asleep."

"Take the win. So what exactly do we need here?"

"We're all set on diapers, and formula and bottles. But we need something for him to sleep in, and a half dozen of those little onesies. And something that makes him stop crying would be nice."

"It's a baby supply store, not a magic lamp. I think you're stuck with the crying."

"Hey, I raided the coffee can in my closet. I have a wallet full of cash, and I'm open to suggestions," I said.

"In short, their ideal customer. But I'd keep the open wallet part to yourself. So what's our cover story?"

"I was just going to say we're watching him for a friend."

"But you're stocking up on supplies. And we don't know his name or how old he is? You might want to practice that story because you'll probably be repeating it to the cops."

"OK, his name is J.B. He's my brother's baby. And we're doing this as a surprise, because my brother and his wife are just moving to town."

"You are surprisingly good at fabricating. As your former editor, should I be worried?"

"That also covers us in case we buy something large and need to have it delivered."

"You are not buying the giant inflatable baby."

"I meant like a bed."

"I believe they call them cribs."

"I knew that. Hey," I said, snapping my fingers, "what if J.B.'s mom shopped here? They might be on some kind of registry. The store might even have an address on file. They have these places all over the country."

"Possible. But without a name, there'd be no way to check."

"Unless he's local and someone recognizes him."

"Not to burst your bubble, but don't all babies kind of look alike?"

He had a point. At birth, all four of us kids looked nearly identical. Like little old men. Even Annie. Dad claimed we looked like his father—our grandpa Vlodnachek. I've seen the family photos. Unfortunately, he was right.

"OK, but I wanna see what this car seat sells for. If they only sell a few of them, that could be a lead."

"OK, Nancy Drew," he said, picking up a onesie that was styled to look like a tuxedo. "Hey, check this out. You could take J.B. to your next cocktail party."

"Oh, he would look cute. How much?"

Trip checked the tag. "Ouch! Let's just say you could save your money and rent a real one for his prom. I thought Nick said this place was affordable. Or has the Cookie King moved into a higher tax bracket?"

"Trust me, money's as tight as ever. But for some reason, tiny baby things come with giant price tags. Cheap is relative."

"Says the woman whose favorite designer is 'Clearance Sale.'"

"I'm not cheap, I'm thrifty," I said in a bad Scottish accent.

"Well, hello! Welcome to Mega Baby! And who's this little cutie?"

I turned and saw a middle-aged woman in a pastel pink golf shirt and khakis. Her name tag read SHERYL.

"Hi, Sheryl," Trip said smoothly. "This little guy is J.B."

"Well, isn't he precious!" she said.

And she was right. Asleep, he looked like an angel. He still had that little smile on his face. I wondered: Was he dreaming about his mom?

"So how old is little J.B.?"

"How old does he look?" I asked. It slipped out before I could catch myself. Blame the sleep deprivation.

Trip shot me a look. "J.B. is Alex's nephew. We're helping his parents get settled in the area. And

Auntie Alex is worried that J.B. is too small for his age."

I nodded mutely. Face it, if I opened my mouth again there was a pretty good chance something stupid would fall out. Honest, but stupid.

"Oh, he looks like a big healthy boy!" Sheryl enthused, beaming at the cherubic little bundle. "I'm guessing you might want to go for the six-month size. He looks like he's about three months, but that will give him plenty of room to grow."

"That sounds perfect," Trip said. "Let's pick up some onesies, then we can look at a bassinet."

"Oh, he's much too big for a bassinet," Sheryl informed us. "No, you need a crib. And you want the safety bedding. But no pillows. That's important. And I see you already have the Tykumi car seat. Good choice."

"Do you sell those here?" I asked, finally finding my voice. Even if it did sound more like a reporter than a mom. Or an "aunt."

"We don't. But it's a really good brand. They're Danish. And very high end. You don't see them as much in the U.S., unless you order them online. But we have some that are very similar—TravelSafe— when he's ready. And this one should fit him for at least a few more months."

"Good to know," I said, sliding an eye at Trip. "Let's check out those onesies. Oh, and do you have something that might, uh, keep him from crying?"

Chapter 14

As we pulled into the driveway, I felt strangely refreshed. And hopeful.

Maybe it was because J.B. had slept through most of the trip. Including a stop at the barbecue joint. Maybe it was the cherry cobbler à la mode. And maybe it was because we bought a little wind-up swing that Sheryl swore would put a smile on the face of any baby.

At this point, I'd have settled for mild disapproval or silent disdain. As long as he stopped crying.

We also got a crib. But they were delivering that tomorrow. And assembling it.

I'd remembered the Ikea bookshelves I put together myself when I first bought my house two years ago. They still listed to one side. And we weren't sleeping a baby in those.

So unless Nick had acquired a new superpower during his years in Arizona, I figured we'd better pony up $50 and let the pros handle this one.

Besides, it was a lot cheaper than an E.R. visit.

"I can't believe Nick's back with your car," I said.

Face it, a set of wheels like that and no J.B.? I didn't think we'd see Nick again until at least midnight.

"And I don't see any dings or dents," I said, unfolding myself from the bucket seat of Nick's little Hyundai. "At least, not from here."

"I'll get out my magnifying glass and halogen lamp later. First, we get the little guy inside," Trip said.

While he carried J.B., I gathered up two giant Mega Baby bags stuffed with onesies, blankets, bibs, drool cloths, and toys. OK, I might have gone a little nutty.

We even got one of those little yellow plastic baby tubs, so we could give J.B. a bath. I figured if his family didn't want it, we could use it for Lucy.

And Trip rented a pram so we could take J.B. out to see if anyone recognized him.

Four racing bikes sped by, this time going the other way. They never slowed, but again one rider raised an arm in greeting. I waved back.

When Trip came back down the walkway, he had a big smile on his face. Kind of like me with the cherry cobbler. Nick was two steps behind him.

"I made an executive decision," Nick announced.

"That's one way to look at it," Trip said over his shoulder as he hefted the tub out of the backseat.

"What kind of executive decision?" I asked, warily.

"Look, we were running flat out last night. And we failed. We're not up to this."

"You can't give him to the county! I can find his family. It might take me a few days, but . . ."

"Oh, hell no, I'd never do that," Nick said, putting his hand on my shoulder. "I just figured we needed a little help. A little backup. An expert."

"What. Did. You. Do?" I asked, fearing the worst.

"Relax," Trip said, marching up the walkway. "It's Baba."

"Oh thank God! I thought you called Mom."

"No, I'm tired, not suicidal. Besides, Dad was a colicky baby. So Baba's got a couple of tricks up her sleeve."

"You realize this means we have to eat her cooking?"

"I do. And if I can sleep nights, I don't care. Besides, we can spell her here and there with the cooking. And there's always fast food."

Baba, our dad's mother, was ninety pounds of Russian dynamite. Not quite five feet tall and who knows how old, she was a strike force of one. Literally. She'd recently saved me from a psycho killer armed with nothing but common sense and a cast-iron frying pan.

There was almost nothing she couldn't do. Except cook.

Baba's culinary skills were in a category all their own. And that category was "dreadful." But she made every morsel with love. So we smiled and asked for seconds. And kept the pantry stocked with snack food.

I slapped him on the back. "Good move."

"Really?" He looked touched. Or possibly just tired.

"Yeah. If anyone can baby whisper J.B., it's Baba. And if not, at least it's another set of hands."

"Oh, and Ian called. He's hoping you can stop by this afternoon for tea."

Trip waggled his eyebrows. "And does that T stand for tango?"

"Could you hear Lydia Stewart's heavy breathing in the background? Because every time I get within fifty yards of Ian Sterling, she's right there. Like a Versace-clad linebacker."

"Nope," said Nick. "He didn't say anything about her. Just wanted to have you over for a nice afternoon tea whenever you got back."

"What does one wear to afternoon tea with the lord of the manor?" Trip teased.

"A schleppy T-shirt and an expression that says, 'I've been up all night'?" I replied, glancing down at my jeans. They weren't pressed, but they were cobbler-free and presentable. I could probably use a little makeup, though.

"I was thinking a nice sundress and some sandals," Trip countered. "But it's your party."

Nick pulled the oversized bags out of my arms. "You go get ready. I'll haul this stuff. Man, you should have seen Baba in the convertible. We had the top down and the tunes cranked up the whole way from Baltimore."

"She was OK with it?"

"She loved it! Couldn't wipe the smile off her face. Even though she nearly lost her hat twice. Said it felt "like being a little bird.""

I knew Baba. I'm guessing having a little alone time with her youngest grandchild—who, until recently, she hadn't seen for a year—might have had something to do with the exuberance. Or possibly the fact that we'd cried "uncle" and admitted we needed her.

But who knows? Maybe Baba really was a secret muscle-car junkie.

Chapter 15

I ended up taking Trip's advice—big surprise—and went with the sundress and sandals. I still felt like roadkill thanks to our J.B.-induced rager. But from the outside at least, I looked like a normal person.

And Baba approved the outfit before I left. Even as she tucked in the stray tag at the neck. "You find baby?" she asked me, out of earshot of Trip and Nick.

"Right on the kitchen table," I said. "I walked out there in the morning, and he was sleeping. In his little carrier thingie."

She sighed. "First you find husband. Then you find baby." And with that she toddled off toward the kitchen.

Now, in the shadow of Ian's graceful Victorian, I knocked on the heavy oak door. Nothing.

I knocked louder and waited. It was a B&B as well as Ian's house. Should I just walk in? Somehow that seemed rude. And invasive.

Finally, the door opened.

"Alex, how nice of you to come! Come in, please. I've fixed us a little tea in the solarium."

"Nice!" I said. "Thank you." Was it my imagination, or did he look a little the worse for wear? Those beautiful blue eyes were slightly bloodshot. And his hair could use a comb. But he was still perfectly pressed, and he smelled good. Woodsy mixed with something exotic.

Thanks to the Prestwicks, I knew that Lydia Stewart had booked into the inn. Maybe she was still here. And getting her own special kind of "room service."

Knock it off, I chastised myself. One kiss did not a relationship make. His private life was none of my business.

The Cotswolds Inn, as usual, was spotless. Sunlight streamed in through the glass in Ian's solarium. And thanks to my brother's endeavors, there was a lingering scent of chocolate chip cookies. Just as Ian had predicted when he'd bought the place, it was the perfect setting for afternoon tea. Or a nap.

I shook my head, rousing myself, and composed a mental to-do list: Get some caffeine. Make pleasant small talk. Stay awake for the next hour.

"Here we are," Ian said, swinging into the room with a large silver tray bearing a big yellow china teapot, matching cups, and a large plate of Nick's cookies.

Suddenly, I realized what was missing.

"Is your father here? I haven't seen him since the party."

Ian's smile vanished. He actually looked startled. He sank heavily into a chair and rubbed his eyes.

Gone was the bon vivant innkeeper. And flirty neighbor. I sensed I might be glimpsing the real Ian Sterling. Possibly for the first time.

"I was hoping it wasn't that obvious," he said. "I've been trying to keep up pretenses, but . . ." The sentence trailed off, and he brushed a wayward lock of hair off his face. "He's gone."

"Gone? You mean on vacation? Or back to London?" I hoped he didn't mean something even more permanent.

"I'm not sure. Just gone. The night of the party. It's like he vanished into thin air."

I remembered the freezer in the basement with a sense of creeping dread.

"Did he say anything? Leave a note?"

"Nothing. He had been acting a little off lately. Small things. Odd phone calls. Errands that had nothing to do with the inn. And we've been fully booked lately with both rooms and events. We were even talking about taking on some help. So it's not like either of us had much in the way of free time. And he started keeping his door locked."

"Well, this is an inn. With people wandering around, that's probably a good thing."

"His rooms are on the fourth floor. A bedroom and a study. He locks the bedroom, yes. But never the study. It's where he goes to . . . get away from it all. It's a very private space, and it has a bit of a view. That's why he selected it."

"It's been more than twenty-four hours," I said. "You could file a missing person's report."

"He's a grown man. It's been one day. Your constables aren't going to take it terribly seriously. But I know him. I know he wouldn't do this. I know something's wrong."

"Is there anything I can do?" I regretted the offer the moment it was out of my mouth. But what else could I say?

He looked straight into my face. With those bluer-than-blue eyes. "I'm already making some phone calls. But I'm a little thin on the local front. Would it be possible for you to make a few discreet inquiries? Off the record, so to speak. Anything that might help me get a lead on where he might have gone?"

If Harkins had been a city councilman who'd disappeared with a bag of cash and a stripper girlfriend, I might know where to look. But a regular everyday missing person? Totally out of my depth.

"I'm not a detective. I'm just a freelance writer." A freelance writer who was barely keeping the bills paid.

"You're a reporter. I've read your stories. You're good. And you really know how to dig up information. You have local sources. That's what I need." He sounded desperate.

"And there's something I failed to mention," he confessed.

OK, here it comes.

"In my father's previous life, when he lived in the U.K., he had a rather colorful past."

"How colorful?" I asked.

"He spent some time as a guest of the Crown. Nothing serious. Nothing violent. What you Yanks call 'white collar' offenses."

"What did he do?" I was so tired, the reporter part of my brain kicked in automatically.

"He was a bit of a miscreant. But that was decades ago, in his youth. He's a changed man. Has been for years. Straightened out his life and never looked back. And the truth of it is that, until recently, we'd been out of touch. My mother raised me. She and her parents, really. I'd see my dad occasionally. When my grandparents would permit."

"They didn't approve of him?"

"Didn't see him as a fitting husband for an earl's daughter. And by the time I had become an adult, he'd all but disappeared. But I've gotten to know him over the past few years. He's a damn fine man. And an honest and moral one, to boot. I trust him. And I can't say that about many people."

He rubbed his eyes, then looked at me again. I could tell he was sizing me up. As a reporter, it's a look you see a lot. Often from other reporters.

"There is a bit of a snafu. Something I hesitate to mention. Something we really do need to keep private."

Of course there is.

"My father is here legally on a work visa. And he's applied for permanent residency. But if I report that he's missing, that could throw a wrench into it. He could be sent back. Permanently. He wouldn't be able to reapply for at least ten years. And he's not a young man."

"Damn." That put little J.B.'s crying fits into perspective.

Ian put his forearms on the table, leaning toward me. "I don't expect you to track him down. I just need a little more information. From someone with some local contacts. And I need to get that information without tripping any alarms or alerting the wrong people."

"Does he have credit cards or a cell phone?"

"The phone is still in his room. And the credit cards haven't been used. Neither has his bank card. His belongings appear to be here—including his driver's license and passport. Even the Bentley. Wherever he is, he's either on foot, or he's taken some form of public transit."

I didn't have the heart to tell Ian: when the car, cards, and cash were at home, and the missing person wasn't, the story usually didn't have a happy ending. And if that was the case here, how on earth would I break it to him? I realized I was holding my breath.

Out of the blue, I wondered, "What would Aunt Margie do?"

I looked across the table. The tea—and the cookies—sat untouched. That was a new one for me.

But this was the guy who had sent over a basket of baked goods after reporters tracking me had trampled half the block. And didn't hold it against me when I crashed his grand opening garden party with a couple of murderers and a platoon of police. He even brought over a home-cooked meal after the cops carted away the bad guys. Plus, he was loaning my brother a fully licensed kitchen so that Nick could keep his fledgling bakery up and running. And he was a really good kisser. So what could I say?

"Of course I'll help."

Ian beamed. "I don't know what to say. Other than thank you. And somehow, that doesn't seem like quite enough."

"Don't worry about it. I'll make a few phone calls this afternoon."

It wasn't like I had anything else to do.

Chapter 16

OK, I wasn't totally honest with Ian.

Yes, I was planning to make a couple of phone calls to see if I could get a lead on Harkins's current whereabouts. But there was one other thing I had to check first: the basement.

That freezer was bugging me.

So after we said our good-byes and Ian excused himself to go look after one of the guests—not Lydia, thank God—I slipped quietly into the front hall.

I gingerly tried the knob to the basement door. It turned easily. As I oh-so-quietly eased the door open, I spied a light switch on the wall. So far, so good. Because loudly tumbling down the stairs would definitely cost me my ace reporter status.

I shut the door silently, hoping the thing would open from the inside when I was ready to leave. Then I crept down the steep stairs, grabbing that railing for all I was worth.

When I got to the bottom, there was the white chest freezer, right where it had been the night of the party. And I knew it was on because I could hear the faint electrical hum. I touched the top with my fingertips. Cool.

I didn't want to look inside. If Harkins was there, how would I break it to Ian? It would kill him. And it wouldn't be great for his business, either.

Crreeeaaakk! Skreeek!

I jumped.

The sounds had come from the far side of the basement. Where it was dark. The old house settling? Or something more?

Rather than one large room, the Victorian's basement was divided up with what looked like walls, half walls, and unfinished walls. I could barely make out what appeared to be some old furniture, too. Ian's "bits and bobs for the inn"?

"Is someone there?" I asked, my voice cracking.

Silence.

The single lightbulb over the landing flickered.

Oh, great. Any minute, I won't just be standing in a creepy, deserted basement. I'll be standing in a creepy, deserted basement in the dark.

"Anybody there?" I called halfheartedly. My mouth was dry. Fear or dust, take your pick.

Nothing. Not so much as a peep from the ghost baby.

The light blinked off and on again. Longer this time. And I realized that, if I was going to see what was in the freezer, I was going to have to do it quick. Before the bulb gave out.

"Here goes nothing," I said, putting both hands on the top of the chest and yanking it upward.

I winced.

His eyes were closed, his lashes coated with ice. He reminded me of photos I'd seen of mountaineers summiting Everest. For some reason, that's the detail that stuck with me. The eyelashes.

I forced myself to look.

Not Harkins. A total stranger.

So who was he? How did he end up in Ian's freezer? And did Ian know he was here?

The dead man was wearing a white golf shirt and navy slacks, with a tan windbreaker. No logos. He had a crew cut. Probably blond or sandy brown. I'd have guessed he was in his midthirties. But it was hard to tell.

There was a reddish stain in the middle of his chest. About the size of a baseball. Gunshot?

Just how long had he been here? Had Harkins shot him, then fled?

At this point, Ian was going to have to call the cops, work visa or no. Besides, I was beginning to wonder if that story was total BS. And exactly what had Harkins done in jolly old England that had gotten him tossed into jail?

Ian never did answer that question.

I dropped the freezer lid and pulled myself up the steps. Just as I hit the top, the lightbulb popped.

It was time to have another talk with my friendly, neighborhood innkeeper. And I had a feeling this time it would be a little less friendly.

Chapter 17

Turned out, operating a B&B was a lot harder than I'd ever realized. Even without a body in the basement.

When I reached Ian, he was on the run. Literally. Tending to the needs of one guest ("Can we get some pink hydrangeas in our room, too? Like the ones in the side garden?") and another ("The bath water is hot, but not 'steaming hot.' Can you fix it?"). And somehow, announcing "By the way, there's a body in the freezer" in a tearoom now teaming with a local book club seemed rude.

When the produce and linen delivery guys showed up at the same time, I accepted Ian's offer to wait in the library.

No way I was going back down to the basement by myself. Especially in the dark. I didn't even want to be basement adjacent.

I was guessing the cops would just carry out the whole thing—freezer and all. Neater that way. And less hassle for Ian.

It wasn't like he was ever going to use that freezer again.

I looked down and realized my hands were shaking. So who was the dead man? I was fairly certain I'd never seen him around the inn. Or at the cocktail party.

Then it hit me: What was I going to tell Nick? He needed Ian's kitchen to keep his business afloat. With a dead body downstairs, the cops could close down Ian, too. If it were me, I'd take my chances with shuttering the bakery for a few weeks while we retrofitted my kitchen. But that was Nick's call.

The library looked much the same as it had the other night. I wondered if Rube was still in residence. And if so, why? He lived a short hop away in Georgetown. Escaping to Baltimore for the weekend, I could see. Or the mountains. But why a local B&B? Or maybe it was true what they said: the rich really aren't like you and me.

"So sorry to keep you," Ian said, striding into the room and closing the doors behind him. "Is this about my father? Have you found something already?"

"Uh, not exactly. It could involve your father, but I'm not sure."

I gave him the basics. Icy freezer. Icy body. Not Harkins. Possibly there since the party. Or before.

He looked troubled. But not as flustered as I'd expected. My read: He hadn't known about the body. Yet, somehow, it wasn't a total shock, either.

"You're certain it wasn't my father?"

"Totally. This guy is a lot younger. I'm guessing early to midthirties. Blond or sandy-brown crew cut. Wearing a white golf shirt, tan windbreaker, and navy slacks. Sound familiar? One of the guests? Maybe someone who came for tea?"

"Not familiar in the least." His face was a mask. "And he doesn't sound like anyone I've seen around here. How in the blazes did he get inside the freezer? It's not even supposed to be plugged in."

"I know it doesn't suit your plans, but we need to call the police," I said quietly.

"I know," he said, nodding. "If you don't mind, though, I need to leave my father's name out of this."

"They'll need to question everyone here. The fact that he's missing could be a red flag." Unfortunately, I'd learned that one the hard way.

"If they can narrow down the time frame for when the man died, that could rule out the need to talk to Dad."

"It could," I said.

Or it could throw him right in the soup. Which was where I'd put my money if I were betting.

"I could just say he's away for the week," Ian said blandly. "Fishing, perhaps."

"Look, I know I'm the last person who should be giving advice on the subject. But it's never a good idea to lie to the police. Eventually, everything comes out. And in this case, that could be a good thing. It was for me."

Ian's expression was stoic. Unreadable. But his

eyes were now a stormy blue, like the sky on the night of the party. I could see the wheels turning.

"How long has the freezer been in the house?" I asked.

"Delivered last week. From an appliance store," he said.

"So, conceivably, the body could have been in there since then. Or even before, if the guy is somehow connected to the appliance store."

"We opened the freezer when they brought it in. And it was empty, save for some paperwork and a few wire shelving racks. We had them deposit it downstairs near the entryway until we could clear a space in the back. But no one ever plugged it in. I am certain of that."

"Someone did. Probably the same someone who put the body in it. We need to turn this over to the cops."

"Could you tell how he died?" Ian asked.

I shook my head. "Some kind of injury to the chest. Could have been a gunshot."

Ian's face relaxed slightly. "My father hates guns. Won't touch them."

"Harkins is a good guy. That's a given. But we still have to call the police."

"Agreed. But I want to see him first. The dead man. If he is one of my guests, I want to know."

"The basement bulb is burned out, so we're going to need flashlights."

"Again? That is the third bulb just this week. Between the plumbing and the electric, I'm beginning to believe this house truly is cursed. Wait, 'we'? 'Flashlights'?" he said, emphasizing the "s."

"Trust me, it's not something you want to see alone."

"Yes, right." He nodded. "Thank you for that."

Five minutes later, armed with flashlights, we were standing over the freezer. I took a step to one side. Ian lifted the lid and looked down. I kept my eyes on his face. Call me crazy, but I suspected that the guy knew a bit more than he was telling.

"It's empty," he said, with obvious relief.

"What?" I mumbled, startled.

"There's nothing in here. Certainly no *one*," he said, pointedly.

"That doesn't make sense," I said, staring into an empty freezer. "I was down here twenty minutes ago. There was a man in there. A man with a crew cut and a big red stain on his chest."

"I don't know about you, but I could use a brandy," Ian said. "Would you join me for one in the library?"

"Ian, we have to call the cops!"

"And report what? That our freezer is missing a dead body? We don't know who he is, or where he is, or even what he is. For all we know, it could have been some sort of a sadistic hoax. The lighting down here is rather dim. It could have been one of the mannequins we employed for the murder mystery weekend."

"Pretty realistic mannequin," I said, remembering the eyelashes. "Do you know where they are now?"

"Afraid my father took care of that part of it. No idea where those supplies are now. Luckily, we don't host another one for a few weeks. Alex, I'm not doubting you. I'm saying that in the past week there have been some odd things happening here—almost like a series of practical jokes. But vicious. Things I've fixed—broken again. Water spigots left on. Water mains turned off. Lightbulbs smashed or missing. That fuse box and our generator the other night. This morning, someone actually deposited a dead rat on the patio. One of the white ones that you see in a laboratory. Right in front of the French doors. Luckily, I spotted it before one of the guests did."

"You think someone is sabotaging this place?"

"I don't know what else to think. It can't be a coincidence. Then you see a body? A human body? But now it's vanished. Like a trick. It could reappear later. Or perhaps it was never genuine in the first place. I think someone is having some rather cruel fun at the inn's expense."

"Do you think it has something to do with your father's disappearance?"

"No idea. But that seems quite a step up from malicious mischief. Alex, I can handle the inn. But I need to make sure that Dad's all right. I've made some inquiries among his crowd in London. But nothing's borne fruit. Not yet."

I sighed. "I haven't forgotten. And I will help you. That was the real reason I was down there."

"What do you mean?" he said sharply.

"I realized the freezer was up and running the night of the party. Even though it wasn't supposed to be. And when you said your father went missing that same night, I was worried. I had to check it out. I'm relieved it wasn't him. But it was someone. I take it you still don't want to call the cops?"

"Not until we have something we can actually show them. And other than a laboratory rat in the rubbish bin, right now I have precisely nothing."

I wasn't going to argue with him. He was right. The police would show up, take our statements and leave. Probably within fifteen minutes. Ten, if Ian didn't offer them coffee.

I also didn't like the idea of Nick working in Sabotage Central.

I might have promised Ian I wouldn't narc to the cops about his father. But I'd said nothing about ratting him out to my brother. So to speak.

When I got home, Nick would get the full story. Every detail. Including the now-missing contents of the basement freezer. And I was hoping he'd put his own safety ahead of his new career.

I also prayed he'd forget that, in a similar situation not long ago, I'd made a very different choice.

Chapter 18

I took a pass on Ian's offer of a brandy in the library.

I just wanted to go home, bolt my doors (for all the good it would do), take a long, hot shower, and put a serious dent in Nick's stockpile of limbo cookies.

Alas, it was not to be.

I noticed Trip's car was gone when I arrived back at Chez Vlodnachek. I hoped he was finally sampling the Cajun place. He'd earned it.

Nick opened the door before I hit the porch.

"We have to talk," we both said in unison.

He grinned. "OK, you look like you could use a beer. How about I bring two out here? You can tell me your news. Then I'll tell you mine."

I sagged onto one of the plastic lawn chairs that served as my "outdoor furniture." Nick seemed pretty upbeat. But if his news was "Hey, we found J.B.'s family," I didn't think he'd stand on ceremony.

We Vlodnacheks tend to blurt things out. Which made for some very entertaining holiday meals.

"How are Baba and J.B. getting along?" I asked when he reappeared and handed me a can. I hadn't heard any crying, so that was probably a good sign.

"It's like he's a long lost Vlodnachek. She loves him. And he loves her. She told him Russian fairy stories and sang to him, and he was enthralled. He just nodded off."

Maybe Trip was right. Maybe J.B. was a Vlodnachek after all. If he was, Nick didn't seem to have a clue. How could I ask him about that *and* tell him the truth about his spooky new workplace?

I decided to take the same advice I offered him: one crisis at a time. "He's sleeping? Really sleeping?"

"Yup. She took out one of your dresser drawers and fixed it up with blankets. Like a bassinet. He's tucked in safe and snug. With a little smile on his face. Now, what is it you needed to say?"

"I found a body in Ian's basement freezer."

"Ian's got a freezer in the basement?"

"Really? That's your takeaway?"

"Well, he doesn't seem like a body-in-the-basement kind of guy. Are you sure?"

"Yes, I'm sure. I saw the guy. It was awful. Then the lights went out. And I went to tell Ian. But by the time we got back, it was gone."

"The freezer too, or just the body?" Nick asked.

"Just the body. What is it with you and the damned freezer?"

"Well, if your guy's thawing out, he's gonna be pretty easy to find."

"Jeez, you're right," I said. "Look, the real story

is there are all kinds of strange things going on at the inn."

"Yeah, I know."

"What do you mean, you know?"

"I was there all Friday afternoon and most of the evening baking. I hear things. Man, last night I was so beat I was imagining shadows in the garden."

"I'm not talking about the ghost baby," I said.

"What ghost baby?"

I ignored the question. "Ian thinks someone is sabotaging the inn. Broken lights, messing with the electrical system, water left on—or turned off at the main. This morning he found a dead rat on the patio."

"Yikes! I hope Simmons doesn't hear about that. He actually stopped by when he heard I was baking over there. Claimed he was required to do a spot check."

"On a Saturday? He seems awfully invested in shutting you down."

"Yeah, for some reason, I think this one's personal. Ian ushered him out, and that's the last we saw of him."

"Ushered him out?"

"I'd say 'tossed,' but it was so much more polite. Like Ian was inviting him to leave."

"Yeah, he does have that reserved British demeanor thing going for him," I said.

Three racing bikes streaked down the street. Reflexively, I waved. Two of the three riders returned the gesture.

"Anyway, I heard some of the guests talking,"

Nick said. "A couple of people who checked in this week vanished."

"You're kidding! Who?"

"One was a woman. Possibly some celebrity. Very mysterioso."

"Walked out on the bill?"

"Rumor is she was fully paid. And collected her stuff. But cut her stay short and just disappeared."

"Who was the other one?"

"Some insurance salesman. Supposedly checked in, paid for a week, and nobody's seen him since."

"I don't suppose he had a crew cut?" I asked.

"No idea," Nick said, taking a sip. "I overheard a couple of guests talking. They didn't describe him. I don't know if they ever saw him. They were just repeating the dirt they heard around the inn. And all they said was that he sold insurance. You think he's your corpsicle?"

"I don't know. Ian didn't mention any of this. Just the pranks. He put it all down to 'malicious mischief.' Or possible sabotage."

"I got the feeling that the disappearing guest thing wasn't that uncommon," Nick said. "No one skipped out on the bill. They just decided not to stay. For whatever reason. And that's not exactly something you advertise to your other guests."

"Yeah, a couple at the party theorized that the woman was an actress recovering from plastic surgery. Apparently, she was never seen without a big hat, sunglasses, and a scarf."

"So she healed up, opted for a discreet checkout, and went home," Nick concluded.

"That explains one of them—but what about Insurance Guy?" I countered.

"Checked in, didn't like his room, and left? If he never actually stayed there, it's not like he'd even have to check out. They'd just credit his card. Maybe the reason Ian didn't mention it is there's nothing to mention."

"Nick, there was a body in the freezer! A real human body."

"What did Ian say when you told him?"

"Not much," I said. "Harkins is missing. Almost two days now. He was just relieved it wasn't him. And when the freezer came up empty, he tried to play it off like one more prank. He even suggested it could have been a mannequin from one of their murder mystery weekends."

"Are you sure it wasn't?"

"Yes! I mean, the light wasn't great. But yes. It's not like I haven't seen a body before."

"True that. I don't suppose it could have been left over from the last psycho killer?"

"Nope. The freezer was just delivered last week, according to Ian. And there was something in his reaction. Or lack of reaction. I can't quite put my finger on it. Not like he actually knew about it. Just that he wasn't all that surprised."

"British reserve again?"

"I dunno. Look, whatever's going on over there, it's way past the point of practical jokes or even sabotage. I don't think it's safe for you to be working at the B&B."

Nick took another pull of his beer, but I could see the amusement in his eyes.

"I'm sorry," he said, smiling. "You're going to tell me where it's safe to work? At the last job you had, someone was stabbed right there in the office."

"Yes, and when I learned that, I left."

"You kept going back until they fired you. And every night after that."

Why did I think he was enjoying this?

"And it damn near got me killed," I admitted. "You're smarter than I am."

He grinned. "Look, I appreciate that you're worried. And I'll keep my eyes open. Who knows, we might learn a little something just by my being there. But this is my business. My actual business. It has nothing to do with you or anyone else. It's mine. And it's going really well. In spite of Simmons. There's no way I'm backing off now."

"You think this is funny?"

"I think now you know how Baba and I felt every time you took off for your night job at that office."

"If we retrofit my kitchen, we could have your bakery back up and running in a couple of weeks," I pleaded.

"I've been interviewing contractors," Nick countered. "More like one month, minimum. Realistically, at least two. And I don't have the cash to pay for it yet. Soon, but not yet. Remember I told you I had some good news?"

I nodded numbly. How much worse was this gonna get?

"The client I saw this morning? The one I made the cookies for? She has a friend who runs a little café in Baltimore. Near the Inner Harbor. Turns out she sampled some of my stuff at Ian's tearoom and loved it. She put in a standing order. Every week."

Crap. I was so happy for him. And scared. What could I say?

"Nick, that's wonderful. Really, really wonderful."

He beamed. "I've literally tripled my business. Angie's even willing to pay extra for the delivery. And some weeks when she's in the area, she'll pick up the stuff herself. And she's far enough away that I don't have to feel guilty about fueling Ian's competition."

"A toast," I announced, raising my beer can. "To your continued success. It can only get better from here."

No lie.

"Thank you!" he said as we clinked cans.

That's when it hit me. I should have thought of it sooner. But then, I should have slept last night, too.

"Competition!" I shouted.

"Huh?"

"You blamed one of your competitors for siccing Simmons on you, right?"

"Yeah," Nick said. "But I still don't know who it is."

"What if the pranks around Ian's place are more of the same? Not your competitor, but one of his?"

"Killing someone's a little extreme," he said.

"Maybe that's not part of it. Maybe we're looking at two separate suspects. One who's trying to eliminate a competing business. And the other who, for whatever reason, is eliminating people."

"That makes a lot more sense," Nick said, cocking his head to one side. "I mean, if you really wanted to scare Ian's customers, why hide the body?

You'd want to leave it right out in the open for maximum impact. Like the patio rat. Soooo, does that make you feel any better about my working over there?"

"Oh, much. Because instead of one maniac running around Ian's inn, there might be two."

Chapter 19

Nick was satisfied with the status quo at Ian's. That made one of us.

I decided that if he could stick his fingers in his ears and pretend everything at the B&B was fine, I could go over there and quietly nose around a little.

Hey, we each have our strengths.

So the next afternoon, while Nick grabbed a nap (and after Baba and I walked Lucy and J.B.), I traded my jeans for a summer skirt, put a dozen limbo cookies in a big mason jar, and headed over to the inn.

If anyone asked, I was there to see Rube. And bring him some cookies.

Ian wasn't at the front desk when I walked in—so far, so good.

Guests tended to congregate on the patio and in the library. I thought I'd hit the library first.

"Well, hello there! You're Alex from the neighborhood, right?"

Emily Prestwick was knitting on the sofa.

"Good memory! And nice to see you again. How's the sightseeing?"

"So good we decided to extend our stay another week. So far, we've hit the Botanic Garden, Kennedy Center, and the Corcoran Gallery—and spent several lovely afternoons at the Smithsonian. This evening we're taking in Georgetown."

"There's a new Cajun place I've heard about in Georgetown," I said, sitting in a side chair. "File Gumbo. It already has a Michelin star. And I have a foodie friend who really loved it. Especially the bananas Foster beignets."

"That sounds perfect," she said, clicking those needles lickety-split. "Frankly, I'm happily eating my way around the District. And the food is so good at this place. I'm afraid we're getting spoiled. This morning, eggs Benedict. And it was absolutely delicious. Bill is off giving a talk to one of the local garden clubs. Of course, I had to catch afternoon tea. Some lovely Ceylon with the most marvelous homemade scones, clotted cream, and strawberry jam. Served on the patio. And, of course, the garden is just beautiful. You should join us. Georgie will be there, too. We can make it a girls' tea."

I remembered the newlyweds and nodded. "I'd love to. My brother bakes the scones. And they are really good."

"Lovely! And it ought to cheer Georgie a bit. Between you and me," she said, lowering her voice, "I think she and Paul are already having problems. I've seen them apart more than I've seen them together."

"Yeah, he seemed like kind of a jerk," I said. "So

how have things been around the inn? I hear they're still working out some of the bugs?"

"Oh, the usual thing. A few snafus with the electricity. And someone overflowed a tub. Or was it a toilet? I don't remember," she said, as the needles flew.

Same stuff Nick had mentioned. Minus the midnight shadows.

"No more ghost baby?" I said.

Emily shook her head, smiling. "Heavens, no. But at least my Bill has a whimsical side, bless him. I feel for poor Georgie. That dolt of hers has no imagination at all. And no sense of humor. I just hope he's not violent."

"Any interesting new guests?"

"A congressman. If you call that interesting. Frankly, I don't. From out west. Idaho, I believe. Word is he's waiting for his local housing to be readied."

Man, this place hadn't been open long. And it had its share of problems, if that freezer body was any indication. But for some reason, it was already pulling in movers and shakers. Hand it to Ian—he was good at what he did. Whatever that was.

"I've got to stop by and see another friend," I said, getting up. "But save me a seat for tea."

I did want to talk with Rube before I left. The guy could read people like no one else I'd ever met. And he didn't miss much. Maybe that's what made him such a good writer. If there was a saboteur creeping around this place, Rube might have a few ideas.

But my first goal was to get into Harkins's room and look around.

I knew Ian had said he'd looked for clues. But it was possible he didn't know what he was looking for. It was also possible he was lying.

There's an old saying in the newsroom: if your mother says she loves you, ask for proof.

I headed up the stairs. While the staircase into the lobby was stately and wide, it narrowed as it gained altitude. By the time I hit the third-floor landing, the air was getting thin.

I honestly had no idea how I was going to get through Harkins's locked door. I'd noticed that even the guest doors had more than your typical bedroom door push-lock.

Too bad. With two older siblings, I could beat those things by the time I was five. Nick could do it by three and a half. Although Mom left that milestone out of our family Christmas letter.

The phone vibrated in my pocket. I pulled it out. Trip.

I'd meant to call him before I left. Rule No. 1 in the newsroom: always let someone know where you are and when you expect to return. It won't necessarily keep you safe, but it will give the cadaver dogs a place to start.

"Hey," I whispered as I ascended the summit, "any idea how to beat a locked door?"

"Where are you?"

"The B&B. Heading for Harkins's room."

"One dead body this week not enough for you?"

"Apparently, if it falls into a freezer in a basement and nobody hears it, it doesn't make a sound. So it doesn't count."

"Seriously, what are you doing there? Besides the obvious."

"Nick's bound and determined to keep coming over here. So I need to find out what the heck is going on. And if I get a lead on Harkins in the interim . . . What's that noise? Are you watching a movie?"

"I'm YouTubing a video on how to pick a lock. But if you get caught, we were sharing fashion tips. I know a place where you can get some silver earrings that will look great with your new handcuffs."

"Thanks for the vote of confidence."

"I don't suppose Nick's there, in case you need a hand?"

"Nope. And I planned it that way. He needs the rest, and I need to keep him out of this. Well, this is my floor. Two doors."

"The lady or the tiger?"

"Hey, as long as it isn't the murderer or the dead body, I almost don't care."

"So how many bodies is it that you've found now?"

"How many have I found, or how many do the police know I've found?"

"Should it bother me that there's a difference?"

"Talk about sharing your number. OK, here goes nothing."

I turned the knob. Didn't budge. Definitely locked.

I reached for the other door. The knob turned in my hand. "I'm in—I'll call you back."

"You've got fifteen minutes," Trip said. "Then I'm calling the cops myself."

"Deal."

I didn't know it from the hallway, but this room occupied one of the turrets on the back of the house. The outer wall was rounded and made up of a half-dozen long windows. It smelled of oil paint and turpentine. There were a half-dozen easels all over the room. Different paintings. Different styles. Different artists.

The room was like an art museum. I walked softly from one canvas to the next, studying them. If I hadn't been carrying a jar of cookies, I would have instinctively clasped my hands behind my back.

They were amazing. I'm no art connoisseur. But growing up, my parents dragged all four of us kids to every art museum, gallery opening, and exhibition in town. To me, these looked like the real thing.

One was a Van Gogh. Another was a Monet. Waterlilies. And a sturdy Degas dancer warmed up on a third easel. There were also a couple more modern ones in styles I didn't recognize. But the star of the show was in the center of the room. Renoir. And it looked familiar.

Mom and I had seen it a couple of years ago when some big-business muckety-muck lent it—and a few other prized works—to a local museum for the summer. I remember standing in front of it, just staring. Entranced. Kind of like I was now.

Ian's father wasn't some reformed youthful hooligan. Harkins was an art thief.

I heard a soft *thump*.

And it definitely didn't sound like the house

settling. It sounded like someone hiding in the closet. That explained the unlocked door.

I was trespassing. And whoever it was didn't want to be discovered. Even by me. So I didn't wait around to find out who they were. Or what they were doing.

I flew to the hallway, closed the door softly behind me, and jogged lightly down the stairs. When I hit the second-story landing, I stopped to breathe.

I pulled out my phone and hit #1 for Trip. My heart was pounding.

"Should I call a lawyer, or will you be sleeping in your own bed tonight?"

"I'm out, I'm fine. And have I got a story to tell you."

Chapter 20

After my foray upstairs, tea was relatively uneventful.

Emily regaled Georgie and me with stories of the things she and Bill were seeing and doing in DC and environs. I filled them in about some of the local haunts and low-key daily life here in Fordham, Virginia. (Despite the fact that low-key daily life was currently eluding me at the moment.)

Georgie scarfed down sandwiches, scones, tea cakes, and cookies, but said relatively little. Any time either of us mentioned Paul or the honeymoon, she changed the subject.

I did manage to find out that Rube was staying on the third floor. And except for the cocktail party and the occasional meal, he'd been locked in his room most of the time. I concluded that he probably hadn't seen squat and was just hoping he was OK.

But after we polished off another round of tea and a platter of delicious little sandwiches—trimmed with cookie cutters to resemble flowers and birds— I planned to ask him myself.

* * *

And that's where I was fifteen minutes later. On the third floor, I leaned in and put my ear against a door.

My mother would have been mortified. I consoled myself with the reminder that it was for a good cause: the health and safety of my younger brother.

I heard a regular rhythmic clicking sound. And this one I recognized: a keyboard.

Bingo!

I knocked on the door.

The clicking stopped. Dead silence. Then the door opened a crack. One brown eye stared out at me. I held up the jar of cookies. Rube stepped back and opened the door.

"Thought you might need a break," I said.

"Yeah, I thought that was you at the party. What are you doing here? You on another news story?"

"I live across the street. My brother makes the pastries and cookies they serve here. This is some of his work," I said, handing the jar to Rube.

"You're not on a story?" he asked, accepting the jar while eyeing me skeptically.

"Not exactly."

"Uh-huh. That's what I thought. What's the story?"

Was I right about this guy or what?

"It's not a story. It's not for print. It's more of a puzzle. My brother, Nick, works out of the kitchen downstairs. Some weird things have been going on here. Plumbing stuff. Electrical stuff. The outage the night of the party? That wasn't the storm. Somebody messed with the fuse box in the basement. I think one of the inn's competitors might be trying to sabotage the place. I was wondering if you might have noticed something."

Rube took a long hard look at me. Then he popped open the mason jar and offered me a cookie. I took one, and he did the same.

"Damn, these are really good. Your brother made these?"

"He's runs his own bakery," I said, nodding. "Right now, he's operating out of Ian's kitchen downstairs. Until we can get my place retrofitted."

"Boy's got a gift," he said, wolfing down the cookie and reaching for a second.

"So how's your mom?" I asked.

"She's doing great. Right now, she's planning my niece's wedding. In two weeks. I'm walking the bride down the aisle."

"Congratulations!"

"Can't take credit for it. She's a great girl. And that's all my moms. But they have totally taken over the house. I've got a book due the day before the big event. I was losing my mind."

"So you came here?"

"All the peace and quiet money can buy. I want food, I just roll downstairs. Or have it sent up. Non-stop writing. It's great. There's even a patio if I want to work outside with a cold drink. I'm happy, my moms is happy, and my niece is happy. Best of all, I can keep my editor happy by making my deadline."

"I know what that's like."

"Yeah, I heard about your little situation a couple of weeks ago. You come out of that mess OK?"

"Absolutely. And the guy who owns this place,

Ian Sterling—he helped a lot. I don't suppose you've noticed anything going on around here?"

Rube reached for two more cookies. I knew he'd missed afternoon tea, and the way those cookies were disappearing, I was beginning to wonder if he'd missed brunch, too.

"Man, it feels like I haven't been out of this room in forever," he said finally.

"What's this book about? I mean, if I can ask?"

"Off the record? You don't share this with anybody."

I nodded, putting my right hand up like the Girl Scout I never was. "I swear."

"A seventeenth-century scullery maid discovers a plot to kill the king. She tries to foil the assassination with the help of a roguish duke, who's actually the king's love child."

"And they fall in love?"

"Hell, yes, they fall in love! This is a romance novel. Turns out, the duke wasn't really born out of wedlock, but his mother died in childbirth. And he's secretly the prince of Wales. They save the king—and Rosie marries the duke and becomes a princess. Or she will if I can ever finish the damned book."

"So I guess you wouldn't have noticed if anyone was skulking around the inn?"

Rube went quiet and still.

"The night of the party. Before the lights went out? I was dog tired. I decided to turn in early. I said g'night to your friend Ian. Then I headed upstairs."

He paused, and I could tell he was replaying whatever it was in his mind.

"I was on the stairs when the lights went out," he said. "I was so beat, I couldn't decide whether to keep going up or turn around and come back down. When I turned, I saw someone coming out of that little side door in the entry hall. Learned later it goes down to the basement. Didn't know that at the time. Thought it was a bathroom."

The basement? Rube might have actually seen the saboteur. Or possibly the murderer.

"Who was it?" I asked.

"It was pitch black. The lights had just gone out. And my eyes hadn't adjusted to the dark."

"But?"

"I couldn't swear to it. But I think it was that kid on his honeymoon. Paul Something-or-other."

Chapter 21

I vowed that I'd keep Rube's secrets. And asked that he do the same about the possible identity of the saboteur. We sealed the deal with me promising more of Nick's cookies. Or whatever freshly baked goodies my brother might have available.

I could see Paul as the prankster. I couldn't see him as the killer. But Emily had been worried he might turn violent. So I was wondering if Georgie had shared something specific.

Which meant she was my next stop.

I didn't have any cookies to break the ice this time. But with the meal she'd put away at afternoon tea, I didn't see how she'd have room for any. I found her out on the patio, in sunglasses, stretched out in a chaise longue reading a book. Teatime was over, and the place was almost deserted.

How exactly did you accuse someone of sabotage with absolutely zero proof?

"Hey, Georgie," I said finally. "You and I need to have a quick talk. I know what's going on."

Even behind the glasses I could see her face crumple. She nodded, mutely.

"Who are you working for?" I asked.

She pulled off the sunglasses. Her hazel eyes were red and puffy. She'd clearly been crying, and fresh tears rolled down her damp cheeks. I pulled a napkin off the table next to her drink and handed it to her.

"How did you know?" she said, blotting her eyes and dabbing her nose.

"Who's behind it?"

"The Alexandria House Inn and Spa. The owner. His name is Hamilton Stephens."

I knew Ham Stephens. Ironically, he was tight with Lydia. They ran with the same old-money crowd.

"But it wasn't supposed to be like this," she said, sobbing. "I swear."

"Tell me. What were you supposed to do before it got out of hand?"

"Paul and I aren't really married. We're actors. When we can get work. The rest of the time, I wait tables. Mr. Stephens saw us in a play at the Fairfax Theatre. He hired us. We were supposed to pose as a honeymoon couple. He'd pay for ten days at the inn. Everything included. Meals. Room service. Taxis. Everything. And Paul said it would be like live theater. We'd create characters and get to live them twenty-four hours a day. That's why Paul always wore that stupid baby's breath in his lapel. He felt that's what his groom character would do. To me it was just a chance to take a real vacation. I never could have afforded it otherwise."

"What did Ham Stephens want you to do?"

"Just take some notes. On anything that wasn't perfect. Like if the service was slow, or the guests were too loud, or a meal was cold. Like a Yelp review, only we were just looking for the bad stuff."

"So what happened?"

"For the first few days, everything was great. I mean, really great. I was having a blast. But Paul was worried. He was the one who had to report in to Mr. Stephens every day. He said the guy was getting angry because we weren't finding anything. Really angry."

"Why not just go home?"

"That's what I thought. Then Paul said, 'Don't worry, we just need more data.' That's what he called it. Data. He said Mr. Stephens believed that if we just hung around a few more days, we'd start to see flaws. 'Cracks in the veneer,' he called them. But that wasn't true. Later, I found out that Paul was doing things. Making things happen."

"Sabotage?"

"Yeah," she said, inhaling deeply. "He'd stuff paper into people's toilets when they were out, or turn off the water pipes. He even did something to the water heater one time. But they got it up and running just a couple of hours later. Paul was so pissed."

"How did you find out what he was doing?"

"He told me. He said it was his idea, and it was the only reason Mr. Stephens was letting us stay."

She started snuffling again. "I didn't want that. I just wanted to go home. But Paul said if I did that, his cover would be blown. And he warned me that Mr. Stephens knows a lot of people in the local theater community."

"Where's Paul now?"

"I don't know," she bawled. "I haven't seen him in hours. He never showed up for brunch. And when I went back to the room after tea, his stuff was gone. I don't know what to do."

"Is your bill paid up?" I asked.

"Yeah, Mr. Stephens paid it with a credit card that belongs to his driver. I was supposed to say it was my father's card. We're scheduled to check out Tuesday morning."

"What's your real name?"

"Georgette Lange. I live in Herndon. Paul's last name is Hartnett. But I think that's just his stage name. I know he lives in Arlington."

"Pack up your stuff and go home this afternoon," I said. "Don't worry about Paul. You've got to think of yourself. And you want to get out."

"Are they going to arrest me?" she asked. When she wiped her nose, I could see her hand was trembling.

"You made a couple of bad choices, but I don't think you did anything illegal," I said. "I'll talk to Ian. Even if this was criminal, I don't think he'll press charges. But he might want to talk with you about Ham Stephens. That part's up to him."

"Mr. Stephens'll kill me."

"I don't think Ian will blow your cover. As far as Ham Stephens is concerned, you held up your part of the bargain. There just wasn't anything to report. Go pack. Go home. Get on with your life."

She wiped her reddened nose with the linen napkin. "This place is beautiful. But after those first couple of days? All I wanted to do was go home. I just wanna chill out in front of the TV on my smelly old sofa with my roommate and our cat."

"Before you take off, one more question. That insurance salesman who checked in Thursday afternoon—what did he look like?"

Georgie took a deep breath, steadying her voice. "The insurance guy? Sandy-blond hair and freckles. I remember thinking he had even more freckles than me."

"Do you remember what he was wearing?"

She cocked her head to one side. "Some kind of a jacket. Not a suit jacket, but casual. For the weather. Tan, I think."

"Was his hair short or long?"

"Super short. I kinda thought it looked like what's left after you harvest a wheat field."

"A crew cut?"

"Yeah."

"You knew he sold insurance because of what he said to Harkins when he checked in. Do you remember what he said? His exact words?"

"I don't remember exactly," she said, blotting her eyes. "Something about 'You're a smart man. You know you need insurance.' Then he said something like 'But you're lucky—that happens to be my business.'"

Knowing what I now knew about Harkins, I'm betting this guy was into a whole different kind of "insurance." What Georgie had overheard was a threat. Or a shakedown. Shortly after this guy arrived, he was dead in the freezer. And Harkins had vanished.

Chapter 22

Now I had to talk to Ian.

The real question: Just how much was I going to tell him? Did he know about the mini museum with millions of dollars' worth of fine art in his father's "study"? Given the presence of someone in Harkins's closet, were the paintings even still there? Or had they disappeared—like the body in the basement?

And who was that man who had been threatening Harkins? Did Ian know him? Did Ian kill him? Did Harkins kill him? If so, was that why he ran? Or had Insurance Guy killed Harkins? Could Ian have killed Insurance Guy in revenge—and stashed his body in the basement?

I had a good idea what Insurance Guy really was, but I still didn't know his name. Why did I think Ian might? Was that why he wanted to see the body? Or did he know that, by the time we returned to the basement, it wouldn't be there?

Too many questions, too few answers.

When I walked into the lobby, Ian was at the desk, fielding a phone call. He typed something into a small computer console.

"We're looking forward to seeing you then, Mrs. Martinez. And let me know if you change your mind about having someone pick you up at Reagan National. Of course! Have a lovely day!"

He tapped a couple of keys, then looked up at me. "Well, hullo! Nice to see you again. I trust you enjoyed mid-morning tea?"

"It was very nice," I said. "But that's not why I'm here. We need to talk."

"Is it about my father? Have you learned where he is?"

"No, nothing yet. It's about the inn. Is there a place where we could speak privately? This isn't a conversation you want to have in public—or in front of the guests."

Ian was clearly perplexed. "My private study's just over here," he said, stepping quickly to a door off to the left of the lobby. "Let's talk in here."

He unlocked the door with an old-fashioned brass key, stepped inside, and held the door open for me.

The study was actually a small library, complete with antique, built-in oak bookshelves and a fireplace. It reminded me of the B&B's main library.

The fireplace was set off with a marble hearth, intricately carved woodwork, a heavy vintage oak mantel, and a Renoir.

I was drawn to it, as if pulled. It looked identical to the one upstairs.

The paintings upstairs were minus their frames. And the canvasses sported a light sprinkling of dust. This one had a frame. And it was dust-free.

So either Ian had done a bit of framing and light housekeeping sometime in the past few hours, or this was a different painting.

Bizarre.

I turned to catch Ian studying me. I couldn't read his expression.

"You were right," I said. "Someone has been sabotaging the inn."

"Who?"

"Paul the happy honeymooner. But he was sent here by one of your competitors, Ham Stephens."

"From the Alexandria House? Good Lord, why?"

"I'm guessing he didn't exactly welcome the competition." But was it strictly a tug-of-war over guests? Or did the rivalry have anything to do with the affections of one Lydia Stewart?

"Where is Paul?" Ian asked.

"No idea. Georgie hasn't seen him in a while. It sounds like he cleared out today. Left her high and dry, by the way. And I really don't think she was part of it."

"I can't believe Ham Stephens is such a total snake. Are you certain?"

I nodded. "I just spoke with Georgie. She could be spinning a story, but I don't think so. And there are a few things you can check. Including the credit card used to pay for their stay. According to Georgie, it really belongs to Ham's driver."

"The unremitting gall of the man! He actually hosted a drinks party to welcome me to the so-called local fraternity of innkeepers. He's a gold-plated phony."

"That's a pretty good description of Ham Stephens," I said, grimacing. "He hired a couple of out-of-work actors to pose as newlyweds. Supposedly just to make notes on your weaknesses. Anything that was going wrong, anything that could be used against you. The problem was, there was nothing to report. So Paul kicked it up a notch and turned himself into a one-man wrecking crew. Electric, plumbing, lighting, you name it—he broke it."

"Is it possible Ham didn't know about the sabotage?"

"According to Georgie, Paul reported in to him by phone every day. Paul told Georgie that the sabotage was his idea, and that Ham just greenlighted it. But from what I know about Ham, I think it was more likely the other way around. They could have even planned the sabotage angle from the beginning and just kept Georgie in the dark. She's young, and broke and scared you're going to have her arrested. Or rat her out to Ham."

"I would never. On my honor. I would like to speak with her, though."

"I think she's expecting that. I told her you might. I also told her the best move was for her to pack up and leave this afternoon. For what it's worth, that's all she's wanted to do since Paul started in on the sabotage. She was just looking for a free vacation—a couple of days with all expenses paid at a nice inn. Then it spun out of control, and she didn't know what to do. Apparently, Ham is plugged into the local theater scene. And Paul used that to threaten her career if she left."

"Poor kid. I'll talk to her before she leaves and tell her 'no worries.' No idea where Paul is, then?"

"Both he and his bags are gone. Georgie says he lives in Arlington and goes by the last name of Hartnett. But she thinks that's just his stage name."

"I don't know whether to be appalled or relieved," Ian said. "I can't let Ham get away with this unchallenged, of course. But I am very glad to know that this place isn't truly crumbling around us. I don't know how you did this—how you put it all together—but thank you. This is quite amazing."

He was standing across the room, staring at me with those blue eyes. I should have been happy. And I did feel that stupid flutter.

But, at the same time, I couldn't help but wonder just how much Ian really knew about his father.

Chapter 23

I might not have told Ian what I'd found in Harkins's room. But I did tell Nick and Trip. As soon as I got home.

Nick deserved to know what was going on over there. Or at least what little I knew about what was going on over there.

His take: It was good news. Since he wasn't an art thief—or shaking down an art thief—he was bulletproof.

I just hoped he didn't mean that literally.

Trip agreed with him. To a point.

"OK, it won't go on LinkedIn's list of best places to work. But as long as Nick sticks to the kitchen and doesn't go poking around, he'll probably be fine," Trip said, as the two of us sipped coffee on my front porch. "If Harkins did kill the guy you found, it sounds like he did it in self-defense. So who do you think was in the closet? Do you think Harkins came back for his stuff?"

"In broad daylight? I doubt it. If he's on the run,

it makes more sense to come back at night. But I want to know more about those paintings. I've been doing a little research."

"Do tell," Trip said, steepling his fingers.

"That Renoir? I saw it a couple of years ago when Mom and I went to an exhibition at the Corcoran. Business tycoons had loaned pieces from their private collections for a special show. The stuff was spectacular. And Jameson Blair owned that Renoir."

"Oh, jeez, not him," Trip said.

"Why? What have you heard?"

"Made his money in acquisitions. Buys companies, builds them up, takes them public, cashes out. Or buys them up and guts them. Either way, has his fat little fingers in a lot of pies. A couple of guys on the business desk have been looking at him pretty closely. They've been hearing rumors that his dealings are a little less than ethical. Or legal. Self-described big shot. Lavish lifestyle. Throws around cash. Planes, yachts, parties. The ladies love him. A little too much. Wife number two found out, and from what I hear, she's hired a really good divorce lawyer."

"He also owns at least three of the other paintings I saw in Harkins's room. And there were two more paintings that I didn't recognize, but . . ."

"But it definitely sounds like Harkins—or whoever—was targeting his collection. The question is why?"

"The question is why was there an exact replica of that Renoir in Ian's private library?" I told him.

"Holy impressionists, Batgirl, are you sure?"

"Exactly the same, save a frame on one and a

little dust on the other. Ian's short-handed. If he was going to tidy up and frame some art, he'd focus on the public areas, not his own library. And believe me, there were bookshelves in that room with dust to spare."

"So the innkeeper isn't a great housekeeper. At least that's something you have in common," he said, pulling a big red rubber bone from the back of his chair and tossing it onto the porch. "Maybe Blair is the key."

"What do you mean?" I asked.

"Harkins could have targeted him for a reason," Trip said. "If we knew more about him, we might be able to fill in some of the blanks about Harkins. Maybe they have a past. Or something in the present that connects them."

"It smelled like turpentine. And oil paint."

"Ian's library?"

"Harkins's study. Those paintings looked like the real thing. But that room? That was an artist's studio."

"So Harkins is an art forger, as well as an art thief. Maybe he did the one in the library."

"Ian said that Harkins selected his rooms because there's a view and they're private. He also said that his father usually keeps the study door unlocked, but lately he's been locking it."

"So whatever this is started recently."

Four bicyclers coasted down the street. The neighborhood racing squad again. The leader waved, and I waved back.

"Ian admitted that Harkins has a criminal past," I said. "But he wouldn't share any of the details. He doesn't have a record over here. Not that I've been able to find. But I wonder about back in Great Britain. What if he was a reformed art forger?"

"If so, sounds like Daddy's fallen off the wagon."

"So how does Blair's getting divorced make him a target for art theft?" I asked.

"No idea," Trip said. "And maybe it doesn't."

"Have you noticed that every time I think I'm closing in on an answer, it just opens up more questions?"

Chapter 24

It's odd how quickly even the weirdest things can start to seem routine.

Over the next couple of days, with Baba in residence and J.B. content and happy, life seemed almost normal.

The Mega Baby guys assembled the crib in fifteen minutes flat. We set it up in my room, and Baba and I took turns getting up with J.B. at night. But Nick usually pitched in with at least one night feeding, when he got back from Ian's in the wee hours of the morning.

Every night, when I heard him come through the front door, I was relieved. Apparently, holding my tongue also meant holding my breath. It was torture. The only thing Nick and I agreed on: not to tell Baba.

Kudos to Sheryl: J.B. loved his swing. Almost as much as he loved Baba.

She'd put him in it, fasten the seat belt, and crank the handle. It would play a calliope tune that sounded (to me, at least) like an ice-cream truck. He'd wave his arms and grin while Baba clapped along to the music, and Lucy raced around the sofa like a demented ferret.

Even the pup was warming to our little guy. One afternoon, when we had him on his little blanket in the backyard, Lucy carefully placed one of her favorite rubber chew toys on his tummy.

Another time, I heard J.B. giggling—and looked up to see her enthusiastically licking his toes.

For my part, I was spending most of my time either answering Aunt Margie letters or trying to get a lead on J.B.'s parents and Ian's father.

And having about the same level of success with all three: zippo.

I was thrilled with my first batch of Aunt Margie letters—convinced I'd totally nailed the tone and cadence of her voice. And her commonsense wisdom.

I e-mailed them to Maya, who e-mailed them to Aunt Margie. A day later, the "edited" version popped up in my in-box. About five words were the same. And three of those were the byline.

Back to the drawing board.

Ditto with Ian's father. I decided to start with what I did know and go from there. So I did a local property search. Turned out the inn was owned by an LLC. Which was fairly typical. That, in turn, was owned by another company out of London. Which was controlled by a corporation in the Caymans. And that's where I hit a brick wall.

Nick had been right about one thing: his late hours in Ian's kitchen gave him a front-row seat to the strange goings on at the Cotswolds Inn. While the pranks had stopped, Nick swore he saw shadows out in the garden after midnight at least once.

Neither one of us went near that basement.

But I had popped over to the inn a couple of times to take Rube some of Nick's best wares. And commiserate on the pace of his progress with the story of Rosie and her duke.

My brother approached Ian with an idea that could prevent future sabotage: installing one of those DIY security systems with cameras you can control from your phone. Ian countered that his guests expected to be able to relax and unwind in complete peace and privacy. And apparently a multiple video camera setup sort of defeated the purpose.

I suspected the real reason had something to do with Harkins's art collection.

While Baba and Nick kept J.B. happy and fed, it was my job to find his mom. And I was getting nowhere. But then it wasn't like I could stick up fliers with his photo announcing "Found Baby."

Could I?

On the off chance that J.B. had been left at the wrong house, I wheeled him and his pram around the neighborhood (and a couple of local shopping centers), until my legs nearly fell off. Other than a few strange looks from the neighbors—including one woman who confided that she "just knew" I was pregnant when she saw me snarfing Reese's Cups at the neighborhood Halloween party—nada. No one seemed to know J.B. Or miss him.

I kept pumping my sources at the local cop shops

for any info on missing people—especially babies, young women, and older men—for my "story." Just in case, I even expanded the geography and reached out to contacts I had in Annapolis, Baltimore, Lancaster, and Philadelphia. Trip agreed to back me up, in case any of the cops checked to make sure the story was legit. None of them did.

Strangely, my first real break on J.B.'s parents came during one of the rare moments I wasn't looking.

Nick had driven Baba to the grocery store. And after a hearty breakfast, J.B. was down for the count. Lucy was dozing next to his crib.

I needed to stretch my legs and get away from Aunt Margie. I didn't dare run the vacuum with J.B. snoozing. So I opted to do a little tidying.

It's amazing what you find when you clean. Under the sofa cushions: three magazines I didn't even remember buying. I arranged them on the coffee table, grabbed the trash bag, moved an end table—and found a stash of treasures. Lucy.

There was one of my heels. Half of the pair I'd warn to the cocktail party. (Now a bit gnawed around the toe.) A wayward piece of carrot (Nick's attempt to give her healthy teething snacks). A purple rubber bone (her favorite chew toy). And a small scrap of paper.

Thick, creamy stock. Expensive. The top and bottom were missing. Torn off. Or eaten.

The words that remained floored me: . . . *sweet Ian—so sorry to have to do this. But there was no other way. I want you to meet little Alistair. Take good care of him. He's your . . .*

Flowing, beautiful script. Definitely a woman's handwriting.

I flipped it over. Nothing.

I rifled through the rest of Lucy's treasure trove. No more paper.

I scouted under the couch. Dust. Three quarters. And five peanut M&Ms.

They say the road to hell is paved with good intentions. I contend it's peanut M&Ms.

Since I hadn't had any in the house since December, I chucked them into the trash bag.

For the next fifteen minutes, I held my own scavenger hunt. I found two dimes and a nickel. Six bobby pins. A crumpled dollar bill. Three tennis balls. And a fork. (I'm blaming Nick for that one.)

But no more bits of paper.

By now, I figured the rest of the note was either being processed by Lucy's digestive system or had already fertilized the yard.

Sitting on the floor, I leaned against the back of the couch, unfolded my legs, and tried to wrap my head around this new information.

Alistair. J.B.'s real name was Alistair? And he wasn't a Vlodnachek. He was a Sterling!

Ian had a child. Did Ian have a wife? Or a girl-friend? Clearly he had someone. Or had had someone at least a year ago, if Mega Baby Sheryl was right about J.B.'s age.

Alistair's age, I corrected myself.

Damn.

I walked into my bedroom and peered into the crib. He was awake, staring up at me with those beautiful blue eyes. The last time I saw eyes like that, they were the color of a dark, stormy sky.

It fit.

"Hi, Alistair!" I said, trying it out loud. "How are you, little Alistair? Are you having a good day, Alistair?"

He gave me a gummy little grin and waved his chubby fists. Was it my imagination or did he seem relieved that someone finally knew who he was?

Chapter 25

After a quick change for Alistair—followed by a bottle for him and a cookie each for me and Lucy—I was just settling him in his wind-up swing when Nick and Baba came through the front door.

"Miya malenkaya reedka!" she said, scooping up little J.B. He gurgled and gave her a bright smile.

"Oh, now he's your little radish," Nick said, grinning. "And I'm just the hired help who carries your groceries. See how easy we're replaced, Lucy?" he added, reaching down to give the pup a scratch behind one ear.

"Bah!" she said, patting him on the back with her J.B.-free hand.

Alistair, I mentally corrected. How many times would I have to remind myself? To me, he'd always be J.B.—James Bond Vlodnachek, the howling terror of Azalea Avenue.

I followed Nick out to his car. "I think I got a lead on J.B.'s family," I said, as he handed me two Giant food bags.

"For real? Where are they? Who are they? Are they nice people?"

"Right across the street. Ian is his father. And his real name is Alistair."

"You're kidding! How did you find out?"

I told him about the note and Lucy's hoard of loot.

"Man, I don't think I want to be there when you tell him. That is serious. A secret baby? What about the baby momma?"

"No idea. We just got a piece of the note. Thanks to your little goat dog."

"Hey, I puppy-proof this place regularly. Somebody breaks in and leaves a note where she can get it, that's on them. Damn. I wonder how he's gonna take it?"

"I wonder if he knows who and where the mother is. And why she just dumped J.B. over here and ran. I mean, Alistair."

"So when are you going to tell him?" Nick asked.

"Why me?"

"You found the note."

"Yeah, and if your dog hadn't eaten it, the little guy would have been home a week ago."

"The dog ate my homework?" Nick said. "Lame."

"Seriously, what are we going to tell him? And how? Besides, it isn't safe for little J.B.—I mean, Alistair—to be over at that place right now. Hell, it's barely safe enough for you."

"Hey, I'm not the one who found a dead body and stolen art."

"You do realize you're making my case for me?" I said.

"Look, if you want me to sit in, I will. Face it, this

is going to be awkward for both of us. For different reasons. But maybe he won't want the little guy over there right now. So we could make him an offer."

"You mean to keep him?"

"Just until the mother comes back. Or until things settle down over there. Or until Harkins comes home. Man, Ian's having a rough week," he said, setting the bags on the kitchen table. "But we have to clear it with Baba first. Right now, she's doing all the heavy lifting."

"That's not a bad idea," I said. "I mean, with Harkins gone, Ian's working nonstop to keep up with the guests. And you remember what it was like here before Baba arrived."

"Yeah, and I can't imagine anyone would check in and pay money to go through that. The place would be empty in no time flat."

"Ironic," I said.

"How so?"

"Well, Paul the not-so-merry prankster was trying to shut down Ian's business," I reminded him. "But a sweet, innocent little baby could totally succeed where he failed."

Nick grinned. "That's because to really screw up someone's life, you have to be family."

Turned out, Baba loved the idea of a few more days with J.B. Or Alistair. Or her *malenkaya reedka*.

Now all we had to do was tell the father that he was a father.

I figured it was better to do it away from the inn. Fewer prying eyes and ears. And I was sort of hoping that if he saw how happy Alistair was over here, he might be more inclined to let him stay.

I phoned, and Ian agreed to "pop over for a quick chat." But he couldn't stay long. So this was going to have to be one of those "rip off the Band-Aid" conversations.

"Should I brew up a pot of tea, just to break the ice?" I called to Nick, as I ran around plumping cushions and gathering up baby and doggie toys.

"You're telling him he has a kid. I think you're going to need something stronger than tea."

"We've got coffee, tea, generic soda, generic beer, and limbo cookies."

"Yeah, I've got news for you—we're out of limbo cookies."

"Tea it is," I said.

"OK, but if things get dicey, I've got a couple of cans chilled and ready to go."

"Sounds like a plan," I said, just as we heard a knock on the door.

I smiled when I saw Ian standing on the porch. Strangeness at the inn or no, I couldn't help it. His eyes were a calm, clear blue today. So much like someone else I knew. He was holding a big bunch of pink flowers wrapped in newspaper. Idly, I wondered if it was the *Tribune* or the *Sentinel.*

"Hydrangeas! They're beautiful! Thank you!" I said, accepting the bundle. So how would he take the news of his own little bundle?

"There's a riot of them in the side garden," Ian said. "Thought you might enjoy a few blooms indoors, as well. I notice your azaleas are really doing well."

Small talk it is, then. This wasn't going to be easy.

"Well, come on in. Nick's getting us a little tea."

As per our plan, Baba, Lucy, and Alistair had disappeared into my room. But the house still looked like a herd of buffalos had rumbled through it.

I saw Ian eyeing the baby swing.

"More family staying with you?" he asked.

"Not exactly," I started, "That's sort of why . . ."

"Here we are with some tea," Nick said, showing up with a tray. "Hey, man," he said to Ian. "Bet you could use a little break."

"Definitely. The good news is, we're fully booked. The bad news is, without Dad, I'm one man doing a two-man job."

"Have you heard anything from his friends?" I asked.

Ian shook his head. "The ones I was able to reach haven't heard from him in months. A couple of his closest friends are on some kind of photo safari. Tanzania or Zambia. No one seems to know exactly where. And they're not due back for a couple of weeks. I was hoping maybe you'd learned something."

I looked at Nick. Nick looked at me.

"No, nothing about Harkins," I said. "There was actually another reason we needed to talk with you."

"If it has to do with the escapades around the inn, thanks to you, they seem to have stopped," Ian said, accepting the cup I'd poured for him and adding a little cream. Or, in this case, milk. "We haven't had any incidents of mischief since Paul left."

"No, it's not that," Nick said. "Look, there's no easy way to say this . . ."

"We found a note over here this afternoon," I said. "It was meant for you. Lucy actually ate most of it, then hid what was left. I found it just now when I was cleaning."

I cast an eye around the living room. It didn't look like it had been cleaned today. Or this month.

"Was it from my father? Is it about my father?"

"No, it has nothing to do with him," I said, focusing on Ian. "This was from a woman. She needed to leave something with you last week. Friday morning. Only for some reason, she left it here. I don't know why. I'm guessing the rest of the note might have explained that."

I went to the dining room that served as my office and carefully retrieved the note from one of the small drawers in my rolltop desk.

"This is what's left of it," I said, gingerly placing the scrap in his hands as if it were a piece of the Dead Sea Scrolls.

I looked over at Nick. He nodded encouragingly.

"Alistair?" Ian said. "Who is Alistair?"

"He's a baby. About three months old, from the looks of it. He was left on my kitchen table last Friday morning, along with a couple of clean diapers and a couple of bottles of formula. Sleeping in a very pricey car seat."

"A baby?" The guy looked stunned. "It can't be . . . my . . . baby."

"Apparently. Granted, the note's not a lot to go on. Can you think of who his mom might be? Or why she might have left him here, rather than talking with you yourself?"

"Absolutely no idea," he said, staring at the slip

of paper. "This doesn't make sense. I'm careful. Very careful. And fatherhood is most decidedly not in the cards right now, I can assure you."

"Would you like to see him?" I asked gently.

Numbly, he nodded.

"I'll get him," Nick said, jumping up.

I prayed Alistair was in one of his charming moods. As opposed to one of his devil-baby moods. He'd been on his best behavior since Baba had arrived. Some of that may have been because she'd diagnosed him as "gassy" and started feeding him a top-notch brand of baby formula made from goat's milk. But I'd seen what the little tyke could do to well-meaning yet inexperienced caregivers. I had my fingers crossed.

Nick brought him out, wrapped in the little blue blanket he'd arrived in. Which had been washed umpteen times since then.

Ian's eyes were the size of saucers. A theoretical baby was one thing. But now the little guy was right here in front of him. And Papa Ian hadn't even had nine months to prepare.

"Would you like to hold him?" Nick asked.

Ian nodded. I was beginning to wonder if he'd been struck dumb. Not that I could blame him.

"Here you go," Nick coached him. "Juuuuust like a football. Or in your case, a rugby ball. And you have to be careful to always support his little neck. That's the weak spot. Well, that and the back of the head."

"Oh my Lord," Ian breathed. I don't think he realized he'd said it out loud.

For his part, Alistair looked amused. And curious.

Ian lowered the little guy into his lap and looked into his bright blue eyes.

"Good Lord, he looks just like me," he said. "I mean, as a child. My mother has photos. I looked just like this. Like him."

It was the first time I'd ever seen him rattled. A dead body might not have fazed Ian Sterling. But a live baby definitely did.

Alistair, fresh off a nap, a bottle, and some Baba love, looked up and smiled. That's when I saw Ian's face melt.

"He's mine," he said softly. "He actually is mine."

Ian reached out and traced the line down Alistair's soft cheek. The little guy cooed.

"So you're Alistair?" Ian said softly. "Alistair Sterling. I'm sorry we had to wait so long to meet. You are gorgeous, you are. Yes, sir."

Alistair giggled. Poor Ian. This kid had him right where he wanted him. He'd be driving the Bentley at sixteen and cruising off to Harvard or Oxford two years later. I could tell from the look on Ian's face that the little guy would want for absolutely nothing.

"Ten fingers, ten toes, and a huge appetite," Nick said.

Ian smiled. "He smells wonderful," he said, sniffing the top of that downy head.

"Most of the time," Nick said, refilling his own teacup. "More on that later."

"You cared for him? For a week?" Ian said, looking at me.

"We didn't know what else to do. The mother obviously took good care of him. But for some reason, she left him here."

"And she got past two dead bolts to do it," Nick added. "That's got to narrow the suspect pool a little."

Ian gazed blissfully at his new bundle. "I wish I could think who he looks like. But the truth is he favors my side of the family."

He was right about that. If this was a case on *Paternity Court*, it would be a slam dunk. Now if we could just find out who the mother was.

It was time for part two of our nefarious little plan. But I didn't have the heart to interrupt daddy-baby bonding time.

"When he first arrived here, he wasn't this calm," I started. I looked over at Nick, who nodded. "He cried a lot. Almost all the time. Nick and I, we were running flat out to keep up with bottles and diapers and burping and rocking and laundry. There was a lot of laundry."

I looked at Nick for encouragement.

"No breaks, no sleep," Nick added.

"How did you manage?" Ian asked, looking down at the contented baby who was dozing off in his arms.

"Baba," I said. "Nick went to Baltimore and explained the situation."

"Hey, she was happy to help," Nick said. "And she really knows what she's doing."

"When I found the note, when we realized who J.B.—I mean, Alistair—belonged to, we realized it would be tough for you, too. Anyway, we talked it over with Baba. And if you want, she's fine with continuing to look after J. . . . uh . . . Alistair, over here until you find his mom or until things settle down a little at the inn. And, in the interim, she can walk you through some of the basics of baby care. Unless you have a lot of experience with babies."

Heck, for all I knew, back in jolly old England, Ian could have captained a fleet of nannies who served the royal family itself.

"I have precisely no experience with babies," he said, smiling down at the sleeping cherub in his lap. "This is the first time I've even held one. If your grandmother wouldn't mind, that would be wonderful. He's so small. So fragile. I just don't want to make a mistake."

"You're going to do fine," I said, relieved. "You love him. And he clearly loves you. That's what counts."

"I feel like an idiot," Ian said, beaming. "All I brought for you was a bouquet of flowers."

Chapter 26

When I padded out toward the kitchen the next morning, there was what looked like a log under a yellow blanket on the couch. But this log was snoring. Loudly.

I assumed Nick was so tired he didn't quite make it to his bedroom. Since Angie had put in her first order, he'd been working overtime testing out new recipes and techniques.

Baba, Trip, and I were his guinea pigs, and it was the best job I'd ever had. Even the burned stuff was good.

And the poor guy was still helping out with Alistair in the wee hours. So if he needed to sack out on the couch, so be it.

But Lucy wasn't at his feet. Odd.

Maybe she'd taken over his empty bed.

The kitchen smelled like apples and cinnamon. And there was a very large bakery box on the table.

I half expected the note on the top of the box to say "Eat me." Because that's kind of how my life was going at the moment. Instead, in Nick's scrawly hand, it read: *Guys, My latest batch—give it a try and see what you think. Nick.*

I brewed up a big pot of coffee. Between me working at home, Nick's late hours, Baba in residence, and Ian dropping in to see Alistair, we were gonna need a gallon of caffeine.

Plus, I hoped it would go well with whatever was in the box.

I poured a big cup, dumped in some milk, and took a long, satisfied sip. Now all I needed were the newspapers.

On my way through the living room, I noticed that the snoring sofa log had picked up some volume. And turned over. The blanket no longer covered his head.

His bald, wrinkled head.

I blinked hard and stepped closer. It wasn't Nick. It was Marty Crunk!

Oh, hell no!

I ran to Nick's door and pounded.

"Sleeping! Go 'way!"

"Nicholas Edward Vlodnachek, you open this door right now!"

I heard a scuffling sound. And the *click, click, click* of Lucy's nails on the floor.

When the door opened a crack, I saw one bleary brown eye. "What?"

"Why is Marty Crunk sleeping on our sofa?"

"Oh, hell, I thought something was really wrong. Your friend showed up last night. Well, more like early this morning. On crutches. Said his niece was trying to kill him, and he was formally 'requesting sanctuary,'" Nick said, making air quotes. "All he really needed was a place to stay for the night. So I said he could take the sofa."

"He's not my friend. He's my, well, I don't know what he is."

Nick looked puzzled. "And?"

"He's a superstar at the *Sentinel.* I met him working on my current gig. He recommended me for it, actually."

"So he sounds like a decent guy."

"He *is* a decent guy. I just didn't expect to find him on the sofa this morning. He's supposed to be in the hospital."

I hoped he hadn't escaped again. Justin and Arlene were gonna be frantic.

"He's been out for a couple of days," Nick said. "Apparently, that's the problem. His niece is his caretaker. And she sounds like a real piece of work. Look, talk to him when he gets up. I'm gonna let Lucy out for a quick break, then get some shuteye. I was up 'til almost three. Toward the end I was so tired I was actually imagining things out in the garden again."

"How's the baking going?"

"Great! Got a new batch for you guys to try. Fresh apple doughnuts. C'mon, you little fuzz-ball," he said, looking down at Lucy. "Let's get you outside."

"Go back to sleep," I said. "I'll take Lucy duty."

"Aww, thank you," he said, yawning. "I'm beat."

Lucy, who seemed to realize some sort of transfer had been made, looked up at me expectantly as Nick trundled off to bed.

"First, a nice walk in the backyard. Then we hit Nick's doughnuts," I told her.

She wagged her tail all the way to the back door. Some days I was convinced the pup understood me better than anybody.

Lucy and I had a blissful few minutes in the backyard. She frolicked in the ever-growing grass. I vowed to mow the lawn when I had fifteen minutes.

That's when the yelling started. I recognized both voices. Baba. And Marty.

Yikes! I'd forgotten to tell Baba about Marty!

I raced into the living room. She had him backed into a corner.

Naked from the waist up, he held the blanket and one crutch over his midsection—partially covering what looked suspiciously like white boxers. His right arm shielded his face, and his sparse white hair was flying in all directions as he dodged Baba.

For her part, Baba was wielding a large Pyrex baking dish like she meant business.

"Lady, it's OK! Oh! Kay!" Marty shouted, bobbing and weaving.

"Go! Shoo! Leave! You go now!"

"Baba!" I said, putting a hand on her shoulder. "It's all right. He's a coworker of mine from the paper. He needed a place to sleep last night, and Nick said he could stay here. I just found out about it myself."

"Humpff!" Baba said loudly. "Vagrants!" With that, she toddled off to the kitchen.

"Damn, who was that?" Marty asked, as he wrapped my favorite blanket around his midriff like a sarong. A pair of short, white athletic socks completed his ensemble.

"That's my grandmother, and she's in charge."

"Well, sorry," he said, smoothing down his hair. "I didn't mean to step on any toes. I got up to hit the head, and suddenly she was coming at me, screaming like a banshee."

"Neither one of us knew you were here last night. So it was kind of a surprise."

"Shock" would be more accurate.

"Look, why don't you get dressed and come on out to the kitchen. I just put some coffee on, and Nick made some fresh doughnuts."

"That would be great, kid. Thanks. And I'll, uh, apologize to your grandma. For, you know, trying to kill me."

Marty might be a pest. But he was a fast learner.

Still, I was gonna have to burn that blanket.

Chapter 27

Luckily for me, Baba was all wrapped up with Alistair.

Not that she was thrilled about the prospect of hosting Marty. For that matter, neither was I.

Baba held Alistair on her lap while she gave him his bottle, singing softly as she rocked him. I recognized the Russian lullaby from childhood. Lucy, who had already devoured her own breakfast—and a doughnut—was curled up at her feet.

"Would you like more coffee, Baba?" I asked.

"Da!" she said, smiling as she put a drowsy Alistair on her shoulder to burp. "And one of Nick's dough apples," she said.

"Nuts?" I said.

"No, apple," she said decisively.

"You got it." I topped off her coffee cup and put a doughnut on her plate.

We were both just finishing up when Marty swung in on his crutches. This time, dressed, washed, and shaved, by the look of it. He'd even dabbed on a little cologne. Although I suspected he might have "borrowed" it from Nick.

"I . . . uh, just want to say I'm sorry about before. For showing up out of the blue like that. And for scaring you," he said, looking at Baba.

"Humpff!" Baba said, rising and leaving the room with Alistair, who snoozed heavily on her shoulder. Lucy followed.

"I really am sorry," he said to me. "After you live on your own for a while, you sort of forget how to live with other people."

"How about some coffee?" I said. "And my brother made apple doughnuts. They're really good."

He took a seat, gingerly. The new knee, I was guessing.

I poured a fresh cup into a big glass mug and set it in front of him. Shuffling through the cabinet, I even found a glass plate that kinda matched.

"Thanks, kid, this is really great. You saved my life. Literally."

"Two newspapers, pick your poison," I said. "And there's milk for your coffee, if you need it."

"Nah, I drink it black," he said. "Man, you weren't kidding about these doughnuts. These from the kid I talked to last night?"

"Yup, that's my brother Nick. He's staying here while he gets settled. He moved from Arizona last month. And he's starting a bakery."

"Sure beats the hell out of hospital food."

I'm guessing doughnuts weren't on his approved diet. In or out of the hospital.

"Cute baby. Didn't know you had a kid."

"Not mine. We're just watching him for a friend."

Marty's eyebrows went up an inch. But he didn't say a word.

I smelled cigarette smoke. But for the first time since I'd known him, there were no lit cigarettes in his hand.

"Have you quit smoking?" I ventured.

"The patch," he said, pushing up his baby-blue sweatshirt sleeve to reveal what looked like three fat, square Band-Aids. "My doc's idea. We'll see how long it lasts. I've got the gum, too. But it tastes rank. 'Course, I'm just relieved I can taste anything."

"Wow, was it that serious?"

"Oh no, nothing like that. But right after surgery they had me on these meds. Totally wiped out my sense of taste. And smell, too. They said it was only temporary. But, you know. Until it comes back, you wonder. And I do like my chow."

"So Nick said you were having some kind of problem with your niece?"

"Helen? I think she might have been trying to kill me. So yeah, I call that a problem. Hey, you mind if I get a second cup?"

"Take as much as you like. I'll make more if we need it."

"Thanks," he said, easing himself out of the chair and hobbling over to the counter. "Man, it's good to have the high-test again. In the hospital, all you could get was decaf. Instant. And most of the time it was lukewarm. Tasted like brown water. Mighta been, for all I know."

Helen may have been trying to kill him, but I was supplying a post-op patient with an unlimited stream of fat, sugar, and caffeine. If something did happen to the guy, I was definitely on the hook as an accessory.

"So what makes you think she was trying to kill you?"

"Eh, it was a lot of little things. Part of the deal with this thing," he said, slapping his knee, "is you have to do your rehab and move around plenty in between sessions, too. But every time she'd bring me a meal, I'd fall asleep. Breakfast Wednesday was the corker. When I woke up, what I discovered convinced me it was time to get out of that house."

"What's that?"

"It was Friday afternoon."

He took a long slug of coffee, and I did the same.

"The worst part is, I missed two rehab appointments. If I want to get back on my feet—and back to work—I need those. Plus, I don't want to get a clot," he said, grabbing the last doughnut out of the box. "That's the enemy right now. Clots."

"Well, yeah, your health is priority one, clearly."

Was Helen really trying to kill him? Maybe she was drugging him to keep from killing him.

Marty must have read my mind.

"Don't get me wrong. I know I'm no picnic. And Helen has always been a charitable woman. Even if she is a tight-ass."

He shook his head and winced. "Her house rules? No drinking. No smoking. No swearing. No books with drinking, smoking, or swearing. No TV with drinking, smoking, or swearing. No cable TV. And no *SportsCenter*. Even if it wasn't for the nausea, I had to get out of there."

"The nausea?"

"I had to take some antibiotics for a couple of days after the surgery. To prevent infection. Helen had the prescriptions filled, and she kept the bottles. Doled 'em out like I was a kid who couldn't be trusted with candy. I was sick as a dog. Thought I'd picked up a bug in the hospital. But then I finally started feeling better."

"When you shook the bug?"

"When I stopped taking the meds. Anyway, when I came to yesterday, I decided it was time to make a run for it."

"I gotta ask, why here?"

"All I had were the clothes on my back. Helen confiscated my luggage, my wallet, my laptop, and my meds."

"Well, you do kind of have a history of legging it," I pointed out, helpfully.

"Yeah, not with a new knee. Besides, I heard her on the phone with my doc. She's trying to make it sound like I'm non compos mentis. I didn't know where she was going with it, but I knew it was time to get out of Dodge. I remembered you lived not too far away. So I had a friend run your name through our circulation database. Got your address. Bing, bang, boom, here I am."

Lucky me.

"Look, one newshound to another, I just need a place to crash for a night or two, while I straighten this out. And I could help you with the column. I mean, who knows more about writing Aunt Margie than me?"

He looked at me expectantly. Saying "no" would be like kicking a puppy. But if I said "yes," Baba would kill me. Then him. Baba had no problem with the word "no."

Maybe a compromise?

"What about the B&B across the street?" I asked.

"Do they have any rooms on the first floor, because right now I can't handle stairs. And I don't have any money or credit cards, either."

I might have been able to convince Ian to run him a tab. But I knew for a fact that all their rooms were on the second story and above. If the B&B had an elevator, I'd never seen it.

"We've kind of got a full house right now," I said. "I wasn't kidding about Alistair—the baby. We're looking after him for a friend. That's why Baba is here. We don't even have any spare beds."

"Hey, I'm happy with the sofa. It's really comfortable."

He looked so hopeful. And what if his niece really was trying to kill him? Nick was right. Marty was a decidedly decent guy. A little loopy, but decent. He'd given me a chance to boost my fledgling freelance career. And after the week he'd had, he deserved a break.

"As long as you don't mind the sofa. Sure, why not?"

Chapter 28

I figured the quickest way to get Marty off my couch and back to his natural habitat—whatever that was—was to supply him with the resources he needed. I showed him my home office setup.

"Nice!" he said. "I like that rolltop desk. And a landline. You don't see many of those anymore. It's solid, and you always know where it is. Don't know why they ever went out of style."

What does it say about me that I have more in common with an old curmudgeon than my own peers? But I loved my landline. Last St. Paddy's Day, when a drunk in an eighteen-wheeler took out the local cell tower, I was one of only two people in the neighborhood with a working phone.

Of course, Trip pointed out that the other one was a ninety-five-year-old woman with five cats who thinks Nixon is still president.

"So this is where you'll find scrap paper, pens, and pencils. I have more notebooks in here," I said, opening a large drawer in the bottom. "Just help yourself."

"If it's OK with you, I'm gonna call my physical therapist first. I gotta get that back on track."

"Let me know if you need a ride," I said, jogging toward my bedroom. Now for the hard part. I had to break the news to Baba.

I actually thought about saying nothing. But the minute she hit me with those catlike brown eyes, I'd crack like cheap glass. Besides, I owed her.

She was tidying up the bedroom. Alistair was asleep in his crib, and Lucy was snoozing nearby. When she started to make the bed, I grabbed the other side of the comforter that served as my bedspread.

What I'd never tell Baba: Most days, I didn't even make the bed. I just pulled up the big, puffy indigo comforter.

"Marty is a good guy. He just had a knee operation. He's having some problems with his family—his niece. I told him he could stay here for a couple of nights if he sleeps on the sofa. And behaves himself. And wears pants."

She stopped fluffing the bed and looked at me. That look could have burned a hole in the wall. I could feel the heat coming to my face. I'm guessing it was redder than my hair.

"He's afraid his niece is trying to kill him. I know he seems a little unusual. But he just got out of the hospital. He's not exactly at his best. And he really is a nice guy. I'm taking over his column while he's on sick leave. He recommended me."

She picked up the comforter again and started

moving double time. Like I wasn't even there. At this point, I preferred the laser glare.

"Baba, I'm trying to do the right thing. He's a good man. I really do think he's in trouble. Of some sort."

"Little boys tell stories," she said. "Bigger boys tell bigger stories."

"I listened to him. Really listened. I'm not saying his niece is a homicidal maniac. But he honestly does believe she tried to kill him. And she's holding his medicine and wallet and laptop hostage. I just want to get him back to some place he feels safe to recover. Just a couple of days. I swear."

Baba sighed. "Two days, he is gone," she said. It wasn't a question.

"Two days," I said.

Now I just had to make good on my word.

Chapter 29

Trip had a slightly different take on the Marty situation when we met at Simon's for coffee that afternoon.

Right off the square, Simon's is a local institution. It's also one of my favorite spots. And the fact that Mrs. Simon bakes several kinds of pie fresh every morning has almost nothing to do with it.

"Hey, you were looking for one elderly gent," Trip said as we slid into a corner booth. "But you found a different one. Do you think Ian would take him as a replacement?"

"As in 'the part of Harkins is now being played by Marty Crunk'? Somehow, I don't think so. Besides, Marty is solving his own problems. He just needs a place to crash while he does it."

"You OK?" Trip asked, glancing at me over the top of the Xeroxed menu.

"Uh, yeah. Why?"

"Well, I'd imagine the prospect of instant fatherhood has dumped a little cold water on the budding romance."

"Not as much as the prospect of Alistair's mother waiting in the wings," I admitted. "The guy's got a family. A ready-made family. Married or not, as far as I'm concerned, he's off the market. But I'd love to see the look on Lydia Stewart's face when she hears the news."

"I predict she'll be wearing black for the foreseeable future."

"Only because she thinks it's stylish. Hey, maybe she'll hook up with Ham Stephens. Solve two problems at the same time."

"Birds of a misbegotten feather . . . ," Trip started.

"I think that thing she wore to Ian's cocktail party might have actually had feathers. Besides, what I really need right now is more info on Jameson Blair."

"Hmm, today's pie is blueberry crumb," he said. "Definitely going to have a piece of that. Well, I may be able to help you out on the Blair part."

"You're kidding."

"Hey, don't thank me, thank the dynamic duo of Izawa and Polk on the business desk. They've been digging into your friend Blair. And while they have precious little they can actually print, they are swimming in a virtual sea of gossip."

"And you provided a willing ear?"

"I am the soul of patience and discretion itself. Plus, I bought a pitcher of beer."

"Anything that might help us out?"

"Perhaps. Turns out that art collection of Blair's is just as spectacular as you remember. It's also the most important thing in his life."

"Really? I'm guessing that was a surprise to wife number two," I said.

"Not as much as his ongoing auditions for wife number three. But the art is his major hobby. And he's picked up some pricey new pieces in the past few years. Modern stuff."

"Those paintings I didn't recognize."

"Very possibly," Trip said. "Turns out his art collection is probably the least of our problems. Besides amassing art, money, women, and yachts, our soon-to-be-bachelor also enjoys collecting politicians."

"Politicians?"

"That's why Polk and Izawa were poking around in the first place," Trip explained. "The general elections are just over seventeen months out. And they've been hearing that Blair's funneling some major money. Well over the legal limit."

"Damn."

"Anyway, wife number two—Deirdre—thinks she and Jamie-boy are soul mates. Then she finds out he's cheating and wants to hit him where it hurts. So she tells the attorneys to go after the art collection. Blair goes ape shit. Vows to destroy her and anyone connected with her."

"Yikes!"

"Fast-forward to a few months ago," Trip said. "He backs off. Says they collected most of it together, so it's only fair she gets half of it."

"I take it that's out of character."

"To this guy, 'fair' is just his favorite skin color," Trip said.

"If she knew about his political dealings, she might be blackmailing him," I said.

"Polk and Izawa don't think so. She was boiling mad. She'd have gone straight to the authorities if she had anything. She didn't, so she went after the art."

"And Harkins is an art thief," I said. "And an art forger."

"And we're pretty sure he's made at least one copy of Blair's Renoir," Trip said, between sips.

"What if Harkins is working for Blair?" I theorized. "He's making copies of the major pieces in the collection. But what about Insurance Guy? Did Blair send him to keep an eye on things?"

"Could be Blair's special type of insurance," Trip said. "Keep an eye on the forger. Make sure nothing goes wrong."

"Or goes missing," I said.

"Could also be there to tie up loose ends," Trip said, seriously. "If that's true, it makes me a little less anxious about how and why he ended up in the freezer."

"So Blair has Harkins make copies to give Deirdre, while he keeps the real ones?" I said, trying out the idea.

"Maybe," said Trip. "But you'd think there would be some kind of authentication. I mean, she knows he's a sleaze. It's not like she's going to trust him."

"What if the real paintings are already in Deirdre's possession? If she's the one doing the dispersing, she wouldn't think twice about authentication. That would be on him. That also explains why Blair needs someone who's a forger *and* a thief."

"And why the collection is sitting in Harkins's study," Trip said. "They've already done it. They've already swapped the fake stuff for the real art."

"And when Deirdre finally gives Blair whatever pieces he's awarded in the divorce," I concluded, "Jameson Blair is going to be laughing all the way to the bank."

Chapter 30

Before I'd left that afternoon, Baba and Marty had worked out their own kind of truce. He had the dining room. She took the kitchen. The living room, like the DMZ, was split straight down the middle. Though I noticed she gave the sofa a wide berth.

When I got back, Baba was strapping on her sneakers and tucking her purse onto her arm. Lucy was leashed up and ready to go.

"Nicholas is baking. Across street. I'm going to store," she said. "Food. You have charge of house?"

"I'll drive you," I said.

"No. You work. Look after little baby," she reminded me. "If he cries, change diaper. Then one bottle." She held up a single gnarled finger. "Just one. Then pat, pat, pat. Then to sleep. Good?"

"Good! And here, let me give you food money."

She smiled and shook her head vigorously. "No. No. All good. Back soon," she said, giving me a thump on the shoulder. "Take care!"

"You too!" I said, giving her a hug. Lucy jumped up for a little love, and I scratched her ear. She wagged her tail happily, wriggling around to lick my hand.

Was it my imagination or did Baba seem a little more upbeat?

"OK, kid, ready for your first lesson in Aunt Margie?" Marty said. It was more an announcement than a question.

I nodded. "Yup."

"OK," he said, gesturing to a foot-high stack of printer paper on the floor by my desk. "Reach over, and pull one out at random."

I complied, making my selection from halfway down the pile.

"Now, give it a quick read and tell me what you notice," he said.

If this was a magic show, I was the dim-but-lovely assistant.

"OK, now let me take a look," he said, after I finished scanning it. "Hmm, uh. OK, got it. Now, what did you notice?"

"Well, the letter writer is a woman, and she seems awfully invested in her friend's life . . ."

"Yeah, nobody on the face of the earth writes an advice columnist for their friend," Marty said. "You write an advice columnist because you're desperate, because you want validation—or because you're desperate for validation. In this game, 'my friend' is code for 'I did something so stupid I don't even want to admit it anonymously.'"

"Really?"

"Oh, yeah. Look, half this job is reading between the lines. The other half is channeling a little common sense. And, despite the term, it's a lot less common than you think."

"So this woman is sleeping with her mailman?" I felt like a slow six-year-old learning to read.

"Yeah. And the fact that she's writing in at all means she's either afraid of getting caught or she wants to dump the guy."

"How do you get that out of this?" I said, waving the letter in the air.

"Because if she was in the blissful throes of an affair, she wouldn't be taking the time to write me. The fact that she is either means it's run its course, or she's hit a speed bump. And since she's married, having an affair, and living in a high-density urban area—signing the thing 'Having My Cake in Cathedral Heights'—my take is she's afraid someone's gotten wise. Might be her husband. Might be a neighbor. Either way, she wants someone to tell her she can drop the boy toy and go back to hubby. Preferably without 'fessing up."

I hated to admit it. Marty was amazing. "Is she really from Cathedral Heights?"

"Now you're catching on," he said, handing the paper back to me. "Check the e-mail address."

I scanned slowly. At this rate, I wouldn't have been surprised if my lips were moving.

"Navy.gov?!"

"The Navy Yard," Marty said. "Now there's an area where everybody knows everybody's business."

"So why sign it 'Cathedral Heights'?"

"A little extra insurance so nobody recognizes her," he explained. "And probably where she'd like to live. Who wouldn't? Don't worry, kid, you know this stuff. Even if you don't know you know it."

He pulled out another letter, gave it a quick read and handed it over. "Here, look at this. Tell me what you see."

I didn't even know what I was looking for. I closed my eyes and took a deep breath. Then I opened them and read.

"A little self-centered," I said.

"Good. What's the tip-off?"

"He uses *I* three times in the first paragraph."

"Exactly! What else?"

"Seems like a braggart, too."

"Yes! How'd you get that?"

"I don't know. It's just an impression."

"See the part where he says. 'I don't like to blow my own horn, but . . .'?"

"Yeah?"

"Anything before the word 'but' is suspect. Like, 'I don't normally judge, but . . .' or 'I really love my wife, but . . .'"

Marty was a genius. Or Margie. Frankly, I wasn't sure exactly which of them I was dealing with today.

"Did you, uh, talk with Baba while I was gone?" I asked.

"Yeah, we're cool," he said. "She's gonna let me make a pot roast tonight."

"I'm sorry, a what?"

"Pot roast," he said. "You live on your own, you learn to cook one or two things really well. My thing's pot roast. She's gonna get a nice piece of meat. I said I'd take care of the rest. Least I can do with you guys putting me up and all."

When I first moved out on my own, I gave myself food poisoning twice trying to learn to cook salmon. So I guess my "thing" was scrambled eggs. And coffee. And delivery pizzas.

"OK, kid, I looked through the stack," Marty said. "These are the three letters we want to answer today. Give 'em a read, then we'll talk it out. Remember, glean what you can about the person writing the letter. That tells you how much you can trust your narrator. Then look at the problem they present. And take a step back. The world is always bigger than they make it. Last, what's your common sense tell you?"

Suddenly, it all began to click. All the years of reading Aunt Margie. All the weeks of studying the columns. Marty's master class. I could actually do this.

"Wah-wah-wah-*waaaaaahhhhh!*" Alistair.

"Sorry, Marty, I've got to take care of this," I said, bolting from the room.

"Hey, there, little guy," I said as I ran into the bedroom. "It's OK. It's OK, yeah. I know you're missing your momma. And your Baba. And probably your Lucy, too, right? But Auntie Alex is right here," I said, carefully lifting him out of the crib. "Yes, I am."

He looked at me and started crying again. Everyone's a critic.

I laid him on the bed just as the phone rang. Without even looking, I grabbed it off the night table.

Big mistake.

"Alexandra, is that a baby?" My mother.

"The TV. A nature show. Screaming goats."

Alistair didn't agree. Alistair was bawling for all he was worth. I tried waving my hands and making funny faces. I tried bouncing the bed. Nothing worked.

"Alexandra, where did you get a baby?" Translation: Who on the face of the earth would trust you with a helpless infant?

Fair question.

"We're just watching him for a neighbor. Baba had to run to the store, and . . ."

"Your grandmother's there? You invited her, and you didn't invite me?"

"I didn't invite her. Nick and I needed a hand and . . ." There was no good way to end that sentence.

"Oh, Nicholas is in on it, too? Let's just throw a family reunion. But for heaven's sake, don't tell Mom."

"Nobody's throwing a family reunion," I shouted over the squalling. "I'm watching Alistair for a neighbor. He's a little cranky. We asked for advice. And Baba volunteered to lend a hand. That's all." It sounded reasonable to me. But then my eardrums were being liquified by a screaming baby.

"And what, she just flew there on her broomstick? You drove to Baltimore and picked her up! I only live across the District, and I never see either one of you!"

Any wonder why?

"Next time I have a crying baby with a full diaper, I promise you'll be the first one I call. Look, Mom, I've gotta go. If I don't stop this racket, someone's gonna call the cops."

Probably me.

I clicked off and threw the phone onto the bed. As Alistair wailed, I grabbed a diaper and wipes. I bounced him a little, as I dumped the supplies on my bed. Then I spread out one of his little blankets and laid him on it.

All the while, Alistair howled.

I didn't get the whole "baby fever" thing. Sure, I think babies are cute. I also like going to the nature park to look at the hippos. But never once did I want to shove one in the back of my car and bring it home. And I kinda feel the same way about babies.

I eyed Alistair, lying on his little blue blanket. He stared back up at me with wide blue eyes, lips pursed. He'd stopped crying. But he looked as scared as I felt.

"Are you a little hippo? Do you want to be my little hippo?"

He looked panicky. Then he hurled. Some kind of white goop. On the bright side, he was now grinning and waving his hands in the air.

Oh boy. And I'm the mutant for not wanting one of these little guys?

Chapter 31

Marty was right: he made a mean pot roast.

Not only did the house smell wonderful all afternoon, but I snuck a taste, and it melted in my mouth. I called Nick and told him why he needed to come home for a dinner break. He showed up with a dozen brioche rolls, a big cherry tart (his latest experiment), and a half a bottle of Ian's red wine for the roast itself.

"The alcohol cooks off, but the flavor stays," Marty assured us.

I thought Baba would be apoplectic at the idea of sharing her kitchen. Turned out with all her Alistair-related labors, she was relieved to have someone take up the slack.

Shows what I know.

I was psyched. I may not be much of an Alistair wrangler, but I'd blazed through my batch of Aunt Margie letters. And Marty was tickled. I think he liked being able to pass on what he'd learned.

Ian had popped over a couple of times to visit

his son. The little guy was gold whenever he was around. And despite the fact that there was no news about Harkins, Ian seemed to be in a pretty good mood, too.

I invited him for the meal, but he couldn't leave the inn during dinner. So he'd promised to stop by for dessert and coffee. He showed up with a gallon of ice cream.

We were right in the middle of dessert when there was a knock at the door.

"That could be for me," Marty said. "Finally got in touch with the doc's office and found a pharmacy that delivers. They even arranged to bill the doc until I get my new credit cards."

"I'll get it," I said. "I'm closest to the door anyway."

Absent a dining room table, we were scattered all over the living room. Baba and Marty had TV trays in front of overstuffed chairs. Nick, Ian, and I were sharing the sofa in front of the coffee table. Lucy, ever hopeful, was under the coffee table, ready to hoover up any stray tart crumbs. And Alistair was blissfully zonked out in his crib.

I didn't even bother to check the peephole. I just threw open the door,

Big mistake. A couple of months outside the newsroom, and I was already getting soft.

My mother stood on the porch. She was wearing a Chanel suit, L'Occitane perfume, and a sour expression. But it was clear where my supermodel sister got her knockout looks.

She stuck her beautifully coiffed, honey-blond head into the doorway and surveyed the living room. "Glad to know you're not having a party," she said archly.

"You're just in time for dessert," I said, ignoring the jab. "Nick baked a cherry tart. And Ian brought ice cream."

"Ian, Marty, this is my mother," I said, as the men rose to greet her. "Mom, Ian lives across the street. And I'm collaborating with Marty on a project for the *Sentinel*."

Nick jumped up and headed to the kitchen. He was either going to get her a plate or beat it out the back door. My money was on the back door. That would have been my choice.

Baba stayed put and never stopped spooning tart à la mode into her mouth. Her expression was completely neutral. But I noticed a spritely glint in her eyes.

"Dessert I'll skip. But a cappuccino would be lovely."

"We have coffee, Mom," I said. "Or tea."

She wrinkled her nose.

"I've got it," Nick called from the kitchen. "Cappuccino for anyone else?"

Marty raised his hand. So did Ian. And I had to admit, I was curious. "Make yourself at home, Mom," I said, offering her my spot on the couch. "I'll help Nick with the tray."

"What do you mean by offering her cappuccino?" I whisper-shouted to Nick when I hit the kitchen. "And by the way, we've got two more out there who want to try it."

"I'm making six," Nick said. "I'm gonna be baking

all night, so I need the caffeine. And this is too good for you to miss. Plus, I think Baba will love it."

"You do know I don't have a cappuccino maker? Or cappuccino?"

"Yeah, I'm guessing right now, that's the least of your problems. But never fear, Nick the miracle man is here." He had six cups of coffee lined up on the counter, along with a shaker jar of cinnamon. Mismatched mugs, of course. He opened the freezer door and grabbed Ian's vanilla ice cream.

"Did you know she was coming?" he asked, as he spooned a couple of tablespoons of ice cream into each cup.

"I didn't. But I should have. She called this afternoon when Alistair was screaming."

"And you didn't check caller ID."

I shook my head.

"You'd never make it as a man. You always check caller ID." He stirred each of the cups, then gave each a sprinkling of cinnamon. The result was a foamy concoction that actually looked like cappuccino.

"Try it," he said.

"Oh my God, Nick, this is wonderful. This tastes like the real deal."

"It kind of is. It's a little trick I learned recently. Cappuccino is coffee with cream and air and a little sugar. Ice cream is cream with air and sugar whipped in. So in a pinch, coffee plus ice cream equals cappuccino. You don't need a machine. It even makes the foam. Then you top it with cocoa or cinnamon."

"OK, that is more than slightly brilliant."

"Yeah, I'm a mad genius. It's all about the science."

"So what are we going to do about Mom?" I asked.

"What do you mean 'we'? I was just here for the pot roast. I don't have tickets to the floor show. After she enjoys a high-class cup of coffee prepared by her loving son, I'm gonna spend the rest of the night baking at the inn. Whatever's going on over there is a heck of a lot easier to deal with than this drama."

"So not fair."

"Look, I've got a batch due to Angela by Monday. And I think I might have a lead on another client. But they need pies and tarts. So I'm teaching myself to make pies and tarts."

"While you're doing that, I'm going to be Aunt Margie," I said, sipping. "But don't tell anyone."

"For real?"

"A six-week engagement while Marty's on the mend."

"Marty is Margie?" Nick said. "You're kidding! I wonder what Aunt Margie would do in this situation?"

"Somehow, I don't think Aunt Margie would have gotten himself into this mess."

"Mom can't stay here," Nick said, quietly. "Not with Baba here. Those two are like garlic and chocolate. You can have one or the other, but never both."

"First, coffee time. Then you go back to work. I'll figure something out."

"Just in case it's necessary, I call dibs on my own bed."

"Not necessary," I said. "I'm hoping the lack of sleeping accommodations will actually work in our favor."

Nick the hero carried in the tray, and I trailed along behind him. Big surprise, everyone loved the drinks.

"Very good!" Baba proclaimed.

"Thank you!" he said, beaming. "By the way, Marty, that pot roast was fantastic."

"Eh, it's nice to have people to cook for," Marty said. "I'm glad you liked it."

"Now I hate to eat and run," Nick said, "but I have to get back to work."

"Before you leave, sweetie, could you bring my bags in from the car?" Mom said, reaching into her purse. "Here are my keys."

"Mom, we need to talk about that," I said. "I've got a houseful right now. I'd love for you to stay, but we don't even have a spare bed."

"If I didn't have the brand-new knee, I'd give you the sofa and sleep on the floor," Marty said, looking at her with puppy-dog eyes. "A beautiful woman should always have the best of everything."

"He's staying here?" my mother asked, horrified, totally ignoring Marty.

"For a couple of nights while he's recovering from surgery," I said. "Yes."

I snuck a glance at Baba. I could see her brown eyes twinkling over the top of her coffee mug.

"Actually, I think I might be of service," Ian said. "I'm the proprietor of the B&B across the street. The Cotswolds Inn. And due to a last-minute cancellation, we have a room available. The Cheshire Suite. It has a lovely view of the garden. It would be on the house, of course. It's the least I can do, under the circumstances."

"That's very kind of you, Mr. uh . . ."

"Please, call me Ian. Your daughter has been helping me with a few business snafus, and your son's pastries are the star attraction of our teas."

"Are they now?" Mom said, locking her eyes on Nick with a look that declared, "We'll discuss this later."

I may have neglected to inform her when I had—temporarily—been a murder suspect. But apparently Nick was keeping his whole new life under wraps.

I don't know who I felt worse for at this point: me, Nick, or Marty. Possibly Ian. Because the poor guy just didn't know what he was getting into with my mother. Inviting her to stay was like opening the door to a vampire. Once you did, she'd never completely leave. And you'd never have another moment's peace. Guaranteed.

"Well, that's a lovely offer, Ian. My daughter Anastasia spoke very highly of your inn. I'd be delighted to stay there. But I will be paying my own way." Looking at me, she added pointedly, "I'm just so glad that I'm welcome."

Chapter 32

The next morning when I walked into the kitchen, Nick was sitting at the table drinking coffee. He had Alistair cradled in his right arm and a coffee cup clutched in his left hand. The sports section was open on the table.

Alistair cooed and grinned at Nick, who made funny faces, stuck out his tongue, and jostled the little guy. But my brother looked awful. It wasn't just the bedhead, the five-o'clock shadow, or the circles under his eyes. It was as if someone had taken the starch out of him.

I hadn't seen him this way since Gabby left. And I had a pretty good idea who was responsible.

"You two are up early," I said.

"I got a lot less baking done than I'd planned and made it an early night," he said glumly, putting his cup on the table. "Apparently, having a room at the inn also gives Mom free access to the kitchen. She parked herself in there all night. 'Just wanted to chat,'" he said, forming air quotes with his free hand. "Totally threw off my baking mojo. After four burned batches, I finally called it a night."

He took a long sip of coffee. "I work for myself, and I love what I do. But today? I don't want to go anywhere near that kitchen."

"Jeez, I'm sorry," I said. "I was hoping she might go home."

"Three suitcases," he said, holding up the same number of fingers. "She's here for the duration. Wants to help me get my life back on track. Starting with finishing college, then medical school. Or law school. Or business school. Any of the above." He grimaced. "Can you picture me in medical school?"

"I can, actually. You've got the brains and the aptitude. But if it doesn't make you happy, it's not for you."

"I just want my kitchen back."

"Too bad Simmons isn't around," I said. "I'm sure a free-range mother must violate some kind of health-code regulation."

Nick smiled.

"Just talk with Ian. I'm sure there's a 'no guests in the kitchen' policy he could invoke. Or invent."

"Tattle on my mother?"

"It's not tattling. It's setting boundaries. She doesn't belong there. And it's getting in the way of your work—which is vital to Ian's business. Besides, he's only putting her up as a favor to you. Well, us. Look at it this way—the sooner we cut off access to you, the sooner she leaves and he can put another guest in that room. One who doesn't spend all her free time annoying his star attraction."

Nick nodded. I could tell he was considering it. I thought about what Marty said about pulling back and seeing the big picture.

"She's background noise," I said finally.

"Huh?"

"The reason she's talky-talky-talky," I said. "She can't make you do anything. She can suggest. She can persuade. She can push, push, push. But she can't *do* anything. You like running your own bakery?"

"Love it."

"You're good at it. So you're doing it. That decision's already been made. It's not up for debate. She's just background noise. Let her chatter all she wants. She means well. She just wants us safe and happy. Eventually, she'll see that you are, and she'll stop. And if she never does, so what? You're doing great."

His face bloomed into a smile. "I am doing great. Aren't I?" he said, looking down at Alistair. "Aren't I?"

"How about a little more coffee?" I said, getting up. "And some chocolate to go with it?"

"I could use some of that. Any of that tart left?"

"With Marty around?"

"Yeah," Nick said, grinning. "The guy does kind of have a hollow leg. Oh, how about some of that pot roast? I've got brioche rolls in the freezer. We could heat 'em up. It would make for some great sandwiches." He looked down at Alistair. "Yes, it would! You know it would!"

"Now you're talking," I said, dropping the jar of Nesquik on the table, as I topped off his coffee. "Breakfast is served."

Chapter 33

Early that afternoon, Baba took Lucy and Alistair and headed out for "good long walk."

I so wanted to tag along. But Marty was giving me another Aunt Margie seminar. We'd been at it all morning. Even Marty thought I was doing pretty well.

"Don't get too used to this gig," he warned with a grin. "Once I get going on my physical therapy, I'm coming back strong."

"Don't worry," I told him. "Solving other people's problems is way too much pressure."

A light, rapid *tap, tap, tap* on the door startled both of us.

"Are you expecting anyone?" I asked Marty.

"My PT girl," he said. "Terri. She's great. She's gonna put me through my workout. But she's not 'sposed to show up 'til four."

This time, I used the peephole. A cluster of middle-aged women in dresses and suits.

"It's a bunch of women," I said. "But I don't recognize them from the neighborhood."

Bang, bang, bang. Louder this time.

"Maybe they're selling something," Marty said, grabbing the crutches and hobbling toward the door. "I could use a little entertainment. Let 'em in."

I opened the door a crack.

"I'm Helen Westwood," said the ringleader, a short, squat blonde in an expensive-looking lavender suit. "I'm here for Martin Crunk."

"Oh crap, it's Helen!" Marty muttered behind me. The comment was followed by the sound of some fast shuffling and a door slamming. The bathroom. Then the distinct *ping* of a lock.

Oh, great.

"Hi, I'm Alex Vlodnachek. Your uncle has decided to stay here for a few days, while he recovers."

"We know who you are," she said, narrowing her eyes. "You're the one holding him here. Against his doctor's orders."

The rest of the group nodded in the affirmative. And I heard a couple of "uh-huh's" testifying in agreement.

"I'm his niece, and his guardian," she continued. "And I'm not leaving here without him." With that, she planted her pudgy feet on my porch and looked at me defiantly. The Greek chorus behind her nodded in unison.

Good luck, I thought. No one's getting him out of that bathroom without a crowbar.

"Look, I talked with Mr. Crunk. He wants to stay here for a couple of days. He's a grown man, so it's his choice. I'm sorry, but I really can't help you."

Helen held up a cell phone. "I don't want to get the authorities involved, but I will. Uncle Martin has to get back home and back to his routine. His health depends on it. And it's my duty to see that happens."

"Helen's a saint," one woman said.

"Absolutely!" agreed a second.

"The young floozy is a kidnapper," said a third. "She could have him chained to the radiator. That poor old man."

"Probably soaking him for money. She looks like she needs money."

"Did you see what's written on her car? Naughty words!"

"Maybe it's drugs," another one stage-whispered. "She's taking his money for drugs. Or stealing his medications."

"Don't bother arguing with her, Helen," the first one chimed in again. "Just call the police. They know how to deal with perps."

"Yeah!"

"Poor Helen!"

I stepped back, closed the door, and turned both dead bolts.

When I put my ear to the door, I picked up snatches of conversation and tittering. Still, no retreating footsteps.

Next came the phrase that was certain to put a crimp in my day.

"My name is Helen Westwood, and I want to report a crime . . ."

Chapter 34

At least by the time the cops showed up, Marty had exited the bathroom. He'd traded it for a defensive position in one of the overstuffed chairs.

Helen and her ladies swept into the living room with the cops. I stepped in behind the boys in blue and blocked her path. "You and your friends can wait on the porch," I said evenly.

"I'm here to report a crime," she said imperiously. "This is a crime scene. You're a criminal."

"The police can stay. But this is my home. It's private property. And you and your friends are not welcome. You can wait on the porch. Or at the curb. Or in the middle of the street, for all I care. But not in my home."

"Officer!" Helen yelled. "This woman is holding my poor, defenseless uncle. I need to be here to protect him."

"Go home, Helen!" Marty shouted.

"Clearly, she's using undue influence. Drugs or"—she dropped her voice—"s-e-x."

I heard one of the ladies gasp.

"Oh, no!" said another.

I saw one cop look at his partner and roll his eyes.

The second cop, whose name tag read LEWIS, shrugged. "Lady, until we sort this out, why don't you and your friends wait on the porch."

"Out!" I said, pointing to the front door. "All of you! Out! Now!"

"Ooh! Redhead's got a temper," Marty said, grinning.

I glared at him.

Twenty minutes later, the police had determined that Marty was very much in charge of his faculties, his finances, and his life. And that he had plenty of all three. They also confirmed that he worked at the *Sentinel* and even talked with one of his doctors.

"That's amazing," Marty whispered to me, watching the cop chat with his physician. "Took me the better part of an hour to get that sawbones on the phone last time. He calls, and boom, 'Hello, doctor.'"

"So what's with the bunch on the porch?" the other cop asked. His name tag read ZEFKOWITZ.

"My niece and her do-gooders," Marty said. "The ladies are OK, but Helen's a pill. Give her an inch, and she takes over. My sleeping in her guest room for a week after knee surgery suddenly morphed into her being my jailer. I nodded off the first night, and she confiscated all my stuff—even my meds. I felt like I was James Caan in *Misery*. So I left."

"And you're staying here?" Zefkowitz asked.

"Just for a couple of days. The kid here works with me. She and her family have been good enough to put me up. As soon as I can navigate stairs with my crutches, I have a reservation at the B&B across the street."

Uh-oh. I wonder what Mom's going to say about that? Could that be the final straw that sends her packing? If so, way to go, Marty!

"That sounds nice." the cop said.

"They do an afternoon tea that's first-rate," Marty said. "You should take the wife."

If only they knew about the freezer in the basement.

"Hey, if you could get back my keys and my laptop, that'd be great," Marty said to Zefkowitz. "I've got replacements coming for the credit cards, and doc's already sent over my meds. But that laptop's my life."

"You're probably going to have to pick it up," he said. "We can compel her to turn it over, but we can't make her bring it to you. Give us a ring when you're ready to collect it," he added, handing Marty his card. "We can make sure the handoff goes smoothly."

To me he explained, "Better safe than sorry with some of these domestic situations."

When the cops left, I turned both dead bolts.

Helen and her women's brigade were still milling around on the sidewalk. For their sake, I hoped they'd be gone when Baba returned. Baba's reaction to that coven would make me look like a member of the neighborhood welcome committee.

"How come you didn't tell them about Helen drugging you? Or the nausea?" I asked Marty.

"Can't prove it," he said simply. "And without proof, I just sound like a raving old coot. And that's a point for the nice, respectable widow. You know, 'help the crazy man home and look after him.' I'm not taking any chances."

I could see his point.

"How did her husband die?" I asked.

"Mark's not dead. Although for a while there, I think he wished he was. Walked out a couple of years after the wedding. Remarried and lives in L.A. now. Nice guy. I still get cards from him now and then."

"So why does she claim to be a widow?"

"Helen didn't want the divorce. Doesn't believe in it."

"She must have really loved him," I said.

"I don't think she ever loved him Not the way you mean. She felt that marrying him meant she owned him. And Helen doesn't believe in returns. Like one of those old-timey shops with a handwritten sign by the register: ALL SALES FINAL."

We both contemplated that for a moment.

"So why would she want you . . . out of the way?" I finally said.

"Don't know. Makes no sense. That's another reason I couldn't tell the cops. There's no motive."

"What about inheritance?" I said, starting with the obvious.

"Nah, she doesn't get a penny. I got a will. I'm leaving everything to ten different charities. Three of 'em for dogs. Helen'll love that. She hates dogs."

"Could she *think* she's in line to get anything?"

"Don't see why. I've never promised her anything.

Or even implied anything. I've always told her I was leaving everything to charity."

"What about your house?" Shopping for a home two years ago had been an ugly reality check. I'd quickly learned that, in the right neighborhoods, even a modest house could be worth a fortune.

"Mortgaged to the hilt," Marty confessed. "Two loans. Took out the second one four years ago when I did some home renovations. Hell, my estate will be lucky to break even. If the executor is smart, he'll just give it back to the banks and let them fight over it.

"Besides, she's got her own money," he added. "The kid's a whiz with investments. Took the little bit her dad left her and made a pile."

"Did she ever invest anything for you?" I asked.

"Nah, I spend it as soon as I make it. Plus I don't like to mix money and family. That's a cocktail even I won't touch."

OK, blame it on my natural cynicism. Or maybe it's because my own 401(k) is barely breaking even. But when someone claims they made their money from "investments," that's a red flag. It may work for Warren Buffett, but most of us don't play in his league. Call it force of habit, but when I hear the phrase "investment wealth," I think "unexplained money."

"OK, you said she hinted you were losing it," I said. "What happens if you're, uh, incapacitated?"

"I got that all set up, too. Money coming in covers the bills for a while. Not long, but long enough to settle up. And I got an insurance policy for long-term care. But I have a guy who will oversee all of that. For a cut. A pro. It doesn't involve Helen. I may not have realized she had a dark side, but I did know that, without kids or a wife, I had to look out for myself. And, between you and me, that one's been a bitter lemon from the get-go. Even looks sullen in her baby pictures."

Something he said struck a chord. A memory.

"Could she have an insurance policy on you? Life insurance, I mean."

"No reason she should," he said. "I've got my bases covered. And if I have my way, I'll drop dead at my desk at a hundred and two. My retirement account may be crap, but I love my job."

"What does she do for a living?" Other than her being a living saint, according to her girl squad, I knew next to nothing about Helen.

"Thanks to the investments, she doesn't have to work," Marty said. "In her early days, she was an office manager. Very organized, really good at her job. Even then, she did a lot of volunteer work in her spare time. Shut-ins and the elderly, mostly. She'd run them meals or meds. Look in on them. Read to 'em, or watch TV and talk. Still does it, too. That's why I didn't feel half bad about asking to stay with her for a week. I mean, even with the bum knee, I'm totally mobile."

Was he ever. Marty had set a land-speed record lurching toward that bathroom.

"Plus, I offered to chip in while I was there," he

said. "You know, spring for some takeout. Pitch in on the bills. Whatever."

I had an inkling of an idea. But this one was going to take a little more research. Bottom line: Marty was safe here. And as far as I was concerned, he could stay for the duration.

Chapter 35

After Baba, Lucy, and Alistair returned, I phoned Nick. Good advice or no, I was worried about leaving him at Mom's mercy for the last several hours. And more than a little curious why she hadn't shown up here.

No answer. Straight to voice mail.

I hoped that meant he was busy in the kitchen.

With a house full of people, I thought maybe inviting Mom out to dinner—just the two of us—might be a nice move. But with all of the Alistair-related supplies and extra food bills to fortify the army camped out at my house, I was precariously low on funds.

And, for whatever reason, the direct deposits from the *Sentinel* for my new gig were long overdue.

Somehow, I couldn't see my mother, clad in her best Chanel, tucking into a Big Mac at Mickey D's. Or the meat loaf special at Simon's.

So maybe a home-cooked meal with the family would have to do.

After a few more calls to Nick went to voice mail, I started to worry. So when Marty's physical therapist showed up—complete with a massage table—I felt it might be a good time to hit the B&B. Just to make sure Nick was OK.

"Hullo!" Ian said with a warm smile as I breezed through the door. "Everything all right on the home front?"

"The little guy had a nice long walk with Baba and Lucy. Now all three of them are napping," I reported, editing out the part about the police visit and accusations of elder abuse.

"Fantastic!" he said. "I would like to stop by to visit in a little bit if you don't mind."

"You don't even have to ask," I said. "Marty's going through a physical therapy session right now. But he ought to be done in about an hour."

"Perfect. I have to do a little bookkeeping. Then I'll pop over. I can't tell you how much your help—your family's help—means." His face softened. The look in those blue eyes had my heart doing that fluttery thing again. And seeing him with Alistair? When those two were together, they were positively joyful.

What would happen when we found Alistair's mom? Would she and Ian pick up where they'd left off? Would she move into the B&B? Or if she didn't want to be Mrs. Innkeeper, would they sell the place and go back to London?

Stop it! I scolded myself. It's a good thing. Be happy for the man.

So why did I feel that tiny splinter of jealousy?

"I hate to even ask, but has my mother been behaving herself?"

"She's been absolutely delightful," Ian said. "A thoroughly charming woman. It turns out we actually have a couple of the same haunts when we're in London."

"Wow, that's a coincidence."

"Completely," he said with a little smile. "Oh, and you'll be very happy to know that she's taking full advantage of our activities."

"Activities?" I asked. I couldn't picture Mom playing Miss Marple at a murder mystery weekend.

"Since the place is temporarily shorthanded, I've been arranging excursions for the guests. Day trips to see the sights. Through a local tour company. Mercedes minivan, champagne, and snacks. A bit of fun. Today's jaunt was to the Smithsonian. She joined the group. They should be back around seven."

My mother went to that particular museum at least a dozen times a year. Usually dragging a few of her grown children with her. My read on this sudden recent field trip: she was sulking.

"Is Nick around?"

"In the kitchen," Ian said with a grin. "When last I noticed, I believe he was muttering something about galettes."

I walked into the kitchen. It was deserted.

Nick's galettes (I'd have called them tartlets) were cooling on the counter, filling the room with the scent of cherries, cinnamon, and browned butter. It was all I could do not to filch one.

But where was Nick?

I wandered back to the front desk. Ian was gone. And the door to his study was shut tight. I could hear music playing. Mozart. Maybe it helped with the bookkeeping.

That's when I noticed the basement door was ajar.

Cold fear gripped my heart. Nick.

I stepped quickly to the basement door and opened it wide. The stairway was a dark pit.

"Nick," I called softly. "Are you down there? Nick!"

I pulled out my cell and dialed again. Voice mail.

I felt dread in my stomach. My limbs were like lead.

I shoved the phone back in my pocket and flipped on the light. Gripping the bannister tightly, I inched down the stairs. If I was moving, I didn't have to think about where I was going. Or what I might find. Just. Keep. Moving.

When I got to the bottom, it was still there. That damned freezer. I hated the thing.

I mumbled a prayer, crossed myself, and ripped the lid upward.

A bulky man. Dark hair. Not Nick.

Not Nick!

I dropped the lid and sagged. Was it awful that I was so relieved?

When the phone rang, I jumped.

I pulled it out of my pocket. Nick!

"Where are you?" I whispered.

"Giant," he said. "I'm trying something different with the galettes, but I needed a few more exotic ingredients. And Ian's supplier doesn't come again 'til Tuesday."

Even I couldn't believe what I said next. "Why is your car still in the driveway?"

"I borrowed Mom's. Don't tell her."

"Don't worry. We might have bigger problems."

"Baba and Mom getting into it?"

"Not exactly," I said, backing away from the freezer and letting my shaky knees drop me on the bottom step of the stairs.

"Just out of curiosity, when's the last time you saw Simmons?" I asked him.

"Jeez, who cares? It's been at least a week. A glorious, stress-free, Simmons-free week. Come to think of it, he was supposed to touch base Friday. Not that I'm complaining. I mean, the longer I go without hearing that whiny voice, the better."

"Well, I think I found out where he's been hiding."

"Where?"

"Ian's freezer."

"No! Are you sure?"

"Sure it's him or sure he's dead? 'Cause that's yes and yes."

"So how long has he been . . . uh . . . you know . . . dead?"

"Well, let me see, based on lividity and liver temp, I'd say . . . how the hell would I know? I majored in journalism, not medicine."

"Baba would probably know."

"Yeah, she probably would," I admitted. "But since right now you and I and the killer are the only ones who know he's gone, I'd kind of like to keep her out of this."

"Yeah, that sounds fair," Nick said. "I feel kind of bad about what I said about him now. Any idea how he, uh . . . ?"

"There's a kitchen tool sticking out of his chest. Some kind of thermometer. I'm guessing that had something to do with it."

"Where are you?"

"The basement."

"Get out of there! Now!"

"I'd like to. But my legs have other ideas."

"You're going into shock. I'm on my way home. Right now. I'll stay on the phone with you until you're home safe. C'mon, take a deep breath and stand up. Now we're gonna go up those stairs. One at a time. Left foot, right foot . . ."

I hauled myself up the stairs, with Nick's voice in my left ear, my right hand clutching the bannister.

When I got to the lobby, it was empty. But the music was still going in Ian's office.

I knocked on the door. "Ian, Ian, it's Alex!"

"Don't even bother with him," Nick yelled in my ear. "Just get out of there. Run! Go home!"

I could hear him laying on the horn. "Oh, come on, lady! Thirty miles an hour in the left-hand lane? With the blinker on? Move over!"

"Nick, I'm fine! Nick! Relax! I'm OK. Slow down!"

I banged on the door to Ian's study. Nothing.

Whatever else our friendly, neighborhood inn-keeper was up to, he definitely wasn't doing the books.

Chapter 36

When Nick pulled up to the curb in Mom's compact navy-blue Mercedes, I was sitting on the porch steps, limp as a dish rag.

He jumped out and came running up the walkway. "Are you OK?"

I nodded.

"What the heck were you doing in that basement? We had a deal!"

I buried my head in my knees and started to cry. I blubbered until I couldn't catch my breath. Nick sat down next to me on the steps. And waited.

"You . . . didn't . . . answer . . . your . . . phone," I said between sobs. "The basement door . . . was . . . open . . . I was afraid!" The last part came out in one long wail.

I took a couple of deep breaths, trying to regain control. Nick patted my arm.

"It's OK," he said. "I'm sorry. I didn't mean to yell. It's just that you're usually the sensible one."

"I don't feel very sensible," I said, swallowing a

hiccup. "Every time I open that freezer, there's a body in it. And it's always a different body."

"Worst magic trick ever," Nick said, nudging me.

I hiccuped and leaned against his shoulder. "I'm just so relieved," I said. "So relieved I don't even care about Simmons and the rest of it. Is that awful?"

"Nope. Sounds about right to me. Besides, the cops will handle it."

"What?"

"Once you pull yourself together, we'll call the cops. Let them deal with it."

"Nick," I said, taking another deep breath and sitting bolt upright, "what were you doing the last time you saw Simmons? The last time he was in this neighborhood?"

"Watching Ian politely evict him from the inn."

"Yeah, and the day before that?"

"Um, well . . ."

"You were chasing him down the street threatening to boil him in oil and serve him on toast. And trust me, that's the story all the neighbors will remember. And repeat."

"You're saying it looks bad?"

"As someone who's been there, I'm saying you look like Suspect Number One."

"Come on, the guy's a health inspector. He's got enemies."

"I'd be willing to bet none of them were as public about it. Or as vocal. And it's not just that. If he was killed in Ian's kitchen, that thermometer thing could have your fingerprints on it, too."

"What did it look like?" he asked somberly.

"The face of it was about this big," I said, using

my hands to form a circle the size of a small jar lid. "The dial was black, with white notches and numbers—like a speedometer. And the speedometer stick was bright red."

"It's a meat thermometer," Nick said. "I've been using it for bread."

"You've touched it?"

"Lots of times," he said, nodding. "But then it disappeared. I wondered where it'd gone. I was going to ask Ian, but—" Nick shrugged. "The guy's already loaning me a kitchen. Didn't seem right to hassle him over where he keeps his own cooking tools."

I tried to square what I'd seen in the freezer with the image of the happy, new father. Or the welcoming innkeeper.

Shivering, I wrapped my arms around my shoulders. Warm weather or no, I was cold.

"You don't think he did it?" Nick asked.

"I don't know what to think. I don't want to believe it. But how many people have access to that kitchen?" I responded. "Or the freezer? And we know you didn't do it."

Nick smiled. "You really thought I was in there?"

I wiped my eyes with my arm and nodded. "Originally, I just wanted to show up and give you some extra backup with Mom."

"She went to the Smithsonian," he said. "After I told her I was sticking with the bakery."

"How'd she take it?"

"About as well as you'd expect. But after splitting a galette, she had to admit I have some talent. Of course, she used that as ammunition to push for business school."

"Yeah, she doesn't give up. She's almost as relentless as Lydia Stewart," I said.

"And that's another story."

"What?"

"Lydia," he said. "I'm pretty sure she's the one who tipped off Simmons to me in the first place."

"Why?"

"Her friend Janie Parker runs Lady Jane's Tea Room. And until I came along, Janie was the front-runner to supply Ian's inn."

"Where'd you hear that?"

"Ian."

"Janie and Lydia are tight," I said. "Plus it would be one more way for Lydia to bring Ian into her orbit."

Nick grinned. "Yup. And put some distance between Ian and you."

"I'm not the one she has to worry about. Wonder what she's going to say when she hears about Alistair. And Alistair's mom. Hey, if Lydia reported you to Simmons, that means she might eventually notice that he's missing."

Nick shrugged. "Rumor is Simmons was on the take. I've been talking with other people who run food-based businesses. And at least a couple of them suspect their competitors paid Simmons to hassle them. But once he got his hooks in, he didn't let go. He just kept showing up. And he knew things. Insider information. Stuff that had nothing to do with their food work."

"What do you mean?" I asked.

"One guy, Gerry, makes pickles. Everything from relish to those big deli ones."

I nodded.

"He and his wife were having problems."

I cocked my head and stared at Nick.

"OK, OK, truth is, he was seeing someone," he admitted. "Anyway, suddenly there's a surprise inspection. A boatload of fees. Only this time Simmons is demanding cash. Says if the guy doesn't pay up, he's gonna come back every Thursday afternoon. Thursday afternoon is when Gerry would see the girlfriend."

"Simmons was blackmailing him?"

Nick nodded. "Simmons liked to pop in unexpectedly. Listen in on phone calls. Rifle through papers. Basically, trample civil rights."

"How come nobody blew the whistle?"

"How? He decides if their business lives or dies. People put all their time and money—their souls—into these things. Anybody complains to Simmons's bosses, it's just sour grapes because they didn't pass inspection. And you can bet the next time he visited, he'd shut 'em down."

"So what did Gerry do?"

"Came clean with his wife. Dumped the girlfriend."

"Smart."

"Honestly, he couldn't afford the blackmail. If he could have, I think he'd have just paid it."

I shook my head. "Could Gerry have done it?"

"Don't think so. This was a couple of years ago.

Their business is doing great now. They also moved to another county."

"So no motive."

"Yup."

"Lydia sics Simmons on you. Her friend, Ham Stephens, sets Paul on Ian. I wonder if Paul and Simmons know each other? Paul did just up and vanish one morning. I don't think Georgie ever saw him leave."

"You think he killed Simmons and took off?" Nick said. "Weren't they kind of on the same side?"

"Not really. Simmons was out to get you. Paul was out to sabotage the inn. And for Ham Stephens, I think it was personal, too. I always had the impression that he carried a torch for Lydia."

"But Lydia's definitely hot for Ian," Nick said. "Man, you would not believe some of the stuff I've heard her say this week."

"Don't know, don't wanna know," I said. "You mentioned that Simmons showed up at the inn. The time Ian ushered him out. Did he ever come back?"

"Don't know for sure."

I gave him my skeptical look again.

Nick sighed. "There were a couple of times I thought I caught a glimpse of him. Just for a split second. But it was late, and I was really tired. So I wasn't sure."

"Do you remember when?"

"A couple of times last week. The last time was Friday, I know that. Because I remember thinking he wasn't due back 'til that afternoon."

"Do you remember when the meat thermometer went missing?" I asked.

Nick rubbed his forehead. "About the same time."

We sat in silence, both of us thinking. Two racing bikes whizzed down the street. All I saw were helmets, black spandex, and the blur of wheels.

"So Simmons was skulking around, probably listening at doors . . . ," I started.

"Or going through papers," Nick added.

"Poking his nose where it didn't belong," I allowed. "Only this isn't just any old B&B. This is the place where Harkins was forging and stashing art. It's where Harkins then disappeared. It's where Insurance Guy was killed. And it's where Paul the wrecking ball was destroying everything in his path."

"And now Simmons and that meat thermometer are in the freezer," Nick finished.

I nodded. "So Simmons might have learned something. The question is what?"

Chapter 37

To describe our dinner as "strained" was putting it mildly.

True to form, Baba didn't say a word. Mom and Marty did most of the talking. Unfortunately, not to each other.

Luckily, Nick and Marty had saved the day by picking up Chinese takeout from one of Marty's favorite spots. "Little family-run place that makes great dim sum," he promised.

So at least we had something tasty to serve up along with a big helping of family tension.

Nick and I had decided not to tell Mom about Ian's freezer. Instead, we tried to gently steer her into going home. But the more we guided and nudged, the more she dug in her designer heels.

"OK, she can take my room," Nick said during one of our frequent kitchen confabs. "I can sleep on a camping cot in the living room. Or pitch a pup tent in the backyard."

Lucy, who seemed to recognize the word "pup," looked up hopefully.

I grabbed a dog treat from the mason jar on the counter. She took it delicately from my palm, dropped to the floor, and held it with her two front paws as she went to town.

"Putting aside the fact that we don't have a tent or a cot, just how do you propose to explain why she should give up a first-class room with a private bath to sleep in a bedroom that smells like a cross between a bakery and a locker room—not to mention share a bathroom with four other people?"

"I was just gonna say we loved her and wanted her to stay here," Nick said.

"Worth a shot," I said, grabbing a second "cookie" for Lucy.

But Mom was resolute. The more we begged her to stay with us, the less appealing it seemed to be for her. "Besides, I'm probably going home tomorrow," she teased.

"Hey, why don't I come over and spend the night?" I suggested. "It'll be like a slumber party."

If I couldn't get her out of the inn, I could at least stand guard to make sure she didn't venture into the basement. Or wherever people went before they ended up in the basement.

"I'll spend the evening here," she conceded. "But then I'm going back to the B&B to get my beauty sleep. Alone, thank you very much. Besides, you don't want that cute innkeeper to see you in the morning without your makeup. Keeping a little mystery in a relationship is important."

"Uh, Mom, there is no relationship. And believe me, we've got all the mystery we can handle."

Chapter 38

I popped up early the next morning, opened the back door for Lucy, and made a big pot of coffee. The way things were going, we were gonna need it.

When I settled on the back stoop with my cup and my laptop, Lucy was romping in the moist grass. Every so often, she'd stretch her neck and study the birds flying to and fro.

Seeing me, she trotted over and rolled onto her back.

"Does someone want a belly rub?" I said, scratching her silky, white tummy.

Her tail thumped happily. One of the birds screeched, and she sprang into action—racing to the fence and fixating on one of the neighbors' trees.

Lucy was fascinated by nature in all its forms. Clouds, flowers, little hopping bugs, it was all brand-new and wonderful to Lucy. She savored it. Like she was making up for lost time.

I flipped open the laptop. I had a missing Harkins,

two bodies, and no idea what was really going on at the inn.

It was time to take a more professional approach.

Twenty minutes later, as Lucy frolicked—and with time out for the occasional ear scratch or belly rub—I'd typed everything I knew into a file. Heading "The Case of the Cotswolds Inn."

Sherlock Holmes, I'm not.

I reviewed my notes. Precious little. But somehow, setting it down in black and white made me feel better. More in control. And after yesterday's little foray into the basement, I needed that.

Reading and rereading my notes, I had a hunch that wherever Harkins had gone—if he'd gone voluntarily—it hadn't been far. He had a fortune in art squirreled away in his room. He wasn't just going to leave it there. And whatever he'd gotten himself into with Blair, I didn't think he was the type to run off and leave his son holding the bag.

Plus, the Harkins I'd seen was meticulous. He must have had a plan. Even if Insurance Guy had thrown a big, fat monkey wrench into the works. The question was, where would Harkins go?

According to Ian, his father didn't know anyone on this side of the Atlantic. But talk about your unreliable narrators. I was attracted to Ian, no lie. But I didn't trust him. Not anymore.

I don't think Nick did, either. He hadn't shared his plans with me. But I wondered if he'd still be working out of the inn. I hoped not. I also prayed Mom was serious about leaving for home today. The sooner we got her out of harm's way, the better.

Time to take off the gloves. And the blinders. If I was going to keep my nearest and dearest safe, I needed to stop acting like a silly schoolgirl with a crush and start acting like the trained reporter I actually was. Even if I had a sneaking suspicion I wouldn't like what I discovered.

So far, databases, public records, and far-flung sources had gotten me precisely nowhere. It was time to go old school: local contacts and shoe leather.

My partner in crime this morning: Lucy.

Troll the neighborhood alone asking questions and you're a nosy reporter, an unemployed weirdo, or a busybody with way too much free time.

But take a dog—preferably a cute and curious puppy—and suddenly you're that friendly neighbor down the street.

I changed into something I thought marked me as comfortable and approachable. A white T-shirt, jeans, and a Nats cap over a sporty ponytail. Besides, Annie always said you can't go wrong with the classics.

Baba was awake and tending to Alistair. I brought her a tall glass of OJ and told her I was taking Lucy for her morning walk.

"Da," she said, brightly. "*Spasiba!*"

"You're welcome, anytime," I said, kissing her on the cheek.

Before I left, I taped a note for Nick on the fridge. I hoped he'd stay away from the B&B, at least until I returned. But I also knew he was as stubborn as Mom.

This morning's agenda was definitely a new

approach for me. While I'd never actively avoided my neighbors, my odd hours—and some of the even odder things that had been going on in my life—also meant I hadn't interacted with them much. Especially lately.

That would change today. My goal: Actually stop and chat with some of the folks who jogged or walked their dogs before work. I just hoped whatever gossip I could pick up would be more useful than what I'd be netting in Nick's pooper-scooper.

"OK, Lucy," I said as we hit the porch and I clipped on her leash. "We're gonna take a nice long walk." She looked up at me with those trusting, liquid-brown eyes.

"We might even run into some other doggies. New friends for you. But we have to be nice and friendly. This is a secret undercover mission."

I swear she looked puzzled. Either that or she was convinced I'd lost my mind. And I couldn't really disagree.

As we stepped onto the sidewalk in front of the house, four racing bikes flew by. Two of the helmet-and-Lycra guys—I think they were guys— put a forearm up in greeting. I waved back.

OK, not much of a verbal rapport. But at least they were friendly.

Lucy and I trotted down the sidewalk. Two moms running with jogging strollers barreled toward us. "Hi," I said.

"Left!" the first one yelled, ceding four inches of sidewalk.

"'Scuse me," I said, dodging right, as she charged through, followed by her friend.

"Woof! Wooff-wooff! Ruff! Rowr!" Lucy planted her front feet and called after them indignantly.

"It's OK, sweetie," I said, patting her shoulder. "It's all right. They're obviously not dog people. Or people people."

Lucy looked into my eyes. And I swear she could see right through to my soul.

"There are some nice folks out here, I promise. And we'll find them. C'mon, baby dog, let's go see what kind of trouble we can get into."

I spied a couple of guys chewing the fat at the end of the block. One had a golden retriever, the other a Jack Russell.

"Beautiful morning!" I said.

"Hey, I know her!" the one with the golden said, bending to scratch Lucy's ear. "So where's Nick this morning?"

"He's busy, so I'm pitching in to walk Lucy," I explained. Not exactly a lie.

"I never did ask Nick, what exactly is she?" the Jack Russell owner asked, eyeing my young canine.

"She's a Lucy," I said, smiling. "Mixed breed."

Lucy sniffed the Jack Russell, while the golden sniffed her. Then they reversed positions. All three tails wagged double time.

"I'm Jim," said the golden's owner. "This is Frank. Hey, tell Nick we finally got that agility course at the dog park. They just finished putting it in yesterday. We can't wait." He jiggled the leash, and the golden looked up at him lovingly.

"Haven't seen Nick in a couple of days," Frank said.

"He's launching a business. A bakery. He's been putting in some hellacious hours."

"Been there, done that," said Frank. "Lawyer. Hung out my own shingle last year. Now I get to choose my own clients. But I swear I'm working twice as hard for half the money."

As a freelancer, I could empathize. The *Sentinel* still hadn't come through with any cash, despite a string of phone calls. Everyone pointed the finger at someone else, all the while heartily reassuring me that "the situation has already been resolved" and "the money is on its way."

The electronic version of "the check is in the mail."

"Did you hear about the Andersons?" Jim said. "They finally pulled the trigger on the Hawaiian vacation. Two weeks. First-class airfare. Hotel overlooking the beach. The whole deal."

"Oh man, I could use some of that right now," Frank said. "Ain't gonna happen this year."

A potentially empty house in the neighborhood? Promising.

"I wonder who they got to house-sit?" I asked, probing for more details. "We're taking off to visit family for Thanksgiving. I'd love to know who they used."

As if.

"I don't think they have anybody," Jim said.

"If worse comes to worst, I guess I could get one of those DIY alarm systems where you can watch your home via the phone," I said lightly, recalling Nick's recommendation to Ian.

"That's definitely the way to go," Jim said. "And you'll love it. We got one this past Christmas. It's great. A toy for the grown-ups. I'm really surprised more of the homes on the block don't have them. We're one of the few."

Frank checked his watch and remembered he had to call a client. We all said our good-byes. And I promised to take Lucy to the dog park to visit her buds. And give the agility course a try. With a few more sniffs and tail wags, we were on our way.

And I had a whole new idea of how to find Harkins.

If I was lucky, it would just take a couple of phone calls. And a dozen of Nick's chocolate chip cookies.

Chapter 39

I plunked a mason jar full of cookies onto the cheap Formica counter. The woman behind it turned toward the sound.

Just over five feet tall, and almost as wide, she was wearing a blue flower-print dress topped off with a heavy white sweater. It may have been eighty-five degrees outside, but it felt like a frosty fifty-five in the *Washington Tribune*'s circulation department.

"Well, if it isn't the bad penny herself."

"Hey, Annette! Hope your circulation's better than this newspaper's."

"If it wasn't, I'd be in a coma. Whatcha doing slumming down here with us working folks? I thought you were independently wealthy now?"

"An ugly lie. I'm still working. Just freelancing."

"Uh-huh, my first husband used to freelance," she chortled, smoothing her brassy blond perm. "Meant he was free to drink at every bar in town. So what's this?" she said, pointing at the mason jar sporting a big red bow.

"My brother runs a bakery," I explained. "His specialty. Chocolate chip cookies."

I owed Nick big-time. He'd baked these in our kitchen this morning. After I'd told him why I needed them. And promised to take over Lucy's morning walk for the foreseeable future.

"You tryin' to bribe an old lady?"

"Yes, ma'am."

"OK, good. 'Cause I wanna try some of these. What's it gonna cost me?"

I knew I couldn't tell her about Harkins and the freezer of death. So I was ready.

"I'm working on a story about porch pirates. And I wanted to find out which houses in my neighborhood have put their newspaper delivery on hold."

"I heard a nasty rumor you were working for the competition," she said, eyeing me through Coke-bottle glasses with pink plastic frames. Nothing got by Annette.

"Not on this one. I haven't even pitched this story yet. I'm still doing research."

"You don't think it's someone in my department?" she asked, raising an eyebrow.

"Nope. But I want to know which families to talk with," I said. "If they're willing, we might even plant some empty shipping boxes and see if anyone takes the bait."

"Stealing right off somebody's front porch? That's just low. No excuse for acting like that. You gonna tell 'em where you got their names?"

"Anybody asks, I heard it from neighborhood gossip."

"Good girl. OK, what streets do you need?"

Fifteen minutes later, I had a list with a half dozen names and addresses. I also knew that one of the lifestyle reporters was secretly pregnant. And a business writer was cheating on her girlfriend with a photo editor. And the head of H.R. was in rehab. Again.

They say that in jail, cigarettes are currency. At a newspaper, it's gossip and food.

I had to admit, Nick's cookies were pure gold.

Chapter 40

Part three of my plan involved a lunchtime walk with Lucy.

I could have been creeping around in a striped jumpsuit with a stocking cap over my head and a burlap sack on my shoulder. The minute most of the neighbors saw Lucy, they smiled. More often than not, they'd stop to chat. Even if it was just small talk about the Nats or the weather.

And at least three people told me about the new agility course at the dog park. Each time, Lucy looked up at me expectantly.

"OK, we'll go," I said to her the last time. "Tomorrow morning, I promise."

She looked hopeful.

Armed with Annette's list, I was touring the empty houses in the neighborhood. And I now had ten addresses to check. I'd prevailed on Marty (using my porch pirates story) to call his friend in circulation at the *Sentinel*. I'm pretty sure Marty didn't believe me. But I think he kinda felt he owed me. Karmically speaking.

Nice homes where the owners were gone for a week or two? That might be just the spot for a crafty thief looking to stay close but off the grid.

At this point, I wasn't planning on ambushing Harkins. Or even laying eyes on him. I just wanted to rule out a few of the houses on my list. In an hour I was able to eliminate three of them.

I called Trip when we got home.

"Ashamed to show your face in the newsroom?" he said.

"I know it's stupid, but I am currently working for the *Sentinel*. The word is out, and I figured it could be problematic for you."

"Wouldn't even buy me a cheap cup of vending machine coffee? Tsk, tsk."

"I'd invite you for dinner, but you-know-who is cooking," I said, dropping my voice.

"How do your mom and Marty feel about that?" Trip asked.

"Mom's off on another one of Ian's 'excursions.' Georgetown history tour, followed by drinks riverside. Marty's back on his antibiotics, which apparently wipe out his sense of taste."

"Maybe you could get the bottle and pass 'em out to the rest of the table."

"How would you feel about a nice evening walk, followed by coffee and fresh cherry galettes?" I asked.

"At my favorite Fordham bistro?"

"If you mean my front porch, yes."

"And when you say 'walk,' you mean . . ."

"Scoping out empty houses looking for Harkins. Or evidence of Harkins. I figure a couple with a dog looks respectable. And I've been out alone twice today already."

"And you explain peeping in the windows how?"

"Lucy's Frisbee. I just happened to toss it too close to the house."

"So you're inviting me for an evening of casing the neighborhood, trespassing, and a little light stalking, followed by dessert and coffee?"

"Yup."

"What the heck. Count me in."

Chapter 41

That evening, Trip showed up with flowers "for the lady of the house." And a green rubber bone "for the little beast."

Baba's face lit up. "So pretty," she said, giving him a "pat, pat, pat" on the shoulder. "Thank you."

"For you, anytime," Trip said, giving her a peck on the cheek. To me he said, "You didn't buy me coffee, so you get nothing."

"Hey, if you're helping me, uh, walk Lucy," I said, sliding my eyes over to the sink, where Baba was putting the flowers in water, "I'm already grateful."

"Nice move," Marty pronounced, giving Trip a beefy thumbs-up from his perch at the kitchen table, where he was rocking a very drowsy Alistair. "Very classy."

For her part, Lucy remained glued to Trip's side, her new toy clutched in her mouth. Every once in a while, she'd look up at him adoringly, and he'd stroke the top of her velvety head.

"So where's Nick? I was promised galettes," Trip said, as he hung his gray glen-plaid suit jacket on the back of a kitchen chair. Followed by his baby-blue silk tie.

"The galettes are here. Nick is at Ian's. But he's making it an early night. Trying to do fewer late nights, more regular hours," I said, meaningfully. "He'll probably be home before we are."

"Excellent," Trip said, rolling up the sleeves of his perfectly pressed white shirt. "Shall we walk?"

At that last word, Lucy dropped her toy and bolted for the door. I handed her leash to Trip, who clipped it onto her collar. I grabbed the Frisbee and the pooper-scooper. The list was already folded discreetly in my pocket.

"So what's the first step in your infernal scheme?"

"Two houses on Waterleaf Lane. And another on Magnolia Circle."

"Sounds good. Let's roll."

The neighborhood was quiet this evening, the air heavy and humid. Already it felt like summer. Down the block, a couple of kids chased each other on skateboards, while a lanky guy jogged on the other side of the street.

Lydia's brick Georgian mansion, the oldest home in the neighborhood (because her family originally owned the land on which the rest of ours were built) was gorgeous. I had to give her that. Lush hydrangea bushes, loaded with snowball-sized, dawn-pink flowers, flanked it on two sides.

Oddly, I hadn't seen Lydia in the past few days. The way she was going, I'd half expected her to have moved into the B&B by now. Maybe she'd heard about Alistair.

Lydia might covet Ian, but somehow I didn't see her as the motherly type.

Although look who's talking.

"Why do I feel like whistling the theme from *Bridge Over the River Kwai*?" Trip quipped, as we marched along.

"At least you're not carrying a spear and a shield," I said, wielding the pooper-scooper.

"Too bad you can't twirl it like a baton."

"Where this thing has been, you don't want me twirling it," I countered.

Lucy stopped and sniffed a fire hydrant. Her tail began to wag furiously.

"Looks like one of her friends has been by recently," Trip said.

"Yeah, apparently she and Nick have a whole other life I know nothing about. They're the toast of the neighborhood. And tomorrow morning, I promised to take her to the d-o-g p-a-r-k."

"We're spelling now?"

"She seems to recognize that phrase, and she gets all excited. I don't want her to be disappointed when we don't end up there tonight."

"I'm glad to hear one of you is expanding her vocabulary. What are you going to do when she learns how to spell?"

"Get her a job as an editor."

"She couldn't do worse than that new guy we hired. So what exactly are we looking for here?" he asked as we turned onto Treeleaf Lane.

"Well, I'm thinking if there's an alarm system or cameras, that rules the place out. You know the difference between fake security stickers and the real thing, right?"

"When this is over, we've got to get you an honest job."

"Hey, my job is honest. It's my neighbors who are suspect."

"Suspects, more like. OK, this one's got stickers from Brinks. I'm familiar with the name, so I'm assuming they're genuine?"

"Oh yeah. We're either looking for no stickers or fakey names you've never heard of."

A fleet of old cars, along with a couple of new ones, lined the driveway of the second house. The lights were on, rap music blared from the backyard, and I could smell burgers grilling.

"Not them, either," I said. "They may have canceled the newspaper, but they left the teenager at home."

"Rookie mistake. I wonder how much of this manse the firefighters will be able to save?"

Lucy was pulling Trip toward the curb—and the burger smell.

"Just out of curiosity, do you ever feed this little dog?" he asked. "Because it would appear that the wolf cub is starving."

"She had her own dinner and two helpings of Baba's stew. Whatever that was. Nick says no more food 'til morning."

Lucy threw her weight into the leash and pulled him as far as the curb.

"Well, apparently the little beast does not agree.

She seems to think your neighbors have a burger with her name on it."

"She thinks all food has her name on it." I handed Trip the scooper and Frisbee, reached down, and picked up Lucy, cradling her in my arms. "Don't you, you crazy dog?"

She licked my face.

"C'mon, Magnolia Circle's only two streets over. Then we can call it a night."

"Good," Trip said. "I was beginning to think those galettes were just a ruse to get me over here."

I gently deposited Lucy onto the street when we rounded the corner to Magnolia Circle. It was a short cul-de-sac on the edge of the neighborhood. The houses were larger, and the lots were enormous.

"We're looking for 4112," I said, checking my list. "Normally, they get the *Tribune* and the *Sentinel*."

"So we know they're nice, well-rounded folks," Trip said. "How long are they away?"

"Three weeks," I said as we hiked down the street. "And they left the day before Ian's party."

It was at the very end of the cul-de-sac, with a large yard on one side and a house sporting a FOR SALE sign on the other.

"Nice and private," I said. "No cameras that I can see. And the lawn's overgrown, too. That's a good sign."

"A-1 SECURITY?" Trip asked.

"Fake. You can get those stickers at the hardware store. Or print them out online."

"So how come you don't have any?" he asked.

"I was under the impression that a double dead bolt was real security."

"Silly you," he said. "So how do we get a closer look?"

I took the Frisbee from his hand. "Hey, Lucy! You want your toy? You want your toy?"

"Woof! Woof-woof!"

"Lucy says 'yes,'" Trip said. "Let 'er rip."

I released my arm, and the Frisbee sailed, bouncing off the front of the house and dropping into an overgrown bush right in front of a window.

"Nice shot!" Trip said.

"Oh my, it's gone onto my neighbor's lawn," I said, with exaggerated hand gestures. "You hold the leash, and I'll run and get it."

"OK, Cate Blanchett you're not," Trip murmured. "Just collect the Frisbee and tell me if you see anything."

I pretended to search the bush, moving the branches to one side and the other. I stepped closer, flattened myself against the brickwork, reached out, and shoved the branches aside.

Inside the house, behind the gauzy curtains, a face stared back at me—mouth in a perfect O.

Chapter 42

I didn't even bother to look back at Trip. I ran to the front door and started banging like a madwoman.

"Red! Are you nuts?" Trip said, hustling up the lawn with Lucy. "What are you doing?"

I kept hammering on the glossy oak door. It flew open. But whoever opened it was standing behind it. Invisible.

"Get in here quick!" a familiar voice said. "Before someone sees you!"

I dashed inside. Trip followed with Lucy.

Nick's ex-fiancée slammed it shut behind us. True to form, Gabby was wearing a teased blond wig with an orange headband, a long-sleeved, white stretchy T-shirt that could have been sprayed on, figure-hugging black pedal pushers, and kitten heels.

"Sister girl!" she said, throwing her arms around me. Lucy raced around our legs.

"How are you?" I asked. "Are you OK?"

"I'm fine, sugar. Oh, look at the little girl!" she said, dropping to her knees and greeting Lucy. "You look so good! Yes, you do!"

To me she said, "She's all healed up!"

"She's done great," I told my former, not-quite sister-in-law. "She's got a little scar. But the fur's grown back on her tummy, so you can't see it."

Gabby had rescued Lucy from the streets of Las Vegas. The pup had been foraging for dinner out of a back-alley Dumpster when Gabby found her and carried her home. Lucy, in turn, adopted Nick.

And Gabby stood by us, literally, after Lucy ate a sock, nearly died, and had to have emergency surgery. Hence the little scar. She also helped me nab a killer who'd been trying to frame me for murder.

She'd returned to Vegas—and her former boyfriend, now fiancé—right after the little pup was out of the woods. She even sent me a couple of postcards through Trip. Just to let me know she'd gotten back safe and sound.

"She's so much bigger!" Gabby teared up as Lucy bounced on her, licking her face. "It's only been a few weeks, but she's growing up!"

"Gabby, what are you doing here?" I asked.

"Oh, honey, it's a long story," she said, giggling at Lucy the happy jumping bean.

I looked at Trip. He looked at me and shrugged.

"Does Nick know you're here?" I blurted.

"No, sugar. And he can't find out, either."

We agreed on that one.

When Gabby had taken off nearly a month ago,

my funny, outgoing brother turned into a zombie. He ate. He slept. He showered. Occasionally.

But it was like there was no one home behind the eyes.

It took a long time for the real Nick, the extravert with the easy grin, to return completely. I didn't want to lose him again.

"We were looking for Harkins," I said.

"Hmm, really," she said, looking away. "No one here by that name."

I grabbed her hand. "Gabby, I understand he's in danger. We're here because Ian is worried sick. He needs to know that his dad's OK. Even if he doesn't know where he's holed up."

"Plus, there is something seriously wrong at that inn," Trip added.

"That, too," I said.

"Come on," Gabby said. "We're set up in the den."

I unclipped Lucy's leash, and she dashed ahead with Gabby. Trip and I followed.

The "den" was a huge paneled room with what looked like a two-story window or glass door at one end. I couldn't tell because it was covered with heavy drapes. Which were closed. A couple of mini fridges hummed on one wall. Next to them were stacked a half dozen or so six-packs of Gatorade beside an open cardboard carton of snack food. Potato chips. Cheese puffs. Peanut butter crackers. Five folding chairs were clustered around a card table in one corner. I spotted fold-up cots and deflated air mattresses in another.

"Gabby, what is this place?" I said in a hushed voice. "How many people are living here?"

"A few of us," she admitted. "We've got another one a couple of blocks from here. That's where Harkins is now."

"He's OK?"

She nodded.

"Gabby, what's going on?"

"I want to tell you, sugar. You know I do. But it's not my story to tell. You weren't supposed to find us."

"I'm not gonna tell anyone. You know that. Ian is beside himself. I think he's afraid his father is dead."

"Ooh, the English stud muffin! How are you two doing?"

"There is no us two. I don't trust him anymore. But I do trust you."

Gabby looked away. I could tell she was struggling to make a decision.

"OK," I said gently. "How about I tell you what I know, and you tell me if I'm right? And you have my word: It doesn't go any farther than this room. I won't even tell Ian."

But I wasn't making any promises about keeping secrets from Nick. Not until I knew more.

Gabby looked at me, then at Trip. He nodded.

"Oh sugar, it's been so hard. I wanted to come by and see you guys so many times. But with all this, and the way things ended with Nicky . . ."

"I get it," I said, patting her arm. I kind of did, too. Even though they didn't end up together, she did care for him. But the fiancé—a pro wrestler named "Rodeo Rick Steed"—was, in Gabby's words, her "soul mate."

"I know this is about Jameson Blair and his art collection," I said.

Her mouth made that O shape again. "You know? Ohmygosh, does anybody else know? Does Nicky know?"

"Just the basics," Trip said, pulling out one of the folding chairs and settling in. "And we're the only three who do. Not counting whatever Lord Sir Bed and Breakfast has sussed out himself."

Lucy circled the room, stopping to sniff various points of interest.

"Blair hired Harkins to copy his art collection, then swap it for the real stuff," I said. "The divorce court will let his wife keep half of the paintings. But, thanks to Harkins, Blair will have the real collection—all of it—stashed somewhere. And his wife will end up with half a collection's worth of copies."

"That was Blair's plan," she said, shivering. "He's not a nice man, sugar."

"Then Blair sent a cleanup man," I said. "A little insurance. To make sure Harkins stuck with the plan."

Gabby nodded. "Raymond Bell."

"But Bell's dead. And Harkins is in hiding. Did Harkins kill him?"

"No!" she wailed. "He just found the body."

I looked at Trip, who shook his head infinitesimally.

"Bell was threatening Harkins," I continued. "And Bell just happened to get himself killed? And

Harkins just happened to find him? That's a heck
of a lot of coincidences, Gabby. Harkins could be
lying."

"He's not! Really! But that's why he left. Someone killed Bell. And Harkins knew that everyone
would think he did it. Especially Blair. And he knew
the next guy Blair sent would be even more dangerous. So he hid Bell. Where no one would find him."

"In the freezer?"

She nodded.

"Where did he put Bell after that?"

Gabby startled. "What do you mean, sugar?"

"Bell isn't in the freezer anymore."

I wasn't about to tell her who was.

"So where's Bell now?" I asked.

"Harkins left him in the freezer! Honest. He
should still be there. Could Bell be alive?"

"Trust me," I told her. "I saw him. He's very,
very dead."

Gabby winced. Whatever she did in Vegas—
besides picking pockets, lifting identities, and running an illegal online store fueled with stolen credit
cards—I knew it didn't involve violence. She was
too tender-hearted.

"Bell's body is really gone?" she asked.

"Really," Trip said.

"Could Harkins have gone back and moved him?"
I asked. "Without telling you?"

"Harkins can't go the inn. It's too dangerous.
When he needs stuff, he sends one of us. And none
of us'll go near that freezer."

"The other day? In Harkins's room? When I found
the art?"

"I was in the closet," Gabby said with a small smile. "I didn't have time to lock the door behind me when I heard you coming up the stairs."

"You scared the crap out of me!"

"I'm so sorry," she said, patting my hand. "I wanted to tell you so bad. Oh jeez, if Bell's body is gone, that's bad. Really bad."

"Why can't Harkins go near the inn?"

"In case Blair sends someone else."

"He knows Harkins works there. Does he know who Ian is to Harkins?"

She shook her head. Gabby's hairdo—likely a wig from her extensive collection—was shoulder length, golden blond, and teased on top. Gabby loved her wigs.

But something was bugging me. And it wasn't Gabby's hair. Harkins was acting like a man who was protecting someone. If it wasn't Ian, who was it? Or was it the art?

"Has Harkins finished copying the art?"

"Almost," she said. "But not yet."

"So the stuff at the inn? In Harkins's study?"

"Copies," she said with a little smile.

"Damn," I said. "He's really good."

"One of the best," she said proudly.

If Harkins hadn't completed the paintings, Blair wouldn't kill him. Blair needed those copies. But after? That was a different story. And it could already be open season on anyone Harkins loved. They would be collateral damage. Or leverage.

"Who is Harkins protecting?" I asked.

Behind us, I heard footsteps. I turned and saw a blonde in a turquoise midi dress in the doorway.

Big-boned, with a deep tan, sandals, and a flower in her messy up-do, she looked like a fifty-plus hippie. Her eyes were wide. She looked scared.

I looked at Gabby. She gave the woman an encouraging smile and pulled out the chair next to hers.

"Alex, Trip, I want you to meet Daisy. Daisy, these folks are my friends. My family, really. You can trust them with your life."

Chapter 43

"Is it Alistair? Is the bairn all right? Tell me, please!" She pleaded in a soft Scottish burr, as she looked from me to Gabby.

"Alistair's fine," I said. "How do you know about him?"

She pulled back, as if someone had hit her in the face. Or the heart.

"Daisy is Alistair's mom," Gabby said. "Didn't you get the note?"

"Lucy ate it. Well, most of it. She hid the rest. When I found it, all we could make out was that Ian was Alistair's father."

"He's naught of the kind," Daisy said, indignantly.

Gabby giggled and patted her arm. "Not Ian. *Harkins.* Alistair is Ian's brother."

Now my mouth made that O.

"Alistair is doing great," Trip said, stepping in while my mind slipped into a coma. "Alex and Nick's grandmother, Baba, is really good with babies. And she's staying with them to take care of the little guy. She's crazy about him. Sings to him, rocks him, takes him for walks in the pram. And he loves her."

Daisy put her head on the table and started to cry softly. I didn't know if it was relief or something else.

Neither did Trip, who looked as if he wanted to bolt from the room. Instead, he pulled a neatly folded linen handkerchief from his pants pocket and handed it across the table.

Daisy accepted it and tried to compose herself while Gabby patted her back.

"I'm so glad my wee one is all right," she managed. "Grateful. But l need ta be with 'im. He shouldn't be without 'is mum."

"He's missed you something fierce," I said finally. "The first couple of days, he wouldn't stop crying. That's why we had to call in Baba. And regular formula doesn't agree with him. She started using one with goat's milk. So that part's better. But I can tell he misses you. Sometimes he looks at us like 'who are these people?' He's really bonded with Ian, though. Those two get along great."

Daisy dabbed her eyes and nose with Trip's hanky, clutching it tightly in her right hand. "Aye, thank you," she said. "For taking 'im in and for loving 'im. I'm just bein' selfish. Bein' without 'im is like losin' a part of my own body."

"You're who Harkins is protecting," I said quietly. "You and Alistair."

Gabby nodded.

"Ian doesn't know," I ventured.

Gabby shook her head. "Not if he hasn't read the note."

"We wanted to tell him in person," Daisy said softly. "And we were supposed to be married. Long before now." She started crying again. She took a couple of deep breaths, trying to compose herself.

"But that man . . . that devil. At first, it was just lie low for a while. Now it's like we're being hunted."

"I guess saying 'no' to Blair was out of the question," I said.

"For a couple of reasons," Gabby began. She paused, studying Daisy.

Daisy nodded, then blew her nose. That handkerchief was a lost cause.

"Harkins works with some people," Gabby explained. "Artists, art experts, museum people, thieves, and some law-enforcement guys. Nothing official. Just a loose group. From all over the world. They return looted art. Mostly stuff the Nazis grabbed."

At the word "thieves," my ears pricked up. "Through slightly . . . less conventional means?" I asked.

Gabby's blond head bobbed up and down. "When there's a chance, they'll create a copy. A perfect copy. Then it's switched. And the family gets back the real art that was stolen years ago."

"And the person who had the art . . . ," Trip said sotto voce.

"Never knows there was a switch," Gabby finished.

"That's why Harkins took this job," I tested. It was a statement and a question.

Gabby nodded. "A few of Blair's paintings? He got them from people who snatched them during World War Two. Blair's washed the paperwork. Really well. Looks like a series of normal sales."

"But they're not," Trip said.

"They're so not," Gabby said, shuddering.

"Has Blair discovered Harkins's, ah, art affiliations?" he asked.

Gabby shook her head vigorously. "No, sugar. But he's paranoid. And really control-freaky. He thinks Harkins is pulling the job all by himself. Making the copies and breaking in to do the switch. But he's not."

Daisy sighed deeply. "Cecil's an artist. A verrah talented artist. He hasn't done a forgery in decades. Not for himself. Since 'e got out of prison as a young man. That one was a stupid mistake. Almost a dare. And 'e *paid* for it. Hasn't stopped payin'.' That alliance? Returnin' what people lost? What they had ripped away? That's my Cecil. The real Cecil. And 'e's been doing it now most of his life." A smile flickered on her lips. "His paintings hang in museums all over the world. And private collectors? Rich men with looted art they keep in secret? A lot of those, too. Blair doesn't know Cecil. Just wants 'is copies. And then that devil plans to kill him."

"But if Harkins is going to return those paintings to the rightful owners, there isn't just one set of copies," I said. "This time, there are two."

Gabby's head bounced up and down.

"Three paintings in that brute's collection have been hidden for decades," Daisy explained. "Now 'e was actually inviting Cecil in—givin' 'im access. 'E couldn't say no. Didn't want to. Called it 'a golden ticket.' That's what Cecil said to me, the ould fool. 'This is a golden ticket, Daisy, my girl. And we'll be relievin' that prat of his gold.' Then Bell showed up. Aye, that was bad. We didn't know what to do. I was at the inn. Under another name. Had just arrived with the bairn in the wee hours of that mornin'."

"The ghost baby!" I exclaimed. "That was Alistair!"

Daisy looked puzzled. Gabby grinned.

"It's an old legend," Gabby said. "We just borrowed it. But the next day, Bell showed up. Harkins knew it was too dangerous for Daisy and the baby to stick around. So he started making plans to move them. Next thing we knew, Bell was dead, and we had to jump quick."

"That was the night of the party," I breathed. "And the big storm."

"Harkins wanted Daisy and Alistair to leave—go back to Scotland and wait for him," Gabby confessed, dropping her voice. "But she wouldn't go."

"You can bet the Queen's bloomers I wouldn't go," Daisy said firmly. "I'm not abandonin' meh man. That ould goat was goin' to sacrifice himself. To save us. Not while there's breath in meh body!"

I looked at Trip. He smiled.

"I told Cecil I was stayin' with 'is crew," Daisy said, with tears streaming down her face. "But we both knew it would be too dangerous for Alistair.

If we got caught, 'e could end up with the state. Or worse, if Blair's men found us. But Cecil knew a place where the wee bairn would be safe." Her voice cracked. "And loved."

We all sat quietly until Daisy inhaled a couple of quick breaths and resumed talking. "So I wrote the note, explainin' everythin.' And we left Alistair at your house."

"Then I slipped into the inn, dressed in Daisy's disguise—a hat and scarf and big sunglasses," Gabby said. "And she and Harkins went to separate houses nearby. I stayed a few more days, so it didn't look too suspicious. You know, somebody leaving the minute Bell vanished. But I locked myself in the room the whole time. I even hid in the bathroom when Ian brought up the food trays. Then, after a couple of days, I called the front desk and said I was checking out. Harkins had taken care of booking Daisy. Just putting a name in the computer, really. And Ian had never met her. But in person, I was afraid he might somehow recognize me."

"Gabby, Nick was working in the kitchen!"

"I know!" she said, putting both hands to her forehead. "I was a basket case! I thought for sure I was gonna get caught. And you kept popping up, too."

"The rumor was, you were an actress recovering from plastic surgery," I told her. "'A little nip-tuck,' one of the guests told me."

Gabby flashed a smile.

"Did anyone leave a note for Ian?" I asked. "At the inn?"

"It was too dangerous to leave anythin' at the inn," Daisy said. "The note we left at your house was for you and Ian."

"And Lucy ate it," I said, looking at the puppy, who—exhausted from three very long walks today—had finally curled up and fallen asleep at Gabby's feet.

"How did Harkins know where to go?" Trip asked. "Which houses were vacant?"

"At the inn, he chats with everybody all the time," Gabby said. "Delivery guys, mailmen, water and power workers. Invites them in for coffee and pastries, too."

"So they nosh and gossip, and he learns which neighbors are going away and when?" Trip said.

My former almost sister-in-law nodded.

Ian had done the same thing with me. Was that just another ploy?

"Gabby, how did you get mixed up in this?" I asked. "Did Harkins send for you? Does he know you?"

"No, sugar," she said, sighing. "Not before this. The guy they needed is a friend of a friend in Vegas. But he wasn't available. And wouldn't you know it, having an extra woman on this thing was a big plus."

"So what's the plan now?" I said, practically dizzy.

"Harkins will finish the art, and we'll help him deliver it," Gabby said. "Then he'll disappear with Daisy and Alistair. Blair doesn't know about the rest of us, so we just go back to our lives."

Daisy wiped her nose with the crumpled remains of Trip's handkerchief. "Even if we 'ave to 'ide for the rest of our lives, at least we'll be alive and we'll be together."

I wondered what Ian would think of that. Now that he finally had a relationship—and a business—with his dad, Harkins was going to leave again. This time, with his other family.

Daisy and Gabby gave me their blessing to tell Ian that Harkins was alive and well.

But not where he was. Or even that I knew where he was.

I made the argument for continuing to—temporarily—let Ian believe Alistair was his. No one knew Harkins was Ian's father. So as long as the little guy was a Sterling instead of a Harkins, he had another layer of protection from Blair.

We'd also agreed to keep Nick in the dark. I concurred, but I still felt awful.

Nick already knew about the art, Harkins, Insurance Guy (now the killer formerly known as Bell), and Blair. Basically, as long as Nick understood the inn was still a hot spot for murder and mayhem, that's really all he needed to know.

And telling him that the woman he'd loved (and lost) had been mere steps away as he toiled in the kitchen would be cruel. Almost as cruel as telling him she was camping out just around the block.

By the time we finally left, it was already dark. All the better to keep from being seen.

"I earned my galettes this evening," Trip said, as he cradled a snoozing Lucy on our walk home. I fielded the pooper-scooper. But I never had found that stupid Frisbee.

Let the neighbors wonder about that one when they got home.

We overshot my block and doubled back. Just to make sure we weren't being followed. I figured we had to take precautions if we were mixing it up with former felons on the lam, thieves, and art forgers.

And those were just the criminals on our side.

Chapter 44

Early the next morning, after three very strong cups of coffee, I finally got Lucy to the dog park.

She loved the place. And the dogs. The agility course was a mixed bag.

Lucy ran around it at top speed. And she was fast. She dashed up and down the fixed ramps and raced through the tunnels like a pro. But the weave poles confused her. And when the teeter-totter shifted, she planted her plump puppy rump and refused to budge.

No amount of coaxing could get her to move.

I tried the high, happy voice. Nothing.

I tried softly calling her name. Nope.

She just stared into me with those big dark eyes. So I gently lifted Lucy from her perch and deposited her lightly onto the ground.

Time enough to learn this stuff when she was older. Besides, isn't knowing when to ask for help a sign of maturity? If so, the pup was advanced well beyond her years.

On the walk home, I so wanted to take a turn past Magnolia Circle to visit Gabby and Daisy. But that would be too risky. For them and for me.

Besides, this morning I was meeting with Ian.

Nick and his galettes had an audition at a mom-and-pop sandwich place just outside George-town. And I was taking advantage of his absence to give Ian the good news about Harkins. Leaving out the part about him disappearing forever in the near future.

I thought if I served coffee on the porch, we could at least have a little privacy.

Or whatever passed for privacy at my house these days.

As Lucy and I hit the sidewalk in front of my house, I spotted Nick coming out the front door. Lucy strained at the leash. When I unclipped her, she dashed pell-mell for the porch. And her guy.

"Wish me luck!" Nick said, galloping down the walkway and meeting her halfway.

He must have been serious about snagging this client. He was wearing a navy sports jacket, dress pants, and a tie. I looked down at his feet.

Hard shoes.

Definitely going for broke. I didn't even know he owned leather shoes. The only time Nick wasn't barefoot, he wore flip-flops or sneakers.

"You too, little girl," he said, bending to give Lucy a good-luck pat. "Your daddy's going out to make us some money for lots of puppy food! And bacon!"

"You'll do great. If you'd had any leftovers, you could have sold them to Trip last night."

"Depending on how this morning goes, I may have to," he said, giving the pup a full-on tummy scratch.

"Your stuff is wonderful. If they don't buy it, they're nuts."

"That's the main ingredient in the second batch," he said. "Lemon and coconut. I call them 'tropical tartlets.'"

"You're stalling. Go. Expand your business and come back with good news."

"With my shield or on it. Check."

Which reminded me. "And if you hit the pet supply store on your way home, Lucy needs a new Frisbee," I called after him.

From the driveway, Nick turned and gave a mock salute, before disappearing into his Hyundai.

When I walked into the kitchen, Baba was burping Alistair on her shoulder. He might be a little baby, but he could belch like a trucker after a fried chicken dinner.

"Da, da!" she said approvingly, after Alistair shared his best efforts. Then she carefully turned him over and gently lowered him into her lap. She sang quietly, stroking his chubby cheek.

Alistair really wanted to stay awake. His eyelids struggled mightily. And dropped. Pretty soon, he was snoozing in her arms. It might have been my imagination, but he already seemed a little bigger than when he'd first arrived. He occupied a bit more of her lap. Thanks to Baba, the little guy was thriving.

"Hey, how about I make us some breakfast?" I said. "Nick mentioned bacon on his way out, and it made me hungry. I was thinking I could scramble some eggs to go with it."

"Da, cheese eggs," Baba said brightly.

"Cheese eggs it is."

"Sounds good to me," Marty said, strolling in freshly showered and shaved. I could smell Nick's cologne across the kitchen. And he was wearing one of Nick's University of Arizona sweatshirts with the cuffs rolled up. Even so, it swam on him.

"You want I should throw some bread in the toaster?" he asked.

"Go for it!"

Pretty soon, we were dishing up big plates of cheesy scrambles, crispy bacon, and buttered toast. Jars of marmalade and strawberry jam littered the table.

I spooned a good-sized helping of eggs onto a paper plate, crumbling the bacon over the top. Then I broke up a couple more pieces for good measure. Lucy was growing, too.

With any luck, Nick might have left us a stray galette for dessert. Even if I had to turn the kitchen upside down to find it.

Chapter 45

Just after we'd cleared the breakfast dishes, Baba had decided that, with Alistair out for the count, it was a good time to prep some goulash and scour the kitchen.

For his part, Marty was in the backyard with Lucy, working on her training. She knew "come," "sit," and "stay." And she could kind of "heel," when she felt like it. But "no" was still offensive to her delicate canine ears.

I heard a polite knock on the door.

Ian.

I opened it to find him holding a very large bouquet. Wild pink roses.

He smiled. But his eyes looked tired. I assumed that running the inn single-handedly—along with whatever else he might have been doing—meant some long hours.

"By way of saying 'thank you,'" he said, proffering the bundle wrapped in brown paper. "Thought these might give you and your grandmother a bit of a lift. So how's my little guy this morning?"

"You just missed him. Had a nice big breakfast and nodded off. But come on in. You can still take a peek. He's in his crib."

My living room, as usual, looked like the aftermath of a hurricane. Dog toys and baby toys were scattered everywhere. A stack of Aunt Margie printouts had toppled and spilled onto the floor next to one chair, creating a slippery river of copy paper. Marty's blanket, sheets, and pillows were neatly stacked on one end of the couch. On the nearby table sat his forgotten half-filled coffee mug and a potato chip bag. Empty save for a trail of chip crumbs and salt.

Ian took it all in with barely a second glance. "So how many have you got staying here now?" he asked, smiling.

"Counting me, five. Worried we'll give you some competition?"

I swear those blue eyes twinkled.

"Have a visit with Alistair. I'm going to grab us some coffee and set up on the porch. It's a little more tidy, and we'll be able to talk. If I'm lucky, I might be able to scare up a few of Nick's cookies to go with it."

My brother had practically chained himself to the oven the past few days. When he wasn't at Ian's cranking out goodies for the bakery, he was in our kitchen testing new recipes. And while this morning's galette hunt had yielded only one misshapen lemon-coconut tart—split three ways, thank you very much—I'd also discovered a secret stash of brown butter cookies.

"That sounds marvelous," he said, looking genuinely grateful. "Thank you."

So if Ian was the one with a body in the basement, how come I felt like such a monster? How could I tell him everything was fine, when his father was getting ready to leg it out of his life forever?

When I stepped onto the porch with a tray, Ian had already settled into one of the plastic lawn chairs. Smiling broadly, he looked more relaxed than he had even a few minutes ago. His eyes were a beautiful clear blue.

And he was right. Alistair did look like him.

"He was asleep," Ian said, beaming. "He looked so peaceful, so content, that I didn't want to disturb him."

"Yeah, he pretty much has two speeds. That one's a lot easier to handle. Speaking of which, has my mother been behaving herself?"

"The woman's a delight," he said. "Honestly, she's perfectly lovely. Your father was . . ."

I looked at him.

"Your father was the love of her life, apparently," he added quickly. "I don't imagine it's been easy for her."

"No, I'm sure it hasn't been. For any of us."

Dad had left on one of his business trips almost ten years ago. Only this time, he didn't come back. Heart attack.

It was a knockout punch that nearly splintered

our family. 'Til then, I hadn't even realized how fragile those bonds were.

But glacially slowly and steadily, we'd been knitting them back together, like bones healing after a shattering break. Nick showing up at my door last month? Moving back after years in Arizona? For me, that had been the final piece of the puzzle.

Maybe that's why I hated to see Ian lose his dad.

I plunged ahead. "I put out some feelers on Harkins's situation. And I do have some good news. He's healthy, and he's fine. But he has a few things to handle before he can come home."

"Are you sure? Did you see him? Where on earth is he?"

"Yes, he's fine. But Ian, you're going to have to trust me on the rest of it. I don't know his exact location. He doesn't want me to—or you either, for that matter. He's got a problem, and he's dealing with it. Until he does, he doesn't want to come back. And unfortunately, I don't know when that will be. I don't think he does, either."

"His problem—is it medical?" Ian asked "Is it legal? Is he in jail? Does he need a solicitor?"

I shook my head. "He's perfectly healthy. And he's not in jail, or even in custody." Not yet, anyway.

Ian sat back, clearly perturbed. His eyes seemed darker now. "Does this have anything to do with the paintings I found in his room? Or what you thought you glimpsed in the freezer?"

The last thing I wanted was for Ian to go back to that freezer. Assuming he hadn't put Simmons there himself. But he already knew about Harkins's "colorful" past. Some of it, anyway.

"The paintings are his. But I'd leave them alone. He's got a plan. I don't know what it is, but he needs time. And he is one of the good guys. You can be sure of that."

Ian took a deep breath and leaned forward. "I never doubted it. But I want to help him. I have resources he can utilize."

I chose my words carefully. "He knows what he's doing. But it's a ticklish situation. He needs to be away from the inn—and from you—for your own good. And his. He'll come back when he can." If he can.

"Do you know who's after him?"

"Ian, I've told you everything I can." Now tell me how Simmons ended up in your freezer, I wanted to say.

"This isn't some damned news story," he said, chewing the last word. "This is my father!"

Contrary to every natural impulse, I paused. And measured my words. Gabby and Daisy and Alistair were depending on me to get this right. I couldn't afford to blow it.

"Believe me, I know that," I said steadily. "It's more than that to me, too. You asked me to make inquiries, and I did. You asked me to see if I could get leads on where he went, and I did. Sort of. I still don't know exactly where he is. I know what he's doing. And I know why. Or at least, his side of it. All I can say is that there are some very good people depending on him. And I can't tell you more than that."

I didn't bother to add that I was sorry. That sounded pathetic, even in my head.

During our short conversation, Ian had morphed in front of my eyes—like a shape-shifter in a horror movie. From the happy, relaxed innkeeper-slash-father who'd first shown up with flowers and gratitude to the cryptic cypher who'd demanded answers about his father. But even that was preferable to his current incarnation. He was taut. Face hardened into an inscrutable mask. Mouth in a grim line. Though he was completely still and deliberately calm, I sensed barely contained emotion. Anger. His eyes were dark.

I wouldn't want to be his enemy, I thought, as he sat poised in my lawn chair like a coiled spring.

Chapter 46

It was a pretty good bet that Ian wouldn't be bringing me any more flowers. I was just relieved he left Alistair at my house. Or, more accurately, with Baba.

I'd have to give Nick a heads-up, too. At this rate, I didn't know how much longer he might be welcome in Ian's kitchen.

Which, from my perspective, was just fine. The faster I could get my family away from that cursed inn, the better.

I needed some cleaning therapy. I grabbed the basket that was home to Lucy's toys and started tossing them into it from all over the room. I even scored a three-pointer from the corner. After restacking the growing tower of Aunt Margie letters, I grabbed Marty's sheets and blanket and dumped them into the washer, along with the pillowcases. The pillows went into the cedar chest in my closet. I splashed some liquid soap into the washing machine, slammed the door, and hit the button. Then

I snatched up the potato chip bag and carried it to the kitchen trash.

Baba was stirring a bubbling pot on the back of the stove. I squeezed her shoulders and kissed her cheek.

"He is angry now, but he will stop," she said simply.

"I don't think so. Not this time. And I'm not sure it really matters anymore. Not to me."

She turned and gave me a long look and smiled patiently. I wondered what she saw. The granddaughter with a messy home and an even messier life?

"You are not keeping the father away," Baba said carefully.

No need to explain anything. Baba hears all. Baba knows all. And she has a lot better grasp of English than people think. Which works to her advantage.

If we could ever get her on *Wheel of Fortune*, she'd clean up.

"No. But Ian's father is doing something dangerous. He needs Ian kept out of it. And Alistair. He's Harkins's baby."

Baba smiled. If she was shocked, or even surprised, she didn't show it.

"The man Harkins is going up against is dangerous," I admitted. "He'd come after Ian if he knew about him. Luckily, he doesn't. Same with Alistair. Even Nick doesn't know this. And we can't tell him."

"This bad man will go to boardinghouse?" Alarm crept into her voice.

"Not himself. He might send someone. But he's looking for Harkins, and Harkins isn't there." And Blair doesn't know the art is there. Yet.

Baba nodded.

"Baba, I didn't lie to Ian. But I didn't tell him everything either."

Her dark eyes scanned my face. Waiting.

"Ian's father. When this is over, he might not be able to come home. He might have to stay away for a long time. Maybe forever."

She took my right hand in her two strong ones. "You did not make this. You helped him. With little baby. With telling him the father is alive. Telling him the father loves him."

I nodded.

She squeezed my hand. "Sometime that is all you can do."

Chapter 47

A couple of things were bugging me. And so far, the only mysteries I'd solved were the legend of the ghost baby and the puzzle of who was wrecking Ian's inn. And, technically, Rube had cracked that last one.

I'd found Ian's father. But since he was going to disappear soon, I couldn't exactly put that in the "win" column. Ditto the puzzle of Alistair's parents.

And nobody seemed to be missing Simmons. As far as I could tell (and I'd checked), no one had even filed a missing person's report. If Nick's sources were to be believed, the people who knew him best were more likely to be dancing a jig.

So was he still in the freezer? I wanted to know. But not badly enough to visit that basement. Not while the inn was the nexus of all weirdness.

And what of the freezer's original occupant, one Mr. Raymond Bell? I'd done some online sleuthing but learned very little. There was a man by that name living in Brooklyn. Bushwick. The age was about right. He didn't have a Facebook page. But his Twitter page marked him as a total sports fanatic. Especially football, golf, and boxing. He'd bragged about hitting Vegas a couple of times a year for major bouts. His LinkedIn profile listed him as a "business tech consultant."

Was that what hit men were calling themselves these days?

My head spun.

Regardless of what Baba said, there had to be a way I could help Daisy and Harkins. And Ian.

Then there was Marty. He'd straightened everything out with his doctors. And the cops. He'd even had the banks send over new credit and debit cards. And we were all on a first-name basis with his physical therapist.

But he couldn't handle stairs yet. And Helen was on the warpath. So he was still on the sofa. The weird thing was, I didn't really mind.

Although last night had been a bit of a surprise.

By the time Trip and I finally got home from the safe house, it was late. We'd each polished off our coffee and the galettes on the front porch. Talking quietly, so that we wouldn't be overheard.

Afterward, Trip grabbed his coat and tie, said a big good-bye to the room, and took off for home. I plunked down in a living room chair.

Marty and Nick were sitting on the sofa, each with a beer in his hand. Watching *Collateral*.

"I thought that was only on cable," I said.

"We have cable," Nick said.

"Uh, no, we don't. And if you're 'borrowing' it from the neighbors, they're gonna find out. It's not like using their hose to wash your car."

"Relax, kid, it's all on the up-and-up," Marty said. "My treat."

"Marty, I can't ask you to do that. Besides, it's summer. We don't want to be parked inside in front of the TV. It's bad for the brain."

"You tell 'em, Mom."

"OK, that's beyond mean."

"You don't know the half of it," Nick said. "Today's outing was Historic Georgetown. And I heard she made the tour operator cry."

"Oh jeez, really?" Any minute now, Ian would be posting a No VLODNACHEKS ALLOWED sign on the front door of that inn.

"That mother of yours is a firecracker," Marty said. "Is she seeing anybody?"

"Look, I know you mean well," I said. "And this is very sweet. But I made a conscious decision when I moved in—no cable."

"Poverty is not a lifestyle choice," Nick said.

"No sweat," Marty said. "If you want, I can call and have it disconnected tomorrow. I just had the cable company turn it off at my house and turn it on here. While I recover. I'd be paying for it anyway. This way, at least it's not going to waste."

"Oh. Well, when you put it that way . . ."

Nick grinned. "He's got everything. Executive

deluxe package. Before you walked in, we were watching soccer from Romania."

"Cool it, kid," Marty said. "Something I learned after a few contract negotiations: the secret is to clam up after they say 'yes.'"

Small wonder that this morning I wanted to help Marty solve his Helen problem. If she was really trying to kill him, she had to have some kind of a motive. And since they didn't seem to have all that much regular contact, it was probably money.

But she wasn't in the will. That left property or insurance. Marty swore the only thing he owned was his house. And that was mortgaged to the hilt.

It was possible Helen didn't know that. Or didn't believe it. It was also possible that Marty's house had gone up in value without his being aware of it. Although he seemed like a pretty savvy guy.

I grabbed my laptop and hit the county records. In the old days, answering my questions would have taken more shoe leather and another batch of Nick's baked goods. These days, all you needed was a computer and a little patience. And I had very little.

Five minutes later, I confirmed Marty's story. According to the county appraisers, Marty's house was worth about $5,000 more than the total of both his mortgages. Plus or minus $5,000.

That left one viable motive that I could think of: life insurance.

That one was a lot trickier. I'd worked on a couple of stories that involved insurance scams. So I already knew there was no catch-all database to search for

policies. I also knew there was more than one way
to get information.

I looked up a number in my personal address
book, snatched the phone off its cradle, and dialed.

"Hi, this is Alex Vlodnachek. Is Walt there?"

"Hi, Alex, it's Effie. He's in the break room. Hang
on a sec."

A good friend of both my parents, Walter Hamp-
stead had been our family insurance agent since I'd
been in diapers. And he'd been a great source when
I was working on those insurance scam stories. Walt
lived and breathed the business. But he also felt
that there were a few areas where the industry
could do a much better job. So I hadn't had to twist
his arm too hard to get his help.

I hoped he'd be as willing this time.

"Alex, how's my favorite girl reporter today?"
His idea of a joke. As far as I knew, I was the only
reporter he knew. Male, female, or otherwise.

"Well, Mom's here for a visit, and everyone's still
alive. So that's good."

"How is Eleanor? I haven't seen her since the
Christmas party."

"Doing great. She just got back from a trip to
Europe with Annie. And I don't think they missed
a single art museum."

"Oh, don't tell Dolores," he said, referencing his
second wife. "She's on a campaign to get me to go."
He dropped his voice. "I don't want to spend the
better part of a day locked in a flying tin can. Scares
the beejeebers out of me."

I wasn't afraid to fly. But the idea of six hours trapped on a plane with my mother had given me serious pause.

"But I'm sure that's not why you called," he said. "What's up? Working on another story?"

"Favor for a friend, actually." I wasn't going to lie to Walt. Not if it wasn't absolutely necessary. "We think one of his relatives might have an insurance policy on him. Would it be possible to check?"

"I take it he didn't give permission?"

"Definitely not," I replied.

"Does this relative have a fiscal responsibility for your friend? Bills? Burial expenses?"

"Nope. He's got all that handled."

Walt sighed a heavy sigh. "This is the part of the business I hate. Just hate. Use it the right way, insurance is a fantastic tool, but in the wrong hands . . ."

"Just like medicine," I said.

"What's the friend's name?"

"Marty Crunk. Martin. He works in the newsroom at the *Sentinel.*"

"Oh, you're branching out."

"Yeah, I'm pissing off editors at both papers now."

Walt chuckled. "As long as I've known you, I can believe that. OK, what's the name of this loving relative?"

I'd done a little online sleuthing on Helen, too. And pumped Marty for more info. I gave Walt her maiden name, married name, mother's maiden name (Crunk), and her middle name, just in case she was using that. Walt said he'd try them all.

"People think they're being cute," he said with a snort. "But I gotta tell you, Alex, if I check and find nothing, that doesn't mean there is nothing. Plenty of companies don't share records. And at a couple of those, I don't have friends I can call, if you know what I mean."

"I know, I know," I said. "But at least this gives us a place to start."

Chapter 48

Nick walked in with a big smile on his face, a bouquet of pink peonies for Baba and a brand-new green Frisbee for Lucy.

"I got it!" were the first words out of his mouth.

"Congrats!" I said, clapping. "All hail the new king of pastry!"

Baba sniffed her flowers, smiled widely, and gave Nick a pat, pat, pat on the back. "You are a good boy!" she said. "Good man! Very good!"

"Technically, it's just a trial run," he explained. "A couple of pies and a few dozen tarts and galettes every Monday, just to see how it goes. But if the customers like my stuff, after a couple of weeks, they'll increase the order. A lot. I mean, these people go through pies and tarts like you wouldn't believe."

"What happened to their old supplier?" I asked.

"Six-month sabbatical in Paris. She might be competition when she gets back, but I'll have had half the year to win 'em over."

"Let's hope she falls in love with the place and stays there."

"*Mais oui!* Oh man, I've got to get over to the inn," he said, peeling off his shoes. "I'm way behind."

Crap.

"Nick, we've got to talk," I said, pausing. How could I tell him? "Um, well, the truth is Ian is kind of mad at me right now," I finally said. "Furious would be more accurate."

"Hey, whatever's going on between the two of you, I don't want to know. I've got a business to run. Besides, Ian and I have a deal."

"What kind of deal?"

"I get to use his kitchen. He doesn't hold any of the Vlodnachek craziness against me. Especially that pertaining to the females of the tribe."

"Get that in writing, did you?" I said, giving him serious side-eye.

"Nope. Handshake deal. But I call it the 'Mom clause.'"

I spent the afternoon answering Aunt Margie letters. Toward the end, I was mentally composing one of my own.

Dear Aunt Margie,
    I found a body in a freezer, and I didn't report it for fear my brother might be blamed. But my fingerprints are probably all over that freezer. Because of the first body I found there last week.

*Which is now gone. And I didn't report that one
either. Am I going to jail?*

> *Signed,*
> *I Didn't Do It—Honest*

When the phone rang, I jumped. Remembering
what Nick had said, I checked caller ID.

Ian.

I picked it up and held my breath.

"Alex, it's Ian. I wanted to apologize for my earlier behavior. You did exactly what I asked of you—
more than. Much more than. It wasn't the news I'd
hoped to hear, and I'm afraid I blamed the messen-
ger. I hope you can forgive me."

I was stunned. So not what I was expecting. A
lifetime ban from the inn? Definitely. An announcement that he was barring anyone named
Vlodnachek from the premises and my brother and
mother were waiting with their possessions on the
lawn? Not totally unreasonable. An invitation for a
personal tour of the freezer? Possibly.

But a complete and total apology? Did not see
that coming.

"Ian, I'm sorry. This whole thing is awful. I'm just
so sorry."

"No need for you to be," he said evenly. "I'll just
have to trust that, whatever my father is up to, he
knows what he's doing. And I'll simply have to muster
through on my own over here until he returns."

OK, that last part made me feel really lousy. If

I didn't know better, I'd think he'd done it on purpose.

But he wasn't my mother.

"I know it goes without saying, but if you can stand the clutter, you're welcome over here anytime," I said, hoping to offer an olive branch. "I know Alistair loves seeing you."

"Actually, I'd like to pop by this afternoon," he said, sounding hopeful. "I believe there will be a bit of a lull in a few hours, if that works."

"Any time you want," I said. "We'll look forward to seeing you."

Maybe Nick's business acumen had worked its magic after all.

Chapter 49

After a dinner of goulash, Baba decided that Alistair needed a nice long walk. She leashed up Lucy and set off. I wondered if they'd get anywhere near Magnolia Circle.

Marty planted himself in front of the TV. His afternoon PT session had taken a lot out of him. But he was ahead of schedule with his rehab. He told Terri that was because he'd gotten a cute little physical therapist named Lucy.

I just wanted to curl up and lick my wounds. I changed into sweats and lay on my bed, staring at the ceiling for what felt like forever.

Finally, I gave in and grabbed the phone, dialing Trip. According to my bedside clock, "forever" had been five minutes.

"Let me guess. Another relative showed up and you want to bunk at my house."

"Bunk at your house, no. Eat at your house, yes."

"Goulash again?"

"Oh yeah," I said. "Marty loves the stuff. Lucy loves the stuff. And Nick's eating at the inn tonight."

"I'm guessing Marty'll leave your house about the same time those taste-numbing antibiotics run out."

"I keep thinking there has to be some way to help Ian and Harkins and Daisy."

"Yeah, I've been mulling that one, too," Trip said.

"Your guys come up with anything new on Jameson Blair?"

"Same bastard, different day," he replied.

"I was afraid of that."

"So what did you tell the proprietor of the Bates Motel?"

"Only what I could tell him that wouldn't put Daisy and Harkins in danger," I admitted. "His dad is OK, but he has a situation he has to handle. I feel awful. His father is helping victims of the Holocaust. Now he and his lady and their baby have to go on the run. From some psycho who doesn't want to share an art collection that isn't really his in the first place."

"I know. It's lousy. What if you told Ian the truth? Jameson Blair. His ill-gotten art collection. The fact that Harkins and his merry band are stealing from the rich and returning things to the rightful owners."

"Ian would try to help him. And then he'd have to go on the run when this is over. Because sooner or later, when Harkins finishes copying those paintings, and his team makes the switch, Blair is going to send another hit man to clean up those pesky loose ends."

"I keep wondering what happened to the first hit man."

"We know what happened to Raymond Bell," I said. "We just don't know who did it. Or where his body is."

"What if Harkins refused to pull the job and just went on with his life?" Trip mused.

"Blair would up the ante," I said. "Threats. And eventually he'd find Daisy. Or Alistair. Or Ian."

"I can't believe there's a covert group secretly returning looted Nazi art," Trip said.

"It's brilliant. And elegant. And I want to help."

"I know you do, Red. But you don't have a super-power. You're not a forger. You're not an art expert. And I can't see you as a second-story man. Well, I can, but it's not pretty."

"Yeah, my only talent is digging up information and making it public. And that's the last thing they need."

Chapter 50

The next morning, Lucy and I took a new approach to the agility course at the dog park.

I unclipped her leash, and she tore around the thing at top speed. She raced up and down the ramps. She whipped through the tunnels. She ran a wide arc, avoiding the entire cluster of weave poles. Twice. And totally ignored the teeter-totter.

When she crossed the finish line, we bounced up and down like a couple of maniacs.

"I'm sorry, but your dog didn't complete the course," a woman with a leashed Weimaraner stiffly informed me.

"Sure we did," I said, as the puppy danced around my feet. "We're practicing for the freestyle."

More like Lucy-style. Too bad I couldn't tackle my life the same way.

When we got home, Baba was stirring a suspicious-looking pot on the back of the stove.

More goulash.

Marty was keeping her company in the kitchen, coffee cup in one hand, folded newspaper in the other.

"You got a phone call just now," he said, sliding a torn piece of copy paper across the table. "Some guy named Walt. Left his number and wants you to call him. Gotta say, he sounds a little old for you. What about that British fella across the street? The one who runs the inn? He seems nice."

I ignored Marty-the-matchmaker, gave Baba a peck on the cheek, filled my coffee cup, and spilled in a little milk. Then I looked at Marty and grabbed the Nesquik out of the cupboard. This was gonna be a three-spoonful morning.

Since I didn't want to talk about Marty in front of Marty, I parked myself in my office. Or as the real estate agent who'd sold me this house dubbed it, "the cozy dining room."

The number Walt left was his direct line. He answered it himself.

"I think your friend might have a bit of a problem," he said seriously.

"How big is 'a bit'?" I asked.

"She's got a $250,000 life policy with Founding Fathers Insurance, and $100,000 each with Yorktown National and Occoquan Life."

"Four hundred and fifty thousand?" My mind was numb.

"In each case, it's the max she can get without a medical exam. And those are just the ones we could find so far," Walt said. "I have a few more calls out. But a couple of these companies aren't going to talk to me."

"Will they talk to Marty?"

"That's tricky. His niece—she is his niece, right?"

"Yeah, that part's true."

"His niece is the customer," Walt continued. "So they don't have to talk to him. He's the insured. Best case, the insured and the customer are the same person. When they're not, it's up to the companies and the states to set the rules. So you have a lot of different scenarios. Sometimes, companies will talk with the insured. Other times, they won't. But a couple of people said your Ms. Westwood made it seem like she was doing this for her uncle because he couldn't take care of things himself anymore."

Man, was that ever a lie. Marty had colluded with my brother to order up cable and, at this moment, probably was conspiring with Baba to plan my wedding.

"This guy is sharp as a tack, Walt. Any way we can cancel these—and make sure she knows about it?" As long as Helen had a motive, Marty was a slow-moving target.

"Again, depends on the company. Technically, what she did isn't criminal."

"But what she does next might be."

"Or possibly what she's done before," Walt said somberly.

"What do you mean?"

"How many uncles does this girl have?"

"I dunno. I think just the one. But I can find out. Why?"

"A lot of the places I was able to check didn't have a policy on Mr. Crunk. But they had paid out a claim to the niece. Only these were for different uncles. And a few aunts. Quite a number of relatives. Also different addresses—often different states. Over many, many years. And using mix-and-match variations of her name."

"Helen Westwood is running an insurance scam!"

"That's what it looks like," Walt said. "And that's definitely the kind of thing that could get an insurance company to talk. To Mr. Crunk and the authorities."

Chapter 51

Marty took the news pretty well. Considering.

"Beats thinking I've lost my marbles," he said, shaking his head sadly. "So I guess she's not a whiz with investments after all?"

Walt had e-mailed me a list of the policies he'd found—on Marty and the others—along with all the relevant information. He thought seeing it in black and white might make it less personal for Marty. And a lot simpler for the authorities.

We had the printout on the kitchen table, where we'd been studying it.

"She's not investing, she's gambling," Marty said. "Betting on people's lives. But here's the real question: Is she loading the dice?"

"You mentioned she does a lot of volunteer work with the elderly?" I said.

"Sure. That's her thing. Been doing it for years. Took care of her dad when he was sick. Then after he died, she'd pitch in wherever she was needed. Helen is an upright, uptight pain in the backside, but I was proud of her. Sometimes she even took 'em in if they needed special care after surgery and didn't have anywhere else to go. Wouldn't take a dime for it, either."

"It looks like she's making her money on the back end. You said her dad left her some cash?"

"A nice little house and a nice little pile from insurance," he said. "Enough to cover the taxes and pay the bills for a couple of years. She took good care of the house, then sold it for a bundle and got a bigger place. She's traded up a couple of times. She might even be renting out some of them."

So had Helen killed daddy? Or had his death merely opened her eyes to a new revenue stream? And just what brand of "help" had she really given those many "aunts" and "uncles"?

At least whoever had killed Bell had a good reason. This was just evil.

"Marty, we've got to go to the cops. It'll take a police report and possibly a letter from your attorney to cancel those life insurance policies. Until we do . . ."

"Yeah, yeah, I know. I've got a price on my head." He shook his head and winced. "Just never thought that price would be nearly a half million bucks."

We spent the rest of the morning at the police station. Marty's lawyer met us there. So I waited in the lobby.

It was a nice change from last time.

When I'd run out of magazines (*Police Blotter* and *Law Enforcement Monthly*), I checked my phone messages. I got a jolt when I recognized my older brother's number.

Last I'd heard, Peter and my sister-in-law, Zara, were on a two-week vacation. Somewhere in the Caribbean. Destination purposely omitted.

A successful Manhattan tax attorney, he'd just capped the busiest, most stressful season of the year. They both needed to unwind and decompress.

So why was his cell number popping up on my phone? My heart beat a little faster as I hit PLAY in voice mail.

Peter's baritone boomed out of the cheap speaker, accompanied by a tropical drum band in the background. "Hey, Alex, hope everything is going well. Just wanted to check in. Look, I got a call from Mom. She said something about Nick going to business school? Anyway, she wants some references and recommendations. I'm happy to help, but I'm also thinking if Nick wanted that, he'd have called me himself. And I haven't been able to reach him. So if you get this, just give me a buzz and let me know what's going on. Strictly on the QT."

He paused, and I heard giggling in the background. "Oh, and Zara says 'hey!' Love you, sis! Bye!"

So had Mom called Peter before she and Nick had their little powwow or after?

When Marty reappeared, hours later, he gave me the CliffsNotes version of what happened in the squad room. Bottom line: The cops were investigating. And while they did, Marty definitely needed to stay away from Helen.

"What about the insurance policies?" I asked.

"My lawyer says we can cancel them now and tell her, so she knows she doesn't get a cent. But the cops say that'll tip our hand. They want to get a warrant to see what was in those pills she was feeding me. And what else she might have in that house of hers. But that could take a day or two."

"This is your rodeo," I said. "What do you want to do?"

"If this is who Helen really is, I want to nail her sorry behind. Even if it means shutting my yap and lying low for twenty-four hours."

"Hey, as far as I'm concerned, you've got the sofa for as long as you need it."

He shrugged. "You know what the worst part is?"

My mind reeled. Sleeping on my lumpy couch? Eating Baba's cooking? Finding out that a blood relative could be a serial killer?

"No, what?" I finally asked.

"I gotta get a new place to eat Thanksgiving dinner," Marty said sorrowfully. "Helen may be a rotten person, but she makes the best pumpkin pie I ever tasted."

Chapter 52

When we got home, Marty headed out to the backyard with Lucy. He called it a training session. I think he just needed some puppy therapy.

Baba and Alistair were both down for an afternoon nap. But only one of them was in the bedroom. She was sitting bolt upright on the sofa with a magazine in her hand.

I was dragging. Between late nights with Alistair and early mornings with Lucy, a nap sounded wonderful. But first I wanted to share what we'd learned at the cop shop with Nick.

I figured he was at the B&B. I just hoped Ian's "popping over" concept was a two-way street.

I headed up the walkway to the inn just as a couple of guys in muscle shirts and jeans angled the freezer out the front door.

"Wait, stop!" I yelled. "You can't take that! Put it down!"

"Lady, we got two more pickups this afternoon. This is a charity, but we still got a boss and a schedule."

Behind them, Ian leaned casually against the doorjamb with his arms folded. "That contraption was more trouble than it was worth," he said. "Time for it to go."

"Did you clean it out first?" I asked.

"It's empty. And as far as I know, it always has been. But it's a nuisance, and I don't need the liability."

I couldn't help myself. I rushed the box and pried up the lid. The guys lugging the freezer dropped it on the sidewalk.

Empty.

I looked at Ian, lounging against the doorframe. He shrugged.

In the bright light of day, I noticed something. In the corner of the freezer. I bent and plucked it between my fingertips. A single bud. Of baby's breath.

Like Paul Gerrard used to wear in his lapel. The same Paul Gerrard who'd left the inn and was never seen again.

I held up the bud accusingly.

Ian raised his eyebrows slightly.

"Hey, are we taking this thing or not?" One of the guys asked Ian.

"Taking it, gentlemen. Definitely taking it."

I glared at him. I was also blocking the sidewalk. Unless they wanted to knock me down, that freezer wasn't going anywhere.

One guy looked at me and back at Ian. "Look,

we don't want to get in the middle of no domestic sit-chee-a-shun. You and the missus need a minute?"

Ian smiled, and his eyes actually twinkled.

So why did I want to slap that self-satisfied expression right off his face?

"I'm not his missus! And it's his damned freezer!" I shouted, turning for home.

"Alex! Alex!" he called from behind me.

As I hit the curb, he touched my shoulder. I spun around.

"You're getting rid of evidence," I enunciated through clenched teeth.

"I am making a donation to charity," he said calmly. "That freezer is going to a local soup kitchen. We never used it, and frankly, it caused too much trouble."

"Will they scrub it out first? Because it's had at least two bodies in it that I know of," I whispered, holding the bud of baby's breath in front of his face. "Probably three."

"I understand that. But that was not my doing. And that's why I'm getting rid of it," he said quietly. "We need to turn a page, so to speak. And this . . . *donation* seems to be the most efficient way."

"Freezers don't kill people. Crazy people with meat thermometers kill people. And getting rid of your killer's favorite hidey-hole isn't going to stop them. Have you taken care of *that* problem?" I asked.

"I believe so," he said, looking straight into my eyes.

I wasn't having it. "Who?"

"Beg pardon?" he asked, throwing a quick glance at the two guys leaning on the freezer.

"You heard me. Who is it? Who's going around your inn dropping bodies like dominos?"

"The man you found," Ian started. "The man you saw in there. He was a professional hit man. A nasty piece of goods."

"Yes, Raymond Bell. I know. I also know who sent him and why."

"That man did anything, killed anyone, for money. He had no morals, no scruples, no conscience."

"What about Ralph Simmons? He was just a poor, schlubby health inspector."

Ian looked startled. "Simmons wasn't just a health inspector. He was a snoop. An extortionist. A sleazy little worm. He pried, he peeped, he listened at doors. And he likely heard or saw something he shouldn't have."

I studied his face. He was much better at this than I was. I couldn't read him.

"I did not kill him. I didn't kill any of them."

He said, "Any of them." Not "either of them." Three bodies. Not two.

"What about Paul?" I asked. I wanted to believe him. That was the problem.

"I never touched a hair on that boy's head. As far as I knew, he was a guest! You're the one who found out what he was really doing here. And yes, I do believe he's dead."

"Why was he killed?"

"I don't know."

"If you've taken care of the problem, that means you know who did it," I said. "If you know who did it, you know why. So why was Paul killed?"

Ian sighed. "He wasn't just a saboteur. He was also a thief. When he'd go into the rooms to wreak havoc, he'd steal whatever he could find. Mostly cash, jewelry, and electronics. Small things he could pocket. I'm guessing he viewed that as one more way to unsettle the guests. Let's just say he stole something from the wrong person."

"Who?" I pressed. "And what?"

"It was a gun. A very special gun."

"Whose?"

"Alex, I can't tell you more than that. On my word, on my honor, I didn't kill him. I didn't kill any of them. And neither did my father. This is over. I have put a stop to it. But now we have to let this go."

"Three men are dead. There's been no arrest. No charges. No trial. Not even a funeral. Hell, Ian, I don't even know where their bodies are. Do you?"

He shook his head quickly.

"And your solution is 'Oh, let's give the freezer to charity?' Is that supposed to make it all better?"

"My answer to 'all this,' was to intervene and end it," he said roughly, eyes darkening. "Which I have done, and which I cannot discuss. Not even with you. This is just the mopping up. And why shouldn't at least one decent thing come of this? I don't know about you, but I'm sick to death of the rest of it. Raymond Bell was a monster. No one will miss him. Certainly no one who truly knew him."

"What about Ralph Simmons and Paul Gerrard? They weren't monsters."

Ian's face was inches from mine. I could feel the heat coming off his body. And smell that spicy cologne he always wore.

"They were, actually. Your friend Simmons found Bell's body. In the freezer. Then he came to me for money. A lot of money. Which, frankly, I didn't have. I had no idea what I was going to do. Then he vanished. Just disappeared. And Paul Gerrard—or whatever his name was—was an addict and a bully. He was living on borrowed time even before he stole a weapon and tried to blackmail a killer."

"But Bell's body wasn't in the freezer. Where did Simmons find it?"

"It only left the freezer temporarily," Ian admitted.

"Long enough to gaslight me."

"I'm sorry." His face crumpled. "That little deception was necessary. I needed to keep you out of this. To protect you."

"You couldn't protect Simmons?"

"Simmons had photos. On his phone. Look, Alex, I didn't know about any of these deaths until after the fact. I honestly wasn't that concerned about Bell. His demise was what you might call an occupational hazard. I learned about Simmons and Gerrard simultaneously. And you're right, that was a step too far. So I put a stop to it. And I'm afraid that's all I can tell you."

"That's convenient."

"No, it's not," he pleaded, his voice husky. "It's

really not. I want to tell you everything. To share everything. I don't want anything to come between us."

I stared at him. And I realized two things. I liked him. Really, really liked him.

And I didn't trust him one bit.

Chapter 53

The next morning, I rousted myself at 6:30 and let Lucy into the yard for a quick break.

Alistair, snoozing on my shoulder, didn't budge.

When Lucy scampered back into the house, I handed her a doggie treat and headed back to bed.

I'd taken Alistair duty last night. Partly to give Baba a break. Partly because I couldn't sleep anyway.

I rocked him, I fed him, I cuddled him, and I sang to him. He fussed every time I tried to put him down. Round about 4:30, we'd both fallen asleep. Alistair in my arms, me at the kitchen table.

Now I was paying the price.

Lucy followed me back to the bedroom, the treat still in her mouth. "We'll hit the park after breakfast. It'll still be there. I promise."

As I settled Alistair in his crib, she trotted over, dropped the treat, and turned around three times. Then she curled up and nibbled her cookie until it was gone.

When I got up, it was almost nine, and Baba

was headed for the grocery store. Nick was giving her a ride.

Marty decided to ride shotgun. He actually called "shotgun."

"'Cause of the crutches," he explained to a dubious Nick. "I can't climb in and out of the backseat yet."

After they left, I let Lucy out, drained what was left of the coffee, and made another pot.

Alistair's bottle was ready to go. But Alistair wasn't. Every ten minutes or so, I checked on him. He was in the same position, zonked out in the crib. His little chest was moving up and down. But I was beginning to panic.

I phoned Nick's cell and heard a strange ringing on the kitchen table. It turned out to be my brother's phone. Baba didn't have a cell phone. And if Marty had one, it was probably Helen's property now.

That left one alternative. The fact that I was even considering it meant I was truly desperate.

She answered on the second ring. "I'll have a can of soda, no ice," she called to someone. "Historical accuracy, my foot," my mother muttered into the phone. "It's just an excuse for flies and filth."

"That pretty much sums up the eighteenth century, Mom. How's the tour?"

"Never mind that, what's wrong, Alexandra?"

"What makes you think something's wrong?"

"Alexandra."

"All right, it's Alistair. Baba and Nick are at the store. And I'm supposed to be watching him. He gets a bottle every four hours. I gave him the last one this morning around four thirty. But it's almost ten, and he hasn't woken up yet. And that's not like him. I mean, the little guy loves his bottle."

"Sounds like your uncle Ernie. I will never understand why my sister married that man."

"Mom! It's been almost six hours! What do I do?"

"Rule number one: unless it's sick or injured, you never wake a sleeping baby."

"How do I know if he's sick or injured?"

"Have you dropped him on his head recently?"

"No! Of course not."

"Was he running a fever when you put him to bed?"

"No."

"Is his chest moving up and down?"

"Um, yeah."

"He's fine. Let him sleep."

"But he needs to eat every four hours," I babbled. "He's growing. And it's been more than four hours. Way more."

"You can buy him a watch for his first birthday. Right now, go back to bed, Alexandra. You sound dreadful."

Chapter 54

I slept 'til almost one. I hated to admit it, but Mom was right. I woke up feeling great.

When I walked into the living room. Alistair was in his little swing, and Baba was cheering him on from a chair.

"Hey, kid, let's take a ride," Marty said, swinging into the room on his crutches with a Giant foods tote bag on his shoulder.

"What's up?" I asked.

"I gotta run an errand. Can you give me a lift?"

After a couple of days of Baba's chow, I figured he was looking to score a bacon cheeseburger. Add a chocolate milk shake with a side of onion rings, and that was fine by me.

Ten minutes later, we were driving through one of Fordham's tonier developments. McMansions on micro-lots.

"Physical therapy session?" I asked, feeling even

more self-conscious than usual about the epithets keyed into the sides of my car.

"Definitely therapy. We'll see just how physical it gets. Here, right here," he said. "Pull up to the curb," he said, pointing.

The house looked like a smaller, newer version of Lydia's brick mansion, and it covered most of the lot. What concerned me more were the police cars covering the driveway. And the crime scene investigation van in front of us at the curb.

"Marty, what is this? What's going on?"

"Helen's place," he said, pulling a bag of popcorn and Nick's binoculars out of the market bag.

"Hey, you want some?" he asked, handing off the bag, as he pocketed the lens caps and adjusted the binoculars. "The cops are doing the takedown. They called to give me a heads-up. A little professional courtesy."

We both cranked down the windows. There was a nice breeze. I ripped open the bag, grabbed a handful, and passed it back to him. He took a few pieces and popped them into his mouth, then wedged the bag in the console between us. As field trips go, I've had worse.

Marty checked his watch. "The cops were just getting here when we left your house, so they've already been in there for a few minutes."

A uniformed officer was standing just inside the open front door. Techs were coming and going, hauling out boxes of who-knows-what. The cop at the door stepped aside to let out a cluster of well-dressed, middle-aged women. From a distance, I'd have said some looked mad, others confused.

But I didn't have the binoculars.

They spilled onto the front walk and milled around the door. There were a lot of exaggerated facial expressions and hand gestures. And a lot of shrugging on the part of the door cop.

"Yup, that's Helen's crew," Marty said, chuckling. "They're in for a shock."

I snatched another handful of popcorn, and we watched the steady parade of evidence technicians.

"I bet one of those boxes has my laptop," he said. "Shoulda grabbed it when I had the chance."

"Hey, you can always get a new one," I said between bites. "It's a small price to pay."

Marty nodded as he refocused the binoculars.

"Man, the ladies are really giving that poor cop what for," he reported. "See the one in the beige muumuu?"

I nodded.

"That's Barb. She and Helen are tight. Looks like she's hollering at that young cop. Man, if they're not careful, the cops will call for a wagon and haul 'em all away," he said gleefully.

An hour later, the popcorn was gone. But Helen's girls were still in residence. Even if they had moved farther down the walkway.

Suddenly the cop came to life and started shooing them off the sidewalk. Behind him, two plainclothes detectives, a woman and a man, walked out with someone between them.

Helen. In handcuffs.

"Yeah, that's the money shot," Marty said, cackling. As if on cue, a photographer stepped up from the curb behind us and began clicking.

"*Sentinel,*" Marty said. "I put in a call to the newsroom before we left. Guy they sent's an intern, but he'll get the shot."

Helen's cheering section started wailing loudly. Whether it was because of the arrest or the appearance of a lowly news photographer, I couldn't tell. One woman in a powder-blue suit even sagged, as if she was threatening to faint. When the cops—and her compatriots—totally ignored her, she righted herself.

Helen's mouth never stopped moving. And as they got closer to the end of the driveway, I could hear some of the dialogue.

"Helen, we'll get an attorney! Don't worry!"

"Call Frank Harcourt," Helen shouted. "He'll know what to do."

"Don't worry about anything! We can post bail!" another said.

"Shut up, Doris!" said a lady in a lavender pantsuit. "You want to post bail, you go ahead and do it. Don't be volunteering the rest of us. I'm on a fixed income!"

"Sh-sh-sh, ladies, not in front of the media," Barb chided, gesturing at the college kid with the camera. "Those vultures will use any dirt they can get!"

"Tell him he can only photograph my left side," Doris said, pulling a lipstick out of her purse and dabbing it on carefully. "That's my good side. If he uses my right side, I'll sue."

At that moment, Helen spotted Marty.

"You!" she intoned, with the tenor of a Shakespearean actress. "You did this!"

She tried to break and run for our car, but the heels and handcuffs hobbled her. The female cop grabbed her arm and none too gently shoved her into the back of the police cruiser.

Her male partner walked toward us.

"Hey, did you know somebody keyed your car?" he said, eyeing Marty's side of my wagon.

"Vandals," I explained. "We've already filed a report."

"OK. Anyway, we've arrested Ms. Westwood, and we're taking her in for booking. Her first hearing will be tomorrow morning, so she'll spend the night in jail. It's possible she could make bail after the hearing, but I doubt it. If she does, you might want to get a restraining order. Either way, you can get your lawyer to cancel those insurance policies now. And we will definitely share that information with her."

Marty nodded. "My guy'll be at the hearing tomorrow, too. Just to oppose bail."

"Smart move," the cop said.

"She's got my laptop in there," Marty said, pointing to the house. "Any chance I could take it with me?"

The cop shook his head. "We found a couple of laptops, but we had to seize them as evidence."

He reached into his back pocket for a wallet and

pulled out a business card. He scribbled something on the card and handed it off to Marty.

"Call this number next week. If we've processed it and don't need it for the trial, you can get it back."

Marty read the card and pocketed it. "Thanks, detective."

"Is there anything you can tell us?" I asked. "Does it look like she was trying to kill him?"

"Can't really talk about that right now," the detective said, glancing over his shoulder. The photographer was snapping away at Helen in the back of the cop car. The ladies auxiliary on her lawn had vanished.

"Between you and me, you were lucky," the detective said softly to Marty. "Really lucky. But it looks like some other folks weren't. Our lab's going to analyze some of the items we confiscated. Would you be willing to get hair and blood samples taken, depending on what we find?"

"Hair and blood tests?" I interjected. "Why?"

"Some poisons stay in the system," he said. "Wouldn't be a bad idea for you medically, either. Your doc can do it and share the samples with us."

"Yeah, sure," Marty said. "Whatever's necessary." He looked a little pale. And there was a slight tremor in the hand holding the binoculars.

"Thanks, Mr. Crunk. That'll be a big help. Well, we're all done here," he said, tapping the top of our car.

We sat there, watching him walk away—both too stunned to say anything. It was one thing to speculate about insurance policies and money motives.

It was another to realize just how close Marty had come.

The cops pulled out of the driveway with a sulky Helen cuffed in the backseat.

After we watched the car retreat, I turned to Marty. "You ready to go home now?"

"Nah, I could eat," he said. "How about a bacon cheeseburger? My treat."

Chapter 55

Just after we'd finished our fast-food feast, I checked my cell.

One message. Blocked number.

My heart beat a little faster, as I dialed in to voice mail. Was something wrong with Alistair? Were they calling from the doctor's office? Or the hospital?

Gabby's voice burbled in my ear. "Good news, sugar! It looks like things have solved themselves. We're bugging out tonight after dark. If you get this before then, stop by and say 'hey.' Love you, sister-girl!"

They must have made the switch. That meant Gabby was going back to Vegas. And Harkins and Daisy would be going into hiding. With Alistair.

Damn.

When we got to the house, I leashed up Lucy, grabbed the pooper-scooper, and set off for Magnolia Circle.

From the outside, the place looked deserted. Just

like last time. The grass was a little higher. And it had sprouted a few dandelions. I looked around quickly, unclipped Lucy from her leash, and gave her a gentle pat on her plump behind.

"Go on, run up that hill," I said in the high happy voice. "Charge up that hill, and I can follow my little runaway puppy."

I didn't have to ask her twice. Lucy loved to run. Her legs were getting longer, and she was getting faster. By the time she reached the front step, the door was open.

The pup raced inside, and I followed. Then the door shut quickly and quietly behind us. Gabby.

"You guys are done already?" I asked, as she gave Lucy a well-deserved tummy scratch.

"Not exactly done, sugar. The job was canceled."

"So you don't have to switch the art?"

"Well, yes and no." She grinned. "Come on in. You can meet some of the team."

The last time I'd stopped by, the place had been empty, except for Gabby and Daisy. This afternoon, it was a hive.

A steady stream of people moved in and out of the room. Pushing carts, hauling equipment, boxing up who-knows-what. They flowed around us in what was obviously a well-choreographed dance. I felt like a clump of dust in a high-performance engine.

The air mattresses were gone. The mini fridges were still there. But empty and open. The cartons of snack food were depleted.

Off to the side, three older guys were clustered

around the folding table. Which was littered with cards, poker chips, potato chips, and soda cans.

"I call," one said.

"Yeah, and you know what I call you," another chimed in.

"My last hand," the third said. "I'm busted 'til payday."

"Today is payday, Leo."

"Well then, deal me in."

All three laughed, as one shuffled the deck and tossed out cards like a shark.

"Guys, this is Alex. Alex, these are the guys."

"Well, hello there. Any friend of Gabby's is a friend of ours."

"So what's your skill set?" one asked. "Are you a pickpocket, too?"

Gabby and I shook our heads.

"No, I'm more of a communications specialist," I said.

"I'm Fred, this is Leo, and that's Pete the Pick," the dealer said.

"Ben," the man corrected, sticking out his hand. "Benny to my friends."

"Nice to meet you," I said, shaking his hand. "But why do you go by 'Pete the Pick'?"

"'Benny the Pick' doesn't sound as good. Plus, it makes me that much harder to find."

"Got it," I said.

"Come on, we can talk over here," Gabby said, gesturing at a couple more folding chairs set up by the big, expensive-looking leather sofa.

"First rule of camping in," she said. "You never use their stuff. People notice if there's a new dent in their sofa or if their bed smells like someone else. And if you wash their sheets, that's a dead giveaway."

"What's with the boxes of snacks," I asked, wondering if we might be able to get some of those industrial-sized cartons for Baba's next visit.

"Can't use their fridge, either. People may not remember exactly what they have or where it is. But they notice if it's different. Especially if you clean it out. If they stash leftover takeout, it better be there when they get back. No matter how funky. So we pack everything in and back out again. We also stick to rooms with wood floors, tile, or flat carpet."

"No footprints on the shag?"

She grinned. "See? You'd be good at this."

I'm pretty sure she meant that as a compliment.

"So what happened?" I blurted, as she settled into the folding chair.

"Absolutely no idea," she said, spreading her hands. "Word came down yesterday. Blair called off the job. We can all go home. Even Harkins and Daisy."

I was dumbfounded. "Why?"

"Nobody knows," she said, shaking her head— and today's wig—a sleek blond bob. "But your friend Harkins can't wipe the smile off his face. And Daisy's downright giddy. When this is over, they're both going to the inn. And they wanna pick up their little tyke tonight."

"So you don't have to switch the paintings?"

She shook her head. "Nope. We don't have to." Something about the sparkle in her eyes made me push the issue.

"But the three stolen ones? The paintings that Blair got illegally?"

"Already done," she said, her face lighting up. "Last night."

"So Blair calls off the job, the right families still get their art back, and no one is the wiser?"

"Win-win, sugar. Or, in this case, win-win-win."

"Gabby, that's wonderful! But how on earth did it happen?"

"The switch was easy. We had that planned for a long time."

"Not that! The other part. Blair was rabid. That art collection is his baby. Why would he suddenly drop his demands and call off the job?"

"No idea, sugar. But I think it's like one of those laws of nature."

"What do you mean?" As far as I knew, the only nature Gabby had ever experienced were the wilds of the Las Vegas strip. But then there was plenty about her I didn't know.

"You know in those real-life TV jungle shows, how everything always eats something else? The big animals eat the little ones? And the way bigger ones eat those?"

I nodded.

"Well, it kinda sounds like Jameson Blair might have run into something that was way bigger than him."

Chapter 56

I hated saying good-bye to Gabby.

But, Gabby being Gabby, I had a sneaking suspicion I'd see her again soon. The sooner the better, as far as I was concerned.

I felt like a louse for not telling Nick she'd been in town. But she and I both knew that would be a mistake. And we both loved him enough to keep that secret.

So when I told him the story of Harkins's den of thieves (or whatever they were), I'd just leave out the fact that one of them had been named Gabby.

She was going to clue in Daisy and Harkins, too. Just in case.

But I had one final errand I needed to run before I went home to share the happy news.

I wanted to take one more look around the inn before Harkins headed home. Specifically, Paul and Georgie's room.

Ian had admitted he'd already known Paul was

dead even before I found the baby's breath in the freezer. And who had killed him.

But Paul had disappeared long before we'd learned who he was or what he'd been doing there.

So I was curious. Just how had Ian uncovered it? And had he really learned about Paul and Simmons at the same time?

The freezer was long gone. But Paul and Georgie's room was pretty much as they'd left it. Nick had confided that, because Paul had been using drugs and stealing things, Ian had wanted to give the room "a thorough clear-out," before he let in any guests. Just to be certain there were no nasty surprises. With Harkins still missing, he hadn't had the manpower to get it done. So, temporarily, Ian just closed the door and left it.

Luckily, the inn was deserted when I breezed through the front door. I could smell chocolate chip cookies. So it was a pretty good bet Nick was in the kitchen.

And I knew my mother and most of the guests were off on another of Ian's excursions. This time to Baltimore's Inner Harbor.

Classical music was coming from the direction of Ian's library. But the door was firmly shut. More "bookkeeping"?

I didn't wait for an invitation. I stepped lightly up the stairs. I knew where I was going, though not how I'd get in. Too bad I hadn't asked for a few pointers from Pete the Pick.

Luck was with me. The door to Georgie's room was closed, but not locked.

The linens on the two rumpled beds didn't even

look like they'd been changed. It was as if time had stopped. I walked over to the window. The curtains were open, but it was overcast. Cloudy.

When I heard a snap behind me, I whipped around.

Emily Prestwick.

"Sorry, dear, didn't mean to startle you. Bill and I were just getting on the road to Boston when I realized I'd mislaid one of my favorite knitting needles," she said.

She bent easily, reached around under the bed, and finally produced a long thin object.

"Your room's on three. How did that get here?"

The minute the words were out of my mouth, the puzzle pieces clicked into place. The Prestwicks' extended stay. Her antipathy for Paul. Paul, who had gone through the guests' rooms looking for valuables. And instead found a gun. A "very special gun," Ian had said.

Emily had come to Paul's room. Probably while the others were at brunch. He would have assumed she was there to ransom her gun. That she was unarmed. Just a retired college professor with her knitting. And her knitting needles. Like the one in her hand now. Had its mate killed Paul?

A knitting needle. So much like a meat thermometer. Like the one found in Ralph Simmons.

And that baseball-sized bloodstain on Raymond Bell's chest? It might have been a gunshot. Or it could have been a stab wound. Especially if the weapon was something long and thin.

"You killed all three of them," I breathed, truly bewildered. "Why?"

"Well, my dear, it's what I do. Not for the money, like our late unlamented Mr. Bell. But for Queen and country. And a small government pension, of course."

"But why those three? Why here and now?"

How could a cold-blooded killer also be the stylish raconteur who'd held court at Ian's cocktail party? Or kept Georgie and me giggling at our "girls' tea"?

"I recognized Bell when he arrived. That man is vile. Truly vile. Trailed him and found him going through a room upstairs. Whatever he was here to do, he would cause a lot of pain. That was Bell's specialty. Pain. Damnedest thing. When I came back for his body, it was gone. Someone had moved him into the freezer. I've stayed in some very fine hotels, but none ever offered that level of service."

"Let me guess, the room Bell was going through was on the fourth floor?"

"Excellent. You know why he was here?"

"Yes."

"Well then, you're a step ahead of me," she said. "I just knew he didn't belong here. Not in this house."

"What about Simmons?"

She looked puzzled.

"Pudgy guy, dark, slicked-back hair, meat thermometer?"

"That loathsome creature. Always lurking about. I'm afraid he discovered Mr. Bell. And snapped some rather compromising photos. Do you know he was actually blackmailing Mr. Sterling for what I'd done? I couldn't have that."

"And Paul?" Ian had told me one story. I just wondered if they'd synched their narratives.

"Paul was a weasel. He and Georgie weren't really married. But I'm guessing you know that?"

I nodded.

"Actors. Well, aren't we all? Paul had a couple of nasty little habits. Sabotage, stealing things, and cocaine. Unfortunately, he lifted a little trinket of mine. And I needed it back. He offered to sell it to me. But let's just say our negotiations hit a snag."

"Does Bill know?" They were so perfect together. Home and garden.

"Oh, yes, that's how we met. Years ago. At an academic conference. We were teaching at different colleges. But in the same business, really. He's more in information procurement. I do a little of that, but mostly troubleshooting and cleanup."

"You're spies. You're all spies." It just popped out of my mouth.

"Well, of course. What else would we be?" She said it as though it were the most natural thing in the world.

Emily Prestwick was standing between me and the door. I could scream. But other than my brother in the faraway kitchen and Ian in his library blasting Mozart, the house was empty. Even Rube, who hardly ever left his room, had finished his book and decamped. And everyone else was on the latest of Ian's day trips.

I couldn't get over it. She appeared so . . . normal. She looked like the teacher next door. Or your favorite aunt. Hell, she could have played Aunt Margie.

Physically, she didn't look like much of a threat. But I was guessing Paul probably thought the same thing. And Simmons. And Bell.

Mano a mano with a professional assassin? I'd likely lose that one, even if I was armed. Which I wasn't.

But we were only two flights up. If I could manage to throw myself out the window, I'd probably survive the fall.

"Well, Bill is double-parked, so I don't want to keep him waiting. Take care of yourself, dear."

And with that she stepped toward the door. When she turned, I tensed. Ready to hurl myself through Ian's double-paned, energy-efficient windows.

"You remind me very much of your father," she said with a slight smile. "There might be hope for you yet."

And with that, Emily Prestwick was gone.

Chapter 57

"You're kidding?" Trip said as I finished the story.

He'd been so rapt that his Dutch apple pie sat untouched. And by now, his coffee was probably cold.

"Nope. That's it. That's everything." I slurped my coffee. I was so stressed, I couldn't eat. And so wired I'd actually ordered decaf.

"So what now?" he asked.

"Good question," I said, eyeing his pie and reconsidering the whole no-food thing.

"Don't even think about it," he said, signaling Mrs. Simon across the café. "This is the last piece. But she's got a chocolate shoofly that'll bring tears to your eyes."

"You had me at chocolate."

"So, was your dad a spy?"

"No idea. And Dad is one topic that's pretty much off-limits with Mom."

"Because he was a spy?" Trip prodded gleefully.

"Because it hurts too much. Besides, what do I say? 'Hey, I ran into an assassin Dad used to know. She said to say 'hi'?"

"Shhh!" Trip said. "Top secret. Classified. Eyes only."

Mrs. Simon walked over from behind me, topped off our cups, and took my dessert order. When she left, Trip attacked the pie as if he was making up for lost time.

"Someone work through lunch again?" I asked.

"In a newsroom, lunch is often a theoretical concept."

He stopped eating and looked at me.

"What?" I said finally.

"I know you. You won't be able to resist asking your mother for an explanation."

He was right. "I know. But what the heck do I say? I don't want to hurt her."

"Whatever you do say, you'll be gentle about it. She's tough. She'll be OK. Besides, if it's true, she had to know this discussion was coming."

"She knew puberty was coming, too. Trust me, that didn't help."

He started laughing and had to grab a napkin.

"What I really want to know is who put the brakes on Blair?" I said.

"I know a couple of business reporters who wouldn't mind knowing, either," Trip said. "Assuming I can get you to go on the record."

I glared at him.

"Oh, come on," he coaxed. "You've got to admit, it's at least a little funny."

"What do you mean?" I asked.

"If your father was a spy, his job was keeping secrets. Yours is digging them up and sharing them with the world."

Chapter 58

The next Saturday, the B&B was officially closed for the day. To host the wedding of one Mr. Cecil Harkins to the lovely Miss Daisy Campbell. And the christening of Alistair Campbell Harkins.

Reception to follow.

Daisy actually enlisted me as a bridesmaid. "We're gettin' married in the garden, under the trees," she told me. "Just wear something that makes ya feel pretty."

How cool was that?

Annie loaned me a short, raw-silk number in coral. I didn't even want to ask what it cost. But it made me feel like a million. "It'll look smashing with your hair," my sister promised.

I still didn't completely trust Ian. But I'd put my suspicions on hold, at least temporarily, for the nuptials. Call it an early wedding present for the happy couple.

I'd shared everything I'd learned about Harkins, Ian, and the inn with Nick. Even what Emily Prestwick had said about our dad.

I figured we'd pick a date and ambush Mom sometime in the near future. And definitely call in reinforcements in the form of Peter and Annie.

When I talked to Nick, I left out only the part about our favorite blond pickpocket being part of Harkins's crew. But with a wedding in the offing, I knew she was on his mind.

"How are you doing?" I asked Nick when I found him going over a last-minute checklist in the kitchen.

"OK, considering," he said with a sigh. "It's funny, I keep thinking about Gabby. I guess because she's the closest I've ever gotten to the altar. But we didn't end up together. I know she's happy, though. And I'm moving forward."

I slapped him on the back. "I can't believe you're a godfather."

"I can't believe you didn't tell me Ian wasn't the father. Best episode of *Jerry Springer* ever."

"Hey, I didn't even tell Ian. That one was strictly to protect Alistair. God knows, I didn't do much else for the little guy."

"With Alistair, it really does take a village," Nick said. "And every village needs an idiot."

I stuck out my tongue. "Just for that, I'm gonna sabotage the wedding cake. How'd it turn out, by the way?"

"If anyone asks, simple is elegant," he said.

"How elegant is it?"

"Basically, three progressively larger cakes, stacked. White icing. Actual flowers on top. Pansies from Ian's kitchen garden. Edible in case anyone chews first and asks questions later. And the whole thing's covered with icing swirls. Swirls hide a multitude of sins."

"Sounds delicious." When it came to wedding cake—or any cake—the icing was my favorite part.

"Cake decorating is an art," Nick said. "A true art. I should have had one of your forger friends take a crack at it. 'Cause it was totally beyond me. Hence keeping it simple."

"Simple is elegant. Got it. Lucy prepared for her big moment?"

"Yup. And I've got some bacon as a backup. Just in case."

"Smart."

"Hey, that's why they made me the godfather."

"By the way, when the minister asks if you renounce Satan, the correct answer is 'yes.'"

"Och, I'm too old to be wearin' white," Daisy said, looking in the mirror as she finished dressing in her third-floor suite. "I'm fifty-two, and I've got a change-of-life baby, fer cryin' out loud."

"It's a tradition," I said. "It means you and your guy are starting with a clean slate."

Baba nodded.

"Mutton dressed as lamb," she said to the mirror.

"You look gorgeous," I said. "Like a princess."

She did, too. The long, bias-cut dress skimmed her in all the right places. With bronzed skin and sun-streaked hair piled on her head set off with a half-circlet of flowers, she looked like a Grecian goddess.

"You love him?" I asked.

Daisy grinned. "Oh yah. I'd walk through fire for that man. He's ma other half."

There was a loud rap on the door. "Open up, girls. It's nearly showtime!"

Mom.

I opened the door, and she was standing there, holding a bottle of chilled champagne in one hand and clutching four crystal glasses in the other.

"How did you knock on the door?" I asked.

"Heels are good for more than just stopping traffic. Really, Alexandra."

Mom bustled in and proceeded to uncork the bottle with nothing more dramatic than a little *whoosh*. She filled four glasses. I handed one each to Daisy and Baba.

"To true love," Mom said simply. "Now that you've found it, hang on tight."

Was it my imagination or was she a little misty-eyed?

We clinked glasses. And drank it down. Mom gave everyone a refill.

"I can't thank you all enough for bein' here," Daisy said. "On our big day. And helpin' with the wee one. If it weren't for you all . . . Well, I don't know how I could ever repay ya, so I'll just say 'thank you.'"

"If you really want to repay us, help me get this one married off," my mother said, flexing a sharp elbow in my direction.

Baba smiled.

* * *

The backyard garden was lush and green. After the rain we'd gotten, it seemed like all the flowers were exploding at once.

The vicar and Harkins were stationed under a large tree on the far side of the yard. Ian, the best man, was at his dad's shoulder.

I didn't see Daisy's face when she walked down the aisle. In English weddings, the bride goes first, and the bridesmaids follow.

But I did watch Harkins's expression as she glided toward him on Trip's steady arm. Cecil Harkins looked contented, exuberant, and blissful. All at the same time.

I snuck a peek at Ian. The guy really knew how to wear a tux. But that might have been the champagne talking.

Baba was in the front row with Alistair in her lap. Nick sat on her left, a diaper bag by his chair. Tom, Trip's partner, was stationed on her right, armed with hankies and Kleenex. Just in case.

Lucy sauntered down the aisle next to me, her head high. When we reached Ian, he bent and gently removed the wedding rings from the pocket on the back of Lucy's white lace collar. No bacon necessary.

Then she ran over to where Nick was sitting and hopped up into his lap.

After the wedding, I sat with Trip and Tom, while Nick and Baba stood in front of the vicar, next to Harkins and Daisy.

"I got five bucks says the kid's gonna use 'Campbell' as a moniker when he hits grade school," Marty whispered from the seat behind me. "Alistair's gonna be tough going on the playground."

"I'll take that action," Benny said.

"Make it ten," said Leo.

"Too rich for my blood," said Fred. "I dropped all my dough on a silver rattle. Engraved."

Baba held Alistair, who looked up into her face with curious, blue eyes.

Mr. and Mrs. Harkins hit a home run in the god-parent department.

"Took a bit of a chin-wag with the vicar," Harkins confided later, as we snapped photos. "Absolutely worth it."

When the sun went down, twinkling lights in the trees and the arbors made the garden look like a fairyland. Jazz, swing, and R&B tunes floated on the warm evening air as we danced into the night on the flagstone patio. Nick, Trip, Ian, Tom, and I took turns throughout the evening toting chilled champagne and trays of hors d'oeuvres, caviar, and mini sand-wiches out from the kitchen to the big buffet table.

Nick could say what he wanted about his cake-decorating skills. The wedding cake looked beautiful. And tasted great. Lemon sponge.

My favorite moment? After the bride and groom's first dance, Harkins lifted Alistair out of Baba's arms, and he and Daisy swayed together to the music, cuddling their little guy. Alistair smiled and giggled.

I even caught Marty wiping away a tear.

Chapter 59

The next day, I realized the only battle I had left to fight was with accounting at the *Sentinel*. To get paid. Lots of promises, still no cash.

Daisy and Harkins were off on their honeymoon. The Outer Banks of North Carolina.

They'd elected to take Alistair with them and make it a family vacation. Besides, I don't think anyone was prying Alistair away from his parents again anytime soon.

Marty was still on the sofa. He swore he could maneuver the inn stairs just fine with crutches. And Ian had guaranteed him a room no higher than the second floor. I stepped in to make sure it wasn't Paul's old room.

That one had some bad karma no amount of Febreze or burning sage would ever clear.

I was kind of glad when Terri, his physical therapist, said she wanted to see a little more progress before he was regularly climbing stairs. So he was stuck with us for a few more days.

But that hadn't stopped him from hitting the B&B for a poker night with Harkins and his cronies.

That's where Marty had picked up another interesting tidbit. The spandex biking club? Harkins's buds. Without a car, that's how they were getting around town. No gas, no noise, no auto registration, and, in a residential neighborhood, no raised eyebrows. Best of all, Fred confessed to Marty, they'd blasted past our house regularly, just to keep an eye on things. And if they happened to catch a glimpse of Alistair (and could pass the news on to Daisy and Harkins), so much the better.

Mom had booked back into the B&B for the wedding. This time, for one night only. Trip claimed she wanted to end her visit on a high note. I contend she suspected something was up. But that's another battle for another day.

It turned out Lydia Stewart's disappearance had nothing to do with Alistair, Simmons, or the Freezer of Doom. Nick found out from one of Janie Parker's suppliers that Lydia had gone to New York for a little "freshening up." Complete with a casual wardrobe, perky boobs, and a strawberry blond 'do.

How weird was that?

Still, something had been nagging at me. And it had nothing to do with Lydia's new look.

When Emily Prestwick talked about killing Bell, she claimed she didn't know *why* he had been at the B&B. She'd been more concerned about *where* he was.

"Not in this house," she had said.

So what was so special about that particular house?

Now with no Alistair, no bodies, and no Mom to distract me, my brain started sifting through the weirdness of the past few weeks. And a picture started coming into focus.

Ian's vagueness about his former occupation. The fact that he'd sent Emily back to Boston, rather than turning her in to the cops. The location of his inn—just outside DC. And the ease with which he got movers and shakers to come to his place—and to recommend it to their friends.

Ian was running a meetinghouse for spies.

So was he the one who'd intimidated Jameson Blair? Or did he simply have access to someone who did? Through his web of contacts?

But I hadn't told Ian who was threatening his father. Or why.

I knew Harkins and his friends hadn't said anything. And Emily Prestwick claimed she didn't know. I believed her, too. Because in killing Bell, she'd actually made things harder for Harkins. And Ian.

So who had known about Blair and told Ian?

Then something clicked. How angry he'd been when I wouldn't share everything I'd learned about his father. Then the quick mea culpa. Followed by an even quicker visit with Alistair. Who had slept in my bedroom.

I tried to recall the past week. I'd never talked with Nick about my stroll to Magnolia Circle. But I did discuss it with Trip. A lot. On the front porch over galettes that same evening. And later, on the phone.

I lifted the handset off its charging station, examining it from all angles. Nothing.

I grabbed the phone stand and flipped it upside down, running my hand over the flat aluminum underside. One anomaly: a little piece of beige plastic. About the size of a dime.

I pried, and it came off in my hand.

Clutching it, I walked into the kitchen and grabbed a frying pan out of the cupboard. I tucked the bug into a sandwich bag and gave it a hard whack. Followed by two more. Then I emptied the electronic crumbs into my hand.

Marty and Baba were both in the living room. *Wheel of Fortune.* "I've got to go across the street for a minute," I told them. "I'll be right back."

I flew out the door on adrenaline alone.

When I walked into the inn, Ian was standing behind the desk cradling a bottle of champagne. His face lit up.

"Perfect timing," he purred, reaching under the counter to produce two crystal glasses. "I was just about to head over to your place. It took some doing, but I've managed to locate a very special vintage I think you'll really enjoy."

"No, this time I have a present for you," I said evenly.

When I dumped the electronic confetti into his glass, Ian's expression was pure shock. His face crumpled. "Alex, I can explain . . ."

"No explanation necessary," I said, catching a

whiff of his exotic cologne. This time, it had zero effect.

Not even a flutter.

"You got what you needed," I concluded. "And I'm really glad it ended well. But I'm done. Over and out."

With that, I turned and walked out the front door into the bright June sunshine.

Acknowledgments

What's not a mystery is just how many people it takes to bring a book to life. A very big "thank you" to my editor, Alicia Condon. You always make the story better—and you "get" the Vlodnacheks. You're still my best audience!

I also need to thank the wonderful team at Kensington Books. Special shout-outs to copy editor Pat Fogarty, production editor Robin Cook, and art director Janice Rossi. You guys made this into a real book!

A grateful "thank you and wow!" to artist Michelle Grant. Each cover is better than the last. This one is gorgeous and glamorous. It also makes me smile (and laugh at Lucy) every time I see it.

And last but definitely not least: a huge "thank you" to my agent, Erin Niumata, of Folio Literary Management, who first noticed, read and believed in CONFESSIONS OF A RED HERRING. You are one in a million. The hydrangeas in this one are for you!

Read on for a preview of

RED HOT

the next Red Herring mystery.

Alex Vlodnachek is in the hot seat again.
This time, she has a century-old mystery,
a reclusive billionaire, a secret tunnel
and a dead body to thank. But when a
photojournalist flame hits town—
and checks in to the neighborhood B&B—
that really turns up the heat . . .

I was fine until they discovered the body.

After a couple of months of icy silence, Ian Sterling and I had reached a neighborly detente. I avoided his B&B. He stayed away from my house. And, when we were on neutral ground—like the mailbox or the grocery store—we would wave and smile from a polite distance.

Nick thought we were both nuts. But my brother wasn't the one who found a bug planted in his bedroom.

Long story.

So imagine my surprise when I heard a gentle knock on the door one afternoon, glanced through the peephole, and spotted Ian on the front porch.

I looked down at Lucy. The pup looked up at me. "What do you think?" I whispered.

She appeared perplexed.

I debated not answering the door. But my car was in the driveway. And, more important, my brother was baking peach pies in Ian's kitchen. If something had happened to Nick, I needed to know.

Even if it meant consorting with Ian the spy.

I opened the door a sliver. Lucy stuck her snout through the crack and sniffed the air.

"Hullo," he said, in his clipped British accent. Spotting Lucy, his face relaxed into a smile. "I was wondering if I might speak with you a moment. It's a bit of a ticklish situation."

"Is Nick all right?"

Ian looked puzzled. Clearly, whatever it was didn't involve my brother. "He's fine. No worries there."

He hesitated. I pulled Lucy back by the collar and considered slamming the door in his face. No way he was coming inside.

But my dog had other plans. She wanted to go out and play.

"Could we sit on the porch?" he asked. "I have to tell you something, and there's no good way to say it."

"Is everyone OK? Alistair? Daisy? Harkins?" I loved Ian's family like my own. And my tiff with him didn't involve the rest of the clan. I'd watched baby Alistair while Daisy and Harkins went into D.C. last Saturday.

"Everyone's very well, thank you. Ship-shape, in fact."

I gestured at the plastic lawn chairs and stepped outside, as Lucy trampled my feet racing ahead. Then I closed the door firmly behind me. If Ian was expecting a tea party, he'd come to the wrong house.

Lucy tore around the lamppost at top speed, like

a young filly. Now in her canine adolescence, her legs were growing longer and stronger. And she was getting faster.

She raced around the side of the house. I expected she'd be gone for a few minutes. Lucy liked her privacy.

Ian settled into one of the faded yellow chairs. "As you may or may not know, I'm having some renovations done at the inn. Nothing that impacts the guests or the kitchen. But I'd wanted to finish out some of the basement areas, so that we could make use of the space for storage."

Nick had told me as much. But I wasn't going to admit that to Ian. I said nothing.

"While they were examining one of the walls, the workmen discovered a tunnel."

My eyebrows shot up, and Ian paused. Nick had said nothing about a tunnel.

"We found it just this morning, in fact," Ian added. "We were exploring it, to see how far and where it went. And, I'm afraid, that's when we found it."

He stopped.

"It?" I asked.

"A body," he said. "Almost at the end of the tunnel. Very near a door of some kind."

"Ian, that's awful!" I blurted. "Is it . . . ?"

He shook his head quickly.

What neither of us said aloud: Three particularly nasty characters had disappeared from the B&B about two months ago. None had been seen since. I knew at least two of them were dead. I'd found their bodies. Before they vanished again.

Ian swore he didn't know their final resting place. But I had my doubts.

Out in the yard, Lucy reappeared, refreshed. She bounded up the steps and threw herself at Ian's feet. He grinned and scratched her left ear. She thumped her tail in bliss and rolled over exposing her fluffy, white belly.

I struggled not to smile.

Ian looked at me. Willing my face blank, I waited for him to continue. He folded his hands in his lap.

"This appears to be a woman," he said slowly. "From the clothing. The rest is . . . well, bones."

This news would ricochet around our small-town-slash-D.C.-bedroom-community like a bullet. I wondered what kind of reaction he'd get from our patrician, pain in the association neighbor, Lydia Stewart. She had at least ten years on (and a serious case of the hots for), Mr. Ian Sterling. As head of the neighborhood homeowners group, she was also a stickler for community rules and regs. And a dead body probably wouldn't help property values.

Still, when love-sick Lydia heard about the corpse, my money was on her showing up with a shovel and a can-do attitude.

"The craftsmen actually stumbled upon it," Ian continued. "Almost literally. I'll alert the proper authorities, of course. But I felt it was only cricket to tell you first. A bit of a heads-up, so to speak."

That phone call would bring a swarm of cop cars, a crime scene van or two and—last but not least—a hearse from the coroner's office. Along with a few news crews. And every neighbor within walking distance. The town gossip mill would ratchet into overdrive.

Not exactly a good ad for his pricey B&B.

Still, with Nick operating—temporarily—out of the inn's kitchen, it was genuinely kind of the guy to let me know. At least I wouldn't see the ruckus and assume the worst.

"Well, thanks for cluing me in," I said, standing. "I'd love to hear what the police discover."

Oddly, Ian didn't budge from his seat.

"You need to sit down," he said softly.

I started to protest. The look on his face stopped me. His blue eyes were dark. But his expression wasn't anger. It was concern. I sank into the chair.

"The tunnel?" Ian started. "It leads to your house. Living room or kitchen would be my best guess. The body is on your property."